CHLOE AND THE LIGHTHOUSE

By

C.T. Horvath

ISBN   978-0-9852170-0-6
LCN   2012904037

To Mark, with the greatest of love - Always.

And to Chloe, my little black fuzz ball,
who started it all…

CHAPTER I

My eyes hadn't blinked in days. I was still in shock. Looking around my small one bedroom apartment I noticed the plants that needed watering, the dirty dishes to be washed, and the overflowing pile of laundry. With a steaming cup of tea, Tension Tamer they called it, I drank in the familiar mixture of emotions that played through my head. I thought back to last year and wondered how I had survived or how I would survive. Well, some answers were easier than others. I glanced across the coffee table at Chloe who sat contentedly on her chair. She was smiling. I smiled too while sipping my tea. As she reached forward to swat at a piece of paper on the table, my smile turned to laughter. It took a moment to realize that my laughter had dissolved into tears. I doubted if anyone listening would notice the difference.

One year ago, my beloved father had climbed into his

bed after eating one of my mother's experimental vegetarian dishes, had eagerly picked up his favorite western novel and died peacefully in his sleep three pages from the end of the book. That book had always been one of his favorites. In fact, he was buried with his first edition of Zane Grey's *To The Last Man*. Maybe in heaven he'll get a chance to finish it again, for the twentieth time. I'm sure God would understand. My Dad always said that God smiled on cowboys, so God must have been grinning when he made Zane Grey.

My father's passing set in course a series of events that included caring for my mother as she grieved for her husband, life mate, and verbal sparring partner. After a marriage of over sixty years, she still loved him enough to grieve and sob quietly at his funeral. During the service, her warm brown eyes would gaze periodically up to heaven as if to check to make sure my Dad was there. I was sure he had made it through the Pearly Gates. I also felt he was still around hovering nearby looking at mother and me, silently grateful he would no longer have to endure tuna patties, zucchini cookies, and other foods not fit to be consumed by the gods.

The months that followed the funeral were a whirlwind of decisions and planning, cleaning and boxing, and de-cluttering and discarding a lifetime of memories. Often times, we argued over what to keep and what to throw out. Sixty years of keeping every scrap of paper from my kindergarten finger paint art to press releases when I opened my massage practice ten years ago, lay in piles and boxes in their four bedroom house. It took some doing to convince Mom that she could part with the lot. Many nights I went home tired, not from massaging bodies, but from the arguments and sheer volume of junk. Some things weren't even fit for a garage sale.

After many months, it was decided that with the money

my father left and the money raised from the estate sale, Mom would be moving into the new retirement community in south Denver, home to the active and able-bodied senior. I decided it would be a good way for Mom to meet new friends and have more interest in the community. So, it was finally agreed that in early March, Mom would make the move. Ironically, it was also a year to the day since my father had passed away.

On the night before the big move, Mom sent me a message to come at once because she had something exciting to show me. In the past, this could have meant anything from a new angel for her collection that she had found for two dollars at the local flea market, to a new mystery author she was reading. After tidying up my office, I glanced around at the scented candles, the colorful anatomy charts hanging on the walls, the calm light blue paint and white wainscoting. I looked at the peaceful scenic pictures of landscapes I had collected over the years and the other odds and ends given to me by loving clients. Hard not to smile at how lucky I felt to be doing a job I truly enjoyed, was good at, and provided me with the opportunity to meet such diverse and enjoyable people.

I picked up Chloe, walked to my Honda Fit – the red color still caused me to grin – placed Chloe in her seat, and set off for Mom and Dad's. Yes, I still thought of them as together even though Dad was in heaven talking with his favorite western authors waiting for Mom to show up so she could finally talk to Agatha Christie.

One of the advantages of my office, nestled on Main Street in the tiny South Denver suburb where we live, is that my parents live only ten minutes away. Climbing out of the car, I turned to reach for Chloe who jumped out and raced to the front door. I followed behind her looking up at the red brick house with the white trimmed picture windows. Reaching the front step, I opened the door expecting to smell sugar cookies or hear the blast of an old *Murder She Wrote* on TV. The house seemed too quiet. Chloe raced ahead of me into the foyer, turned left down the hall and headed straight for my parents' bedroom. Chloe was standing next to my mother's bed. Mom was lying in bed across the dusty rose bedspread as if she were napping, except I had a feeling she wouldn't be waking up from this nap. She was lying on her side with her left arm outstretched over the side of the bed as if she was trying to pick something up. I looked down to see Chloe playing with a small scrap of paper on the floor. Half in grief and half in irritation, I snatched the paper off the floor and stuffed it into my jean jacket pocket. I sat down next to my mom and sighed. I thought of all the fights we had over her move, at how much she loved this home she had shared with my dad, and how much she would have missed all the memories stored within the walls. She would rather die within these walls filled with laughter, cooking smells, and dust than start over in a sterile new home filled with nothing more than the smell of fresh paint and carpet. Yes, I understood. I absentmindedly stroked her gray hair and touched her cool cheek. She was dressed in her favorite red velour pants suit. I smiled at her with a heart full of sadness, wiped a few tears from my deep black eyes and dug into my jacket pocket for my cell phone to call the same people my mom had called a year before.

The next few days were eerily similar to the ones of a year ago. Doctors declared her death natural causes due to congestive heart failure. A fancy way of saying she died of loneliness and a broken heart. The same people were invited to the same community church. The same songs sung, same passages read, same pastor, same sermon, same old, same old. I even think the potluck dishes were the same as at my father's reception. The blue haired old ladies looked the same, too.

I floated through those days filled with sadness at the beloved parents I had lost and the warmth of knowing that they were together seated at the left hand of Christ, because only Jesus was allowed to sit at the right hand, as any good Baptist will tell you. I knew without a doubt that my parents sat there comparing authors and arguing over the virtues of Louis Lamour and Dorothy L. Sayers. I know that Dick Francis and Dorothy Gilman would have been mentioned with a deep bow of the head and a heartfelt "God bless them." It was hard to be sad knowing that God was being so easily entertained.

It was after the funeral when Chloe and I were safely tucked away in my apartment that I remembered the scrap of paper shoved so hastily in my pocket. After searching the laundry, I finally found it. I smoothed out the paper and recognized it. It was not a recipe for vegetarian lasagna, but a Powerball lottery ticket. *That's weird.* Mom had stopped buying lottery tickets after dad died, since he left her enough money to happily cruise garage sales from here to eternity. I went to the kitchen to the recycle bin and dug through the newspapers until I found the date that matched the ticket. 05, 14, 23, 43, 50 and 36. I checked the numbers on the ticket again. I checked the newspaper a second time. A third time. I sat down. I checked the numbers one last time. I sat there for a very long time. This is what Mom wanted to show me. Her ship had finally come in and she had already sailed away without it. I finally found the courage to cry, not for the loss of parents, but for the fact that not only did they leave me with loving thoughts, good childhood memories, straight teeth and good moral character, they left me one final gift, a sort of parting gift: a winning Powerball lottery ticket.

I cried into the night and slept long into the next day.

I dreamed of possibilities and ships, smiles and cowboys, mysteries and paths not traveled.

They say that it takes a village to raise a child. In my case, it would take a few select old friends to guide my steps from one old life into the terrifying path of the new and unknown. After confirming for the hundredth time that my lottery ticket was "The" winning ticket, I made my first of several phone calls. First, I called my massage clients to cancel my day's scheduled appointments. There were only three, so I didn't feel too guilty. My next phone call was to my family's attorney, Dennis West. Since I am the last surviving member of my family, minus some distant cousins and aunts, he is the family attorney for Chloe and me. I told Dennis that yes, it was urgent, no, it could not wait, and that yes, I could be there in fifteen minutes.

Marching down Main Street, I paused to check out the displays in the windows, and caught a reflection of myself. Five foot five inch frame with a more than ample chest; curves in mostly good places, toned arms, dark olive skin, and big beagle, almost black eyes. My mom use to tell me that beauty and smarts make a lethal combination and that I should be careful how I used mine. Smiling at that memory and smoothing my straight dark brown hair, I hurried to Dennis' office. His small office was nestled in a charming Victorian house on Main Street a few short blocks from mine. He has a cheery assistant who is always smiling and chatty who rushed me into Dennis' office. I told him to sit down, and carefully explained my newfound ticket and the matching wealth. Then I explained it again. After the third time, Dennis still hadn't blinked. I asked his secretary for a glass of water for Dennis and an uninterrupted hour for myself. After sipping his water, he finally blinked. I started to suspect that Dennis was in shock, which was a shock to me as well. Dennis is a stocky man who looks like he could carry a pair of six shooters on his hip, walk down Dodge City wearing a Stetson while never bothering to polish the Silver Star pinned to his jacket. I am firmly convinced that Dennis was a western character like Wyatt Earp in another life right down to his handlebar mustache and his steely gray blue eyes.

Once Dennis realized I wasn't kidding, I wasn't in trouble, and that I was going to be paying him by the hour for services about to be rendered, he came to his senses and got down to business. It's amazing what one can accomplish in an hour when money and life decisions are a motivating factor. After signing nondisclosure agreements, retainer documents, and other documents necessary to handle the dotted I's and the crossed T's, I reached into my wallet and showed him the winning ticket. Dennis stopped blinking again. I asked him to find out all the other ins and outs we had not thought of and to call me when we needed to meet again. I stuffed the ticket back into my wallet, grateful Dennis was blinking again, and left.

My next stop was the South Denver Community Bank up the street from Dennis' office. My favorite banker, Patrick Edgewater, ran the branch and has been a massage client for years. Patrick looks like a tall, redheaded basketball player blessed with the analytical mind of a Midas-touch mathematician. Patrick knows more ways to make and invest money than I know muscles. I asked for a private meeting in his office. I must say that Patrick took the news far better than Dennis. Patrick slowly began to grin which grew into a smile and finally erupted into childlike laughter. I reached into my wallet and drew out the ticket. Patrick's laughter left him like air out of a basketball.

Taking a deep breath, he said, "So, I'm losing my favorite massage therapist."

I laughed. "Well, I haven't given it much thought, but

I think I might be going on a long vacation to think things through."

"Well, Katy Hawkins, my dear, what can I do for you today?"

"Well, oh favorite banker, I need a safety deposit box, so I don't get mugged for this small piece of paper and I need to know what to do with the winnings." Patrick turned into a big orange tom cat and began to purr. I smiled as Patrick imagined what his paws would do with my winnings. The next half hour was spent talking annuities, high yield saving accounts, trusts, and other financial terms no one could comprehend. I asked Patrick to make up, print, and sign a nondisclosure agreement stating that what we talked about stayed in this office and that any and all representation would be confidential. I also added a statement claiming I would be giving him a small percentage to help me when the time came. The purring grew louder and vibrated throughout his office. After shaking his paw, um, hand and promising to return when I received the check, I left feeling like Alice after meeting the Cheshire Cat.

My final call was to my friend, steady client, and conveniently, my financial planner who helped me set up an IRA when I started my massage practice ten years ago. She also helped with the money inherited after my dad's death and would be handling my mom's estate when it cleared probate. Holly is not only a financial wizard, she is a highly talented soprano who sings in two community choirs and solos at local churches. I thought of past Christmas mornings spent singing "Happy Birthday" to her while the rest of the world was singing "Joy to the World." Holly was born on Christmas night, which is why her mother kindly named her Holly. After Holly's third divorce, she took back her maiden name and is now known as Holly Daze. Her mother had a strange sense of humor.

Holly's fuzzy blond hair hides a sharp mind, sharper wit, infectious laugh, and a warehouse of financial information. Her only eccentric oddity is her ever-changing herd of cats that saunter their way into her life and house. Holly is a cat magnet for the lost, half starved, injured and lonely cats and kittens in our community. I think they can sense her feline aura sniffing her out from a thousand yards in high wind. She is also Chloe's favorite chew toy.

I had called Holly first thing this morning and asked her to meet me at the Tea Cozy, a cute little tea shop with tasty quiche, pastries, sandwiches and tea. She arrived at noon, her short blond hair messy from the typical Denver breeze and her clothes covered in cat hair. Lunches with Holly usually consisted of her proud mama stories about her four grown sons who she raised all alone with little help from her occasional husbands. After the son updates, she tells me of the latest cat she had found and loved back to health that is now residing in a warm sunny spot in her home. And she would always be able to wow me with the latest person she had persuaded to adopt one of her "adoptables" as she calls them. Adoptables are the cats and kittens who have thrived in her house, eaten her food, shared her bed, eaten her plants and were now ready to go on to bigger and better things – namely any person Holly comes into contact with. Holly can persuade a hay fever sufferer to work in a horse barn. She once persuaded a nice wealthy couple with antiques and cat allergies to adopt two short hair "antique gray" litter mates. Last she heard, the kittens were cats and were mentioned prominently and generously in the couple's will should the day come when they will be parted from their "heirloom feline companions." Their words, not Holly's. She is a passionate miracle worker for the cat kingdom. I believe her God is a large, longhaired ginger colored tom with six toes and wide green eyes.

After the sons and cats stories, we settled into business. Girl talk. Holly asked me what was new. Well, after a small explanation, a lovely crab and chive quiche inhaled through the wrong wind pipe, Earl Grey coming out of her nose, Holly was able to breathe and talk between coughs, throat clearing, and nose blowing to remove the last tea leaves from her nasal passages. I would say she took the news rather well.

"My God! Imagine the amount of cat food you can buy!"

"Yes, and imagine all the money launderers who are going to be hot on my heels when the news gets out!" I always believe in cutting to the essentials.

Holly's blue eyes grew large as she leaned in close to the table piled with used paper napkins, tea leaves, and chunks of chewed quiche. "So, what are you going to do? What have you done? Who is going to represent you? And have you thought of retirement plans you plan on investing in?" Holly believes in cutting to the essentials, too.

"Well, I've contacted Dennis, my favorite lawyer, and he has agreed to represent me for a small outrageous fee to handle all my legal affairs. I also contacted Patrick, my favorite banker, to arrange for his financial services – also for a small outrageous fee. And you, my dear Miss Holly, are the final leg of this Holy Trinity. Will you be my personal money launderer," she grimaced, "and help me find nooks and crannies in which to stash this money while I figure out what to do with the rest of my life?"

Holly sat back in her chair and hummed. I imagined her leaning forward and lapping milk out of her tea saucer. "I would love to represent you. That way I can keep track of your finances and make sure you aren't spending the money on anything frivolous like new cars, boats, and designer clothes."

Why did I have the feeling that my winnings I hadn't even claimed or received yet, were no longer mine? The rest of the lunch was enchanting, one part friends catching up and one part strategy session to handle the many ways to save, invest, and donate the millions to come. One thing was for sure; Holly wanted to help me give back to others as they have given to me. I looked forward to the good intentions, misguided reality, and volumes of misunderstanding that would pave the way on this new adventure.

CHAPTER 2

Exactly one month later, I held my first Support Triangle meeting. A support triangle is similar to the food pyramid except without the calories. Dennis, Patrick and Holly would be my three legs to help me with my winnings and offer any and all advice. We met at a high priced and fancy restaurant on Main Street where we established trusts, foundations, and began to build a buffer of legal maneuvers to separate me from the outside world of less desirable peoples and parties wanting me and my money. The next morning, I went to the Lottery office and produced my winning ticket. I don't remember much of the rest of the day except lots of loud voices, shouts, lights, photographers, reporters, noise and lots of people trying to touch me and be my friend. After officially holding the check for the LARGEST POWERBALL LOTTERY JACKPOT IN HISTORY, minus about 47% for taxes, I fled from the building feeling like the hounds of hell were on my heels.

The next few days were continuous meetings with my Triangle of friends, partners, and strategists. Dennis would handle all claims for the money from charities, beggars, shysters, and want-to-be friends and lovers. Patrick handled setting up my bank accounts so I could have a steady stream of money to use when I decided what to do with the next seventy years of my life. I do believe it's better for a thirty year old to inherit tons of money than a teenager. Hopefully, I wouldn't go completely insane and buy a small foreign country, a yacht as big as the space shuttle, or enough clothes to fill the Grand Canyon. Holly made sure that the majority of the money was stashed in investments to provide maximum return. A trust was also established so that I could give to the few charities I believed in and knew personally. I have always been the type to know where my money goes and to see it in action. So, Holly sat at her home office surrounded by three tiger striped kittens she found in an alley behind her hairdresser and started donating to the few local "no kill" cat shelters. She also donated to a few horse rescue facilities for which I had volunteered. The rest sat waiting for me to move forward, decide my future and get on with my life. The trouble was I was too scared to move.

Through all this, Chloe sat patiently waiting at home. She would greet me every day, jump into my arms and expect nothing more than dinner and a lap to sleep on. Her black sable fur shined in the sunbeams as she chased her play mice. Her golden eyes looked at me with love and acceptance that I was just Katy Hawkins, her guardian and confidant. While the phone rang with offers to support causes, people, diseases, political parties, marriage proposals, and other foul and preposterous offerings, she kept me safe by sitting with me purring contentedly and occasionally biting my toes. My

Triangle may have had my money – at least on paper, but Chloe had my sanity. And she cared for and nurtured it in her tiny black paws.

After two days, I disconnected my home phone, changed the number on my cell phone, sent good-bye letters to my massage clients with referrals to other massage therapists I had known and trusted, and decided it was time to flee the ringing phones, money hounds and the greedy hoards looking to line their pockets. It was time to leave behind the mayhem and get out of Denver for a while. So, I sold my furniture except for the few keepsakes from Mom and Dad, stored my books and the rest of my massage life in boxes, and paid for a year's worth of storage at one of those lock it and leave it storage facilities.

One of the mainstays of my childhood was the many trips my parents and I made to California. Vacations every summer were spent flying to that warm sunny state and driving Highway 1. Sometimes I went with them and sometimes I stayed with my parents' close friends. To my parents, these trips represented freedom, sunshine, laughter, good food and adventure. I remember my folks explaining the ritual to me in detail. They would arrive in Santa Barbara, rent a car and drive until they saw some reason to stop. Usually it was a gift shop or bookstore for Mom and a local piece of history or scenic wonder for Dad. They would just go where the wind and impulse took them and let fate lend a hand. The magical part about those trips was that Mom and Dad looked young, even as they aged. They left behind their petty bickering, silly arguments, and worn smiles and let the sunshine and surf infuse their marriage with light and healing. Of course it took me years to figure this out. With those memories of magic in mind, I decided that Chloe and I needed to continue that tradition.

On the first day of May, Chloe and I flew first class to

California. Patrick, Dennis, and Holly dropped us off at the airport. They stood looking like friends saying goodbye for the last time. I felt blessed for their friendship, honored for their individual expertise and scared that I would never see them again – except by phone or fax. Chloe just lay curled in her pet carrier blinking casually with her paw on a pink fuzzy mouse. She is the best traveler.

After landing in San Diego, I experienced my first sense of wealth and privilege. At the Hertz rental counter, I chose a green Jaguar coupe, upgraded to the best possible rental package and told the slightly confused but nice attendant that I wanted the car as long as I wanted and that I hadn't decided if I was bringing it back. I'm sure my huge credit limit on my new credit card, which was just shy of the national debt, and a crisp one hundred dollar bill tip meant I could have my way with the car people. Having a little extra money can be fun – and habit forming. I stowed the two stuffed duffel bags in the trunk, one for my clothes and personal items and one with Chloe's toys, food, and blankets. I had purchased a small hooded kitty litter box for her delicate six-pound frame and stored it in the back of the coupe along with an extra bag of kitty litter, water, and bowl of food. Chloe sat beside me on her pillow in her purple harness with matching ID tag and leash. She was my sole heir and I was taking no chances with her getting lost. I also needed to update my will and add a human to look after this most precious of felines. I'd think about that later. It would make Dennis happy to add will making to his billable hours. I pictured him thinking about early retirement or at least an extended vacation at a Dude Ranch.

Off we went on our first adventure as wealthy human and feline sidekick. I didn't feel wealthy, I just felt blessed, well taken care of, scared and humble in a weird pit of my stomach kind of way.

One of the philosophies of travel that my parents passed on to me was that "when on vacation – don't be cheap!" I took that to mean if you want an ice cream cone at three o'clock in the afternoon, then have one. A vacation is a time of renewal, luxury, and a chance to treat yourself to all the fun and frolic you can muster. I had tried to adopt that philosophy into my life as well. So, as I drove, Chloe sat perched on my lap looking out the window and watching the seagulls as they swept over the sparkling aqua ocean. After several miles, Chloe finally settled back down on her pillow for some much deserved napping. I passed towns that were carved into the hills overlooking Highway 1. Some of them were so small, only a few houses dotted the landscape. I didn't have a destination in mind; I just wanted the freedom of the road, with wind, surf, and quiet to seep into my soul. I knew it would take a few days before I would stop cringing every time my new cell phone rang. The ocean would heal those wounds like a salve for sore muscles.

I stopped two hours later at a small village that advertised seafood. The seaside restaurant was cozy and no one seemed to mind that I had a small black fuzzy cat as my dinner companion. After some fairly good clam chowder and a fresh green salad with tiny tasty shrimp, I felt revived and content with my new phase of life. Chloe had nibbled a few of my miniature shrimp and was curled up on the chair next to me smiling.

I decided to drive a bit more as dusk settled in around us covering the sky with deep purples, blues and light gold, which reflected like a tapestry upon the ocean waves. I covered Chloe in her baby blanket, handmade by her godmother, as she settled in for a snooze. As darkness fell, my mind finally cleared and the past regrets and lingering sadness began to leave me and drift out to the ocean to be washed away by the tide. It was peaceful and cool and a perfect time for driving.

The stars had poked through the velvet blanket of sky when suddenly Chloe leapt from under the blanket and started pawing her passenger side window. She began chirping which is her way of saying "pay attention!" I looked at her and out her window just in time to see a simple painted wood sign that said "Comfort" with an arrow pointing off to the right. With Chloe chirping like a magpie, I slowed the Jag down and made the sharp right turn, luckily without any tires leaving the highway. We came to another sign with an arrow pointing to the left for "Comfort" and a right arrow pointing straight to "Uptown." Now being a practical and somewhat metaphysical person, I chose Comfort over being an Uptown girl. The road turned to the left under the highway and led to a small parking lot. From the parking lot I could just make out a small seaside town with about thirty cottages ranging from bungalows to ornate Victorian structures with vibrant and detailed color lining the five tiered streets etched into the side of a cliff. I shut off the car and stared. Chloe immediately jumped into my lap and started pawing at the door handle. I gathered up her leash and my purse and opened the door. Chloe jumped down and took off like a shot. For a cat that weighs less than a Christmas ham, she can pull like a sled dog. She scampered over rocks and sand and stopped at the beginning of a faint path, which led to the small town nestled around the cove and beach. Ahead of us, I noticed a magnificent Victorian house standing three stories tall with several shades of blue acting as accents to the warm pale blue of the main coat. Turrets perched on each end facing the ocean like sentinels. The house appeared huge, square shaped with a side door, clothesline and attached garage at the back. A tasteful, yet ornate sign announced the building to be "The Blue Heron Bed and Breakfast." A smaller hand-painted sign hanging below read: Vacancy. At this point, Chloe sat down on her haunches stared at the Blue Heron and then at me as if to say "Well, this is where I'm sleeping, what about you?" Good question. Though the stars were twinkling above us casting their sparkles upon the ocean, I hadn't thought about where to sleep. Sometimes, Chloe has really good ideas. This was one of them.

I scooped up Chloe and walked purposefully on the gravel driveway toward the Blue Heron. I was just passing the side yard when I heard, "Nice night for a cat walk!" I jumped. Chloe jumped. Thankfully I wasn't scratched to the point of requiring major medical attention. I whirled around and there stood a grandmother. Well, at least that's how she looked. Older, round shoulders, plump in all the motherly places with a handmade shawl over her shoulders, a plain white blouse over a practical khaki skirt accompanied by a pair of brown sensible shoes. Her gray hair was cut short and the style meant maintenance, but well kept. I smiled and felt I had just met Mrs. Claus. She shuffled forward like someone who had spent most of her life on her feet and graciously held out her hand.

"I'm Mabel Moretti and welcome to Blue Heron. It looks like you could use a room," Mabel grinned.

"Hello to you. I'm Katy Hawkins and I would love a room – do you have one available?"

"Come with me my dear, into the kitchen. After the fright I gave you, I bet you could do with a cup of tea and a snack." I followed the back of her head past the side door and into the kitchen. It was like walking into a hug that smelled like blueberries. Mabel had already put the kettle on and was piling lovely lilac colored scones on a plate. I sat Chloe down, unhooking her leash, and plopped into the dining chair offered me. Mabel settled in next to me, her light blue eyes dancing and full of mischief.

"So, what brings you for Comfort?" Mabel asked.

"Don't you mean what brings me to Comfort?" I countered.

"Well, isn't that about the same thing? Some who need comfort actually find it here."

"Good thing the town wasn't named Purgatory or something," I said as I nibbled a blueberry scone.

Mabel laughed, "Well, I think that name is taken. Besides I'd rather have comfort and know where to find it, then to have to find something I don't want. Enough about me, so who is that charming creature I saw you with?"

Scanning the kitchen, I gasped when I realized that I had no idea where Chloe had run off to. We looked around Mabel's kitchen until both our eyes landed on her laundry basket full of clean guest towels sitting on the floor by the dryer. I eased out of my chair and tiptoed to the basket. There nestled in the midst of towels and fine linens lay Chloe sound asleep oblivious to the cat hair she was shedding. Mabel laughed quietly and motioned me back to the dining table. "Let her sleep," Mabel said. "I rather think she found herself a place of comfort. Who are we to intrude? So, is there a story that goes with this little black beauty or is she just passing through?"

"Well, we are both just passing through, but we're a team. Chloe's my only family now."

"That sounds like a good opening for a bed time story, what's the rest of it? Trade you one batch of scones and a pot of tea for one. I like a good story."

"Well, Chloe here is pretty special," I began. "I found her three years ago in a trash dumpster right outside my apartment building. She was about three weeks old and weighed less than five ounces." Mabel gasped while sipping her tea. I continued, having proudly told this story many times before.

"She was a pretty sick little kitten. The first year was filled with doctors, shots and tons of expensive gourmet cat food to try to get her back to health. As you can see she's pretty healthy; however, the time in the dumpster did have an effect her. So, she's small – about six pounds or so. Fit as a fiddle – and fierce. She was feral at first, but good care, a nice warm lap, and tons of understanding calmed some of that wildness in her. She and I have become really close. She would accompany me every day to my massage practice and curl up under the table and sleep. It was so cute. For some clients, she would wake up and get her allotted pets and head rubs. But for other clients she would just stare at them and pretend that they weren't there. Only once were her instincts better than mine. One client, a man, turned out to be a creep and tried to get inappropriate. Out of nowhere Chloe jumped onto his chest and as he lifted his hand to fight her off, her claws flashed and he was left bleeding. The man leapt up, threw Chloe to the ground, grabbed the sheet around him, snatched his clothes and fled. Never heard from him again. I don't think he liked cats. Thankfully, Chloe wasn't hurt and because of her, the creepy guy didn't hurt me either. We've been together every day since."

Mabel's smile deepened and her eyes grew thoughtful and wise. "Sounds to me like you have found a true friend and Chloe has found one in you."

Mabel's words touched something in me, that spot of warmth and home that I hadn't felt in a long time. Tears stung my eyes as I smiled back at her. "Yes, I think you're right. Chloe and I are family and friends in the truest sense of the word. Thank you for showing me that."

Mabel stood up from her chair and started busying herself in the kitchen by taking the plate empty of scones and tea pot to the sink to rinse. Drying her hands on her apron, she turned and said, "Well, let's find you and Chloe a room with a view. I bet you are tired after your trip and Chloe is starting to snore."

I gently picked up Chloe in the still warm towels ignoring the black hair clinging to the fresh laundry and followed Mabel up the stairs to the second floor. At the top of the stairs, Mabel turned and opened a door to the right. Through sleepy, half closed eyes I saw a huge room filled with dusty rose curtains and comforter trimmed in antique ivory lace. The room was situated over the front northwest corner of the house and had a round turret with a huge picture window filled with blankets and pillows. Even through tired eyes, I knew that Chloe would be basking in the warmth of the sun on those pillows come morning. Chloe is never one to miss an opportunity to soak up a sunbeam or two. I noticed a small white porcelain bathroom with dark mauve accents. The rest of the room could wait until I could see straight with a mind that actually fired on all thrusters. I made a move to go downstairs and grab our bags from the car when Mabel stopped me.

"You attend to your wee kitten and I'll see to your things in the car. Welcome to the Rose Suite. Take comfort in knowing you are safe and will be well taken care of. Now, off with you – to bed and to sleep!" And with that, Mabel marched out the door with the sound of her footsteps creaking on the wooden steps as she went downstairs. I placed Chloe on the pillow next to mine on the beautiful queen sized bed and hastily ran into the bathroom. I emerged from the bathroom a short time later to find our bags by the bed and Chloe's litter box in one discreet corner and her bowls of water and food in the opposite corner on a small braided rug. I quickly grabbed my bag, rummaged for an old T-shirt and shed my day's clothes as I did my cares of the world. Smiling and climbing into the heavenly bed, I gently kissed Chloe goodnight as her snoring deepened. I was in Comfort and I was in comfort. And with that, I slept the best sleep I'd had in over a year.

CHAPTER 3

I awoke sometime in the early morning to hear the all too familiar scratching of paws on kitty litter. I'm glad Chloe found her bathroom facilities to her liking. I listened to her digging and then silence waiting because I knew what was next, the lapping of water, the crunching of kitty food, then sun bathing. Drifting back to sleep, I awoke some hours later by a gentle tapping on the door. Calling in a husky voiced "hello" a smiling Mabel walked into the room like a general back from battle.

"Hope you and Chloe had a good night's sleep. I can see she likes the place already," Mabel said as she eyed the few stray pieces of kitty litter that found their way to the floor, the half empty bowl of food and the water dish with one pink fuzzy mouse floating in it. "I take it Chloe would like a fresh water bowl." And with that Mabel marched the bowl off to the bathroom to refresh her water and returned drying the fuzzy pink mouse on her apron.

"Okay, I see I'm the last one up and yes, I'll be paying extra for the kitty litter. But, most importantly, what's happened? You look like an exploded firecracker!"

Mabel grimaced, "I love this old place, but the fixtures are getting to be as old as I am. So, this morning I did battle with the stove – again – and lost – again. I'm about to get my shotgun and put it out of my misery."

"Well, don't do that until I see if I can help. At least I can be a witness at the trial and I'll tell the judge and understanding jury how the stove started it…" I jumped out of bed ran to the bathroom while shouting, "Give me ten minutes and I'll be down to help with the stove." I quickly showered and changed into my usual outfit. I had found through the years that I have a pretty standard wardrobe that I wear. In my head, I call it my uniform: jeans, light or dark colored; denim skirts, long and short, and solid black or solid white T-shirts or tops. I added color in a jacket, zippered sweatshirt or sweater. And of course, the ever present pair of silly socks. One of the eccentricities of being a massage therapist is that clients only look at your feet. So, early on, I developed the habit of wearing silly socks with bright colored cats or other items on them. My clients loved it. So, today, I chose jeans, white T-shirt, lavender sweater and blue socks with steaming cups of coffee on them.

Dressed and well rested with Chloe fed and settled in her window seat, I strolled into the kitchen. It was even more cheery in the morning light if you didn't notice the black scorch marks on the off-white walls by the classic, old style stove. From my unprofessional stove opinion it looked pretty hopeless. And that also explained why Mabel was dusty and covered in soot, ash and grease.

"I hope you don't mind cold cereal, juice, toast and coffee.

I have a few bakery Danishes left over from yesterday. We'll call it even for the kitty litter and a drowned pink mouse."

"I'm glad you can still joke with a dead stove in your kitchen. Have you called the appliance coroner?"

"No, I called Bo, our local Mr. Fixit. If it's broke, he can fix it. But, oh dear, I think this is beyond even his doing. Now dear, don't trouble yourself, sit down and eat. There's little comfort worrying over a dead stove when there's food to be had."

"Speaking of comfort, what is a girl to do in Comfort? Do you have any recommendations?"

Mabel laughed. "My dear, you seem to be enjoying this town of ours – well at least the name. I think you should go out and explore the town. Give the town a chance to get to know you. Are you bringing Miss Chloe?"

"No, I thought I'd do the first adventure by myself and get the lay of the land. Translated into kitty terms that means see what she can get into, over, around and through. I'll take her out for her afternoon bug hunt later."

"Bug hunt?" Mabel gasped. "Never mind, some things are best left to the imagination. I'm sure there will be another good story to tell me later. Now eat! I need to decide what to fix for dinner – with a dead stove. EAT!" And with that, I sat down at the table now familiar from last night's stories and scones, and ate.

After breakfast, I headed upstairs to check on Chloe and take a better look at the room that we shared. From the open doorway, the room was filled in hues from pale pink to light mauve, with ivory and sunlight. The room was adorned with matching Queen Anne cherry wood bureau, vanity, and full-length mirror. The sumptuous and comfy bed was covered with a beautiful rose duvet trimmed in ivory lace that matched the curtains hanging on either side of an enormous picture window encased in the turret like Rapunzel's tower. The bathroom was small but functional with an antique claw footed tub with a shower, porcelain sink, toilet and plush mauve towels. A shower curtain printed in ivory with tiny rosebuds was tied back with a dark mauve braid with long tassels. In short, this place was heaven and comfortable. I spied a small closet and hastily hung up my clothes and stored Chloe's cat things. Before I left, I stood before the antique cherry wood mirror and looked at myself. My dark straight hair was cut to shoulder length and shined with a healthy glow. And my oval face and olive skin were offset by the white T-shirt. I stared at my eyes and still thought they were my best feature – dark brown to the point of black with long curly eyelashes. I smiled at my most prominent feature with the memory of my mother claiming my chest came from her side of the family. I was just less than five foot six and had a good size ten body. A love for good food assured me that I would not be a size four - ever. But at my age, comes the growing of wisdom and self-acceptance. I took one last look at Chloe curled up on the window seat amongst plush rose pillows cast in sunlight, grabbed my small purse and room key and headed for the kitchen door.

Out in the morning sunshine, I took a few moments to stretch my arms over my head and work out the kinks in my neck from sleeping on a new, but glorious pillow. Looking around the town and I marveled at the thought and planning that must have gone into it. The five lanes of houses were chiseled and tiered from the beach up to the hill above where I was sure the highway was. The houses on each street were fairly small bungalows or beach cottages. Some of the houses on Mabel's street matched her Victorian flavor with each house having its own color scheme – as if one neighbor tried to outdo the other. There wasn't a car or garage in plain sight. I spied a few golf carts and giggled thinking of zipping around the town in one of those. Pretty clever.

From Mabel's side door, I discovered a gravel walking path down to the water. There was no beach to speak of, mostly rocks that jutted out from the surf. I strolled to the concrete barrier and stared out at the open ocean breathing in the warm salt air. I was glad that I chose to wear jeans. The sea air and salty spray added a slight chill to the early spring day. But it was glorious. The sun warmed my face and felt good to my soul. I paused long enough to appreciate the wide expanse and view of the ocean and the crashing waves. The wind turned the water from blue to green to frothy white. The knot in my chest began to loosen with each breath and crash of wave. Standing in front of something so vast made my problems melt away.

Turning my face toward the morning sun, I stopped dead in my tracks to stare at the massive structure before me. It was as if some old trading ship or exploration vessel had crashed on the rocky beach and left the enormous stern and part of the hull jutting out from the embankment from the beach. The rear of the ship was positioned a bit cockeyed to true and gave the feeling of drama, peril and bravery. The wide expanse curved and made a perfect focal point with its wooden planks acting as a natural barrier for a good ten feet in front of me. A large park bench was positioned just right to sit and stare at the ocean. In the middle of the stern's planks, was anchored a weathered bronze plaque which stated:

WELCOME TO COMFORT POINT
If you are searching for Comfort, may you find it.
If you find comfort, may you keep it.
If you keep comfort in your heart, you will know peace.
10 June 1774 – The Founders of Comfort

I stood for a long time staring at the words and thought about the founders who claimed this piece of land not just for their homes and livelihoods, but for others who were trying to find their way. I fantasized about the crew and what their lives had been like. Had they survived, how had they lived, were their relatives still presiding in Comfort and what became of the rest of the boat? What a remarkable place, I thought, and felt privileged that Chloe and I were here in this sacred place as if I had stumbled across holy ground. I made a vow to visit this place many more times while staying here and turned to continue on my journey wondering what life would have been like those many years ago, who might have crashed their ship here and what had happened to them.

From the Point, I walked by another set of park benches made of iron that flanked a path leading down to the rocky beach passing by an old shack with a fishnet hanging from its roof and a tacky hand painted sign on the side of the building that said "Sharkey's Bar" with an arrow pointing ahead. I proceeded to the main street section of the little town. Set on what was once a long pier; the shops lined both sides ending at the edge of the pier jutting out into the ocean. Preferring a systematic approach when discovering a new place, I began on the right side of the pier noting that the shops were all connected in one long strip. Each storefront was a little different with pots of flowers, hanging baskets, and various paint and accent colors, all with Victorian touches. Most shops appeared to be two stories with quaint windows on the second floor, probably for decoration, I thought. It made me feel I was in a storybook of a long ago fishing tale.

The first shop was called Comfort Mercantile. Entering through the door was like stepping into an assault of the senses. The place felt bigger than its actual size with its shelves bursting at the seams and jam-packed full of food, grocery staples, paper products, fertilizer, hardware, and a row of toys. A person could buy a gallon of milk, a hammer and a Barbie doll all at the same time. Walking up and down the aisles, I felt completely overwhelmed by the sheer volume of goods. Making my way to the front door, I noticed a Mom and Pop sitting behind the register. Pop looked like he could have been the Gipper's younger brother: salt and pepper hair, good looks, and intelligent dark brown eyes. Mom was sitting behind him absorbed in the book *Zen and the Art of Motorcycle Maintenance.* I smiled at them and mentioned what an eye-popping store they had and the sheer volume of products. Pop just smiled and said, "To me the shop looks a little bare; we're out of a few things. Come back in a week when the new shipment comes in." I didn't realize he was pulling my leg until he winked. Pop introduced himself as "Charley and this is my wife Dotty." Dotty didn't even look up. She just licked her finger and turned the page in her book. I wished them a wonderful day and promised to come back.

Continuing along the right side, I passed Comfort Flowers, which was awash in a dizzying assortment of colors in flowers, plants and shrubs. Comfort Tourist Trappings made me laugh out loud at the name and gasp in delight at the tourist and artsy gifts and knickknacks. I stopped short when I came to a door with a giant nut and bolt hanging over it. Peering through the glass, I noticed a rather cluttered office with various machine parts, carpenter tools, and bins holding every type of nail and bolt imaginable. I tried the door, which turned out to be locked. Only then did I notice the small hand-written note in front of my nose that said, "Gone to Mabel's. Catch me later. Bo." Ah, the Mr. Fixit who should be healing Mabel's stove. I guess I'll meet him later.

The last shop at the end of the pier was named Reinhold

Gallery. This one looked like a one-man show with an obsession. Every single picture, from watercolor, oil, and pencil drawings was of a lighthouse. The same lighthouse! Painted and colored from every possible side, angle, season, and weather. Obviously, the person had a thing for this lighthouse. Funny, I didn't remember seeing a lighthouse. That door was also locked, so I crossed the pier passing another pair of iron benches and stared out at the water. It was beautiful - the sun, the sea, the salty air and the sea gulls calling to each other sounding like laughter. The last few knots in my soul started to loosen. I smiled and headed across the pier to discover the shops on the left side. A Cuppa Comfort sign was artistically painted on a big picture window in bright flaming red. I opened the door and was blasted with smells both exotic and spicy. The deep rich smell of coffee floated though the shop mixed with the soft, subtle smells of tea leaves. Lining the entire left wall were shelves of coffees and teas. Looking at the labels on the coffee, I noticed not one was from a national chain. These weren't just generic coffees; these were works of art and labors of love. The teas were the same. I hadn't heard of any of them. A person could drink a different cup of tea and a different cup of coffee every day and not repeat any for a year, at least. I turned from the shelves and saw red. Mounds and layers of curly red hair tied back with a bright purple scarf. "WOW!" I said out loud without bothering to use my inside voice. The bright green eyes sparkled back at me and only then did I realize that this fiery mound of hair was attached to the most beautiful plus sized person I had ever seen. Though her figure and face were round and fleshy, her skin was alabaster smooth and flawless. Not from scalpels and plastic, but from good genes and attention to the finer things. She was dressed in stunning bright purple velour pants with matching oversized shirt. I smiled and held back a laugh in spite of myself.

"Hi there! Sorry to scare you, but I'm usually not hard to miss. Can I get you something?"

"Hi to you, too. It's a testament to your shop that I was so overwhelmed by the aromas and choices, that I failed to notice someone as, um, well, as striking as you. I'm Katy by the way."

"Welcome, Katy. Glad you like my shop. I'm Cherry. Cherry Kukla."

"Good God! Did your parents actually name you that, or did you get to pick that yourself?"

"Well, both. I was named Cherry because believe it or not, this mound of red hair is real and magnificent, if I do say so myself. But I changed my last name when I turned sixteen and ran away from the last foster home where I was placed. The only good thing about my childhood and the different foster homes and orphanages I lived was watching Kukla, Fran and Ollie reruns. So, I changed my name and became the person I was meant to be. Now, what can I get you?" Cherry asked as her dazzling green eyes studied me.

"Surprise me. With so many choices, I'll never decide, so you choose your favorite – if you will have one yourself and join me." With a sly smile, I teasingly added, "And please tell me you don't have a sister named Fran and a brother named Ollie."

"Nope, parakeets."

"I beg your pardon?"

"I named my two parakeets Fran and Ollie." Her green eyes twinkled even brighter.

"I see, well, it's nice to know that quality children's programming can make a difference in a child's life. I'm glad your name is Kukla and not Elmo!"

Cherry laughed and turned to prepare our tea. She went

about the tea making process like a high priestess preparing for a ritual. We took our tea at one of the tables next to the full-length picture window facing toward the ocean. We sipped in silence.

After a few minutes, Cherry asked, "So, what brings you to town? Vacation? Business? Sight-seeing?"

"I guess I would say vacation mixed with sightseeing. Chloe and I needed to get away from our life for awhile. So we hopped on a plane, rented a car and started driving." I decided to keep Cherry in the dark about the whole lotto story.

"All right, but who's Chloe? Did you leave her at the Mercantile? People do, you know. A kid can hang out there all day and not get bored. And old Charley has enough war and weapon stories to even keep the older kids entertained. There's a rumor that he was a Navy Seal or something and that he and Dotty met while doing a covert operation in some Middle Eastern country. Dotty is a former CIA spy, you know."

"You have got to be kidding me!"

"Nope, this town is full of interesting people. I just think Charley and Dotty are two that you wouldn't expect to be that interesting. So, back to my question…Chloe?"

"Chloe is my cat."

"Excuse me?"

"My little black cat. She travels with me and is my constant companion."

"Well, did you leave her at the Mercantile or is she outside?"

"No, she's back at the Blue Heron investigating her new surroundings. I figured I would get the lay of the land first. You know - make sure the town is cat friendly and that there aren't too many things she can get into."

"Good Lord, don't tell me you walk your cat?"

"Why, yes? It's more of a drag, really… is there a problem?"

Cherry leaned back in her chair and laughed. It started as a small peal of thunder and turned into a rumble followed by an all out storm of the giggles. It passed when Cherry finished drying her eyes, blowing her nose, and taking deep breaths.

"My, my, my, my, my – thank you – I needed that. You have to promise to bring Chloe in here. She's more than welcome and I've just got to see this for myself. Black cat you say? Are you a witch or just a fellow animal lover?"

"Well, I've been called a witch, but I don't think that's what you mean. No, just a cat lover who had a black cat choose her. And you and your parakeets?"

"Oh, Fran and Ollie were abandoned and I rescued them. Story of my life, I was abandoned and rescued through the years and now I do that for birds. They seem drawn to me. I've rescued seagulls, owls, and any number of God's feathered creatures. I hope Chloe doesn't mind that I prefer feather to fur."

"Oh, Chloe is conscientious and understanding. And I will make sure she leaves your feathered friends alone. She prefers bugs anyways."

"EW, enough said! I look forward to meeting the bug-hunting black beast." And with that Cherry stood up, gathered the tea things and bustled back to the counter. She hurried off to help a young couple that had walked in unnoticed. I stood up, waved good-bye leaving several dollars on the table and headed out into the sunshine to finish my exploration.

CHAPTER 4

The shop next door was a bookstore filled to brimming with books, magazines and newspapers. Knowing that I would be in there for days, I strolled past and window-shopped at the next two. Suds and Wicks was a store full of hand crafted soaps and candles. Making a mental note, I vowed to stop by another day and buy some candles for Mabel to say thank you for her attention to Chloe and me. Quilting Comforts was full of quilts, comforters, kits and do-it-yourself projects for the crafty and coordinated, of which I did not consider myself one. I would return here as well and purchase something for Holly who could sew and tackle any of these projects like a pro.

I stopped short at the next window, which was blackened and sooty, with the entire storefront crossed with yellow "Do Not Enter" caution tape. The shop looked like a sad lump of charcoal all burnt and spent. I stared at the sad shell of the former shop.

"Sure is a pity – isn't it?" I spun around and came face to face with the most feminine face I had ever seen on a six-foot hunk of manhood. From the neck down was your average toned runner's body, but attached at the neck was the face that could launch a thousand ships, just as long as the ships had non-masculine names. And the soft, gentle gray eyes and stark blond hair gave added emphasis to the man's beauty. The suit was impeccable light gray linen woven in such a way as to give the appearance that he was covered in fairy dust. The man glowed and sparkled in the sunshine. His shoes were old style black and white wing tips buffed in a glossy polish. And his tie was truly flaming – red. He would never be someone to miss. I figured I had just met Comfort's one man attraction.

"Sorry to disturb, noticed you staring. I'm Gavin Davis, our local gay realtor."

"Pleased to meet you. I'm Katy Hawkins, visiting tourist. Are you gay as in happy or as in not straight?" I asked, noticing that Gavin lisped and hissed like a slow leaking steam engine.

Gavin squealed a giggle and said "I guess both, I'm happy to meet you and I'm so not straight. Does it bother you?"

"Does what?" I asked. Inwardly I was starting to get annoyed by his speech pattern. He sounded like a syncopated slow leak.

"My being gay."

"No, does it bother you?"

"No, I just don't like to upset people. Especially ones I just met."

"Well, I'm not upset, just curious. What happened to this shop? It looks like my mother's pot roast."

"Well, it was torched by person or persons unknown. Case never solved. Sad, too! The girl who owned the place was torched along with it."

"Why would someone do this in a lovely town like this one?"

"Why does anyone do anything? Passion. Someone had a reason for doing it. Only way to live, passion. Well, lovely meeting you, tah-tah, I'm off to a deliciously splendid lunch." And with that, Gavin sashayed off with a walk my mother would have called "with a swing on her back door." But in this case she was a he. Nice to know I got to meet the town's "character" who seemed quite harmless even with his slow leak.

I continued on to the next shop, which turned out to be Gavin's Comfort Properties. A glossy photo of his cherubic face hung on the door next to pictures and details of places for rent, lease and sale. I hurried past Gavin's office with my head down and turned the corner to the right and looked up to see a smaller Victorian cottage with grunts, barks, yips and meows exiting the open door. The full cages were visible from the oversized storefront window. The lively painted sign read Creature Comforts. Right below was written "Everything for Every pet." One glance told me they weren't kidding. Furs and feathers and even a few scaly creatures could be seen, as well as every pet accessory known to man or beast. I smiled and wondered if Cherry was the owner or just a helper and vowed to ask her when Chloe and I returned for a visit to see what was new in their feline department. A few steps past, a round Colonial looking building came into full view. It looked part church, part Masonic Temple, and part Jefferson's Library. Comfort Bank and Trust said the stately sign. I grinned at the building, which was so different from the others. Retracing my steps back to Mabel's and passing Creature Comforts again, I made a beeline for the pier when I noticed I had completely overlooked the corner store. Comfort Food, situated between

Gavin's and Creature Comforts and divided by a small alleyway, turned out to be a smelly, spicy deli with enough cheese, meats and breads to feed most of Denver. With my nose full of delectable smells, I decided to see if Mabel was ready for lunch.

Hurrying back to the Blue Heron, I passed a small house with a ramp leading to the front door. Attached to the house was a large three bay garage filled with bicycles. Not one to exercise on wheels, I had no idea what type of bikes I was looking at except there were many – twenty at least – what looked like brand new to well used. A tall, pale-haired, light-skinned man with thick glasses bent over a bike, wrench in hand, and was oblivious to me watching. He seemed intent on his business, so I did not interrupt. I hurried back to Mabel to see if her stove had been revived or shot and to see what trouble Chloe had gotten into.

Arriving back at the Blue Heron and entering the kitchen, I spied a long, muscled pair of legs wrapped in denim jeans stuck between the stove and the wall. Nice legs, I thought to myself smiling. Mabel was hovering near the stove with an anxious look on her wrinkled face. Then I noticed Chloe. She was quietly attending to the shoelaces that were attached to the nice legs. She had the left boot untied and was alternately chewing and pulling on the right one. The poor legs had no clue.

"Hi Mabel, how's things? Is the stove still dead?" I asked, trying not to look at Chloe's mischief.

"Hi Katy, the goose is officially cooked I'm afraid. Bo here seems to think we should just push it into the ocean and start a new coral bed. Oh, by the way, this is Bo, our local Mr. Fixit. Bo, this is Katy my guest for the next few days, I hope."

A grease stained hand waved from behind the stove and a pleasant deep voice said, "Pleased to meet you."

I smiled inwardly and thought what a nice voice to go

with the nice legs. I motioned to Mabel to get her attention. I then pointed to Chloe who had successfully untied the other shoelace and was happily chewing away at the tips. I raised my hands and my eyebrows as if to ask, "How did Chloe get downstairs and why are you condoning such behavior?"

Mabel smiled and said, "Chloe was making chirping noises shortly after you left. It seems she did not want to be by herself all day. So, I let her out and she's been my company ever since. We've eaten, chased a wad of paper, chewed a hole in my good apron, supervised Bo's work with the stove and now it seems she has found a new form of amusement." At that moment, Chloe decided it was time to see what was inside Bo's pant leg.

"Yikes!"

"Merp!'

CRASH!

"Sorry!" I yelled as I made a grab for Chloe, whose whole body was disappearing up his pant leg. I tugged at her back feet praying that Bo had major medical. I gently pulled at Chloe's lower body and prayed that she wouldn't claw Bo to death with her nails. I wiggled, pulled, and finally succeeded in pulling her out squirming and fussing.

"I'm so sorry, did Chloe bite you?" I asked. "Are you hurt? I don't see any blood!"

"Um, no. No nails, just a tongue. She licked me. I guess she likes my soap. Sorry I yelped, just wasn't expecting it, that's all. No harm done."

"Oh, Lord. I'm so sorry. Chloe has been under a strain lately, she normally doesn't get this close to strangers," I babbled.

"Does she usually run up a guy's pants after she's met them?" Bo asked.

"God, no! This is a first, for her and me. Sorry about your socks. Looks like her claws hooked on them – they're snagged."

"Still, no harm done." Still wedged in behind the stove, Bo asked, "Chloe okay?"

"Not when I get through with her. She's going into time out!" I said.

"Don't be too hard on her. I bet she was just being friendly," Bo said as chuckling came out from behind the stove. I suddenly heard my mother's voice inside my head. "You always make an impression on people, Katy my dear, not always a good one, but at least a first one!" She said this more times than I could count over the years. Totally embarrassed and confused by Chloe's sudden interest in Bo's jeans, I scooped her up and headed upstairs to our room.

The instant our door was closed, I placed Chloe on the floor. She scampered over to the window seat and jumped up. Looking over her shoulder at me, she lifted her leg and proceeded to give her private parts a bath.

"Now look, you black fuzzy varmint, we are guests here and it is not nice to crawl up people's pant leg that we don't know and lick them – no matter how nice and well-formed their legs are. And since when did you start licking people you've only just met? Don't you have manners? Haven't I taught you anything?"

Chloe replied by pausing in mid lick to look at me and say, "Merp."

"Okay, so you thought he was nice and you liked his shoelace, which still does not explain things. You licked him? You've never done that before… what, do you like him or does he smell like roasted chicken? A tasty smell may not be a good basis to build a friendship on."

Chloe finished her bath and stretched her little body rolling over on her back to show me her tummy. That has always been her way of saying, "I'm cute and I got my way." Then she said,

"Merp."

"Just what I figured, you're high on shoelace endorphins. Fine, but just know that your reputation could be mud in a small town like this. Bo will be telling everyone about the Black Claws of Death. And what does he think of me, I ask you? Thanks to you I'm pegged as the Crazy Cat Lady."

"Merp."

"I accept your apology, but you are not getting out of this room for the rest of the day, if I can help it," I scolded.

"Me-yowl."

"Yes, he did seem nice, Chloe. Not that I will ever know, now. So, do you want to hear about my day or not?"

"I would love to, if you can spare a few minutes," Mabel said from the doorway.

"Yipes! I didn't hear the door open! How long have you been standing there?" I asked.

"Long enough to hear you and Chloe discussing legs, licking, and not trusting a yummy smelling book by its cover. It's okay. Bo is a nice man, likes animals and got a kick out of Chloe helping him. So, like he said, no harm done. Now tell me about your adventure."

Mabel sat down in the matching chair next to the closet and I told her my tale while mentally thinking that I would have liked to have spent more time with Bo. I mentioned all the nice people I had met and about Gavin, the hissing realtor. I asked Mabel if she knew what happened to the girl from the burnt art gallery. Mabel sat still for a moment and looked deeply into the fireplace. She finally sighed and said, "Well, that's not a good story to tell, how about it we save it for later. I'm starving, the stove is dead, and I need to figure out how to feed you. How about if I treat us to a lovely lunch at the Deli and I'll tell you the story then? I'll need food and cheesecake to get through it."

"Deal!" I said. "How about if I get cleaned up a bit and I'll meet you downstairs in fifteen minutes?"

"Deal! I'll tell Bo to take that blasted stove out of my sight and I'll see about how to go about getting a new one. Meet you in the kitchen in a bit." And with that, Mabel marched from the room with a stern gaze looking like someone ready to do battle with a major appliance.

I quietly shut the door, grabbed my cell phone off the dresser and placed a call, smiling as I thought of the sneakiness I was about to do.

Holly answered on the third ring sounding breathless and flustered.

"Hello, Holly, guess who? Your favorite client is calling and needs your assistance."

"Katy! Good heavens, you aren't hurt or anything are you? Is Chloe injured, does she need special food, is she eating, drinking and pooping? Talk to me, woman!" Good ol' Holly knows what's important in life.

"I'm fine, Chloe is fine except she just crawled up a guy's pants leg and licked him."

"Lucky girl, I wish I could. Whose pant leg?

"Mr. Fixit. A guy named Bo who is helping to fix a stove that is dead."

"Whose stove?"

"Mabel's."

"Who's Mabel? Wait, why don't you start from the time you left and bring me up to speed. I feel like Abbott and you do not look like Costello. So let's hear it!"

I brought Holly up to date on my Comfort adventure including the town, Mabel, the shop owners I had met, and the nice pair of legs Chloe seemed to enjoy. Holly laughed and hummed sounding pleased with my tale.

"So, you seem to have found a place to discover. Are you thinking of staying awhile?"

"Jeez, Holly, I only just got here. But there is something about this place – small town, nice people, the quiet, the ocean, and Mabel. She reminds me of my mom mixed with Yoda and Italian spices. She's why I'm calling."

"What's wrong with Mabel?"

"She has a dead stove. From what I can tell, it's older than the both of us and had gone home to Jesus. Well, I… um… had a thought. I was wondering… um… if you could… um…"

"Good Lord, Katy! I've known you since you were four and you've never had a stammer in your life. No need to start now. Now out with it!"

"I want to buy Mabel a new stove. A nice one – professional quality one, complete with all the bells and whistles. And I need it now." I said. And waited. And waited. "Hello? Holly? Are you still there?"

A long sigh reached through the phone and into my ear. "Katy? What are you doing, I mean really? You can't just buy people things. They get uncomfortable. They get suspicious. For Heaven's sake, you only just met her?"

"Why can't I buy her a stove?" I wailed. "I have enough money to buy a stove for every house in America and most of Italy, why can't I? Why can't I do something good for someone? Why does a good deed have to be punished?" I was warming up to my cause. "I worked for years to get where I am, Lotto notwithstanding. Who says the world has to be that way? Why can't I help others who just need a little help? You know, that whole give a person a fish, they eat for a day…"

"Buy a woman a stove and she can cook for a village…" Holly interrupted.

"Exactly! Who says I can't be charitable to people and not

just to causes. I know what it's like to have to worry about money and how to pay the rent when it's overdue. Remember? So, I see the struggle in Mabel, so what? If I can help a bit, why not? Besides, it's a tax write-off and… and… and…I want to!" I had spoken!

"Are you through?" Holly asked in a quiet motherly voice.

"Yes," I said in my best "sorry, Mom" voice.

"Now that you've gotten that out of your system, I have a few questions. Are you ready to listen without making my other ear go deaf?"

"Yes, Holly."

"One, gas or electric? Two, how many burners do you want? Three, one oven or two or a convection oven and a warmer. Four, color or stainless steel? Five, any other requests and how soon do you seriously need it?" Holly stopped speaking, but I could feel her through the phone lines. A mixture of frustrated pride and practical caring, a dangerously good mix.

"Well, I don't have the answers right now, but I'm taking Mabel to lunch and I'll have all your questions answered by this afternoon. So, you'll do this for me? Find the perfect stove and have it shipped here as soon as possible?"

"I never said I wouldn't. You never gave me the opportunity. I will tell you that money, especially lots of money, changes people. Remember Katy, you can't buy friends or a new life. Know what your intentions are and never act out of pity. Yes, I remember your struggles and the dark times you went through. I was there, remember? So, let's call this new habit of yours, random acts of kindness. And I see I have no other choice but to get involved and join in on the fun. Those are my terms – do you accept them?"

"Yes, Holly."

"And one more thing, this is going to cost you."

"Jeez, Holly, you already have access to my hoard of millions, what more do you want?"

"A cat."

"Excuse me?"

"A cat. No, make that two. You have to find homes for two cats. I will not put up with yelling and whining from a friend and I will certainly not put up with it from a client. You are both, so two cats. Those are my terms? Agreed?" Holly had won and she knew it.

"Agreed. I'll call you later with the information and you can tell me about your latest adoptables. I had a feeling you'd been busy. Talk to you later, and Holly, I'm sorry for yelling. I just really want to do this!"

"You're forgiven and Hemingway and Xavier will be so grateful."

"Hemingway and Xavier? Let me see...one large white longhaired cat with six toes and one cream colored tabby that you found at the Mexican restaurant by your house. Am I close?"

"How do you do that? And, for the record, I did not find him; the cook at Tres Amigos found him and called me. Call me later. I'll start researching stoves." And with her final word, Holly hung up.

CHAPTER 5

Reaching for my purse and keys, I spied Chloe stretching up on her back feet with her little paws braced against the picture window. She was pawing at something. I rushed over and gasped at the sight. To the right, high up on a jagged cliff, was a lighthouse. Well of course, I thought to myself. All the pictures I had seen at the Art Gallery this afternoon. I knew there had to be a lighthouse around here somewhere. Just not out my front window. I stared at the lighthouse, which seemed to be carved in the crags and cliffs jutting out into the ocean. The tower stood straight as a soldier in dress whites with a spectacular red roof beacon at the top. On the side of the tower away from the rocky edge stood the box shaped house with whitewashed boards that had grown old and dirty from time and the sea. I wondered if the beacon still worked and who owned it. I would definitely have to ask Mabel at lunch.

I was just turning away when Chloe chirped. I glanced back just in time to see a white figure pass on the stairway circling the beacon of the lighthouse. I blinked once and it was gone. Surely nobody lives there. It must have been a reflection of light. Chloe had lost interest, jumped down and went to her bowl of food. I guess she didn't see anything either.

I met Mabel in the kitchen where the stove carcass was being readied for the appliance butcher. Mabel shook her head sadly as we left and headed towards the pier. The Deli was small, but appeared well run. The booths to the left of the door were clean, well-maintained and bright red. I gathered that a few of the locals were eating there by the genuine smiles and waves they gave Mabel and the cautious and curious glances they gave me. The bright Formica tables were steel and spotless on a black and white checkered floor resembling a chess board. The aroma of an old world butcher shop with meats, cheeses, pickles and other smells filled the air and was intoxicating. Mabel and I settled ourselves in a booth by the window, ordered ice teas and got down to business.

"So, Mabel, what are you going to do about a new stove? Any ideas?" I asked somewhat innocently.

"I guess I'll see how my rainy day account is at the bank. It may be sunny out today, but it's pouring in my kitchen. So, I'll talk with my banker first thing tomorrow."

Mabel and I chatted longer about her stove plight and I was able to ask all of Holly's questions plus a few of my own. We both ordered the Deli's soup and salad combo and got busy slurping fresh clam chowder and crunching on a light Caesar salad. When we had finished and were waiting for the cheesecake Mabel insisted we had to try, I cautiously brought up the art gallery.

"I'll trade you one slice of cheesecake for a tale about a

burnt art studio?" I said.

"Ha!" Mabel snorted. "I wondered when you'd get back to that. You are as tenacious as your cat!"

"Well, I am curious. This seems like such a lovely peaceful town that it just doesn't make sense. What happened?"

"Well, to tell the story completely I have to start at the beginning, many years ago." Mabel took a sip of her tea, leaned back in the booth and cleared her throat. "As you may have noticed, we have a lighthouse," Mabel smiled as I nodded. "It's been here for over ninety years and has been passed down from sea captain, to boat owner, to recluse actor to, most recently, Comfort native, James Reinhold. James grew up in a foster home in Uptown. While there, he studied art and went off to some college to refine his techniques. He came back two years ago with a wife and a reputation as a fine and upstanding West Coast artist. His passion is the ocean and his obsession is that lighthouse. He bought it for too much money and planted himself and his new wife there. At about the same time, Megan Harris came to town and started working at the Deli. Now Megan was a tall, willowy girl who moved like reeds in the wind. Megan used to spend her time off painting – watercolors, sketching, you name it and she could do it. Oh my, she was good. A natural talent, they said. Of course James took notice of her and proceeded to mentor her. Think Eliza meets Professor Henry Higgins. James' wife, Anna, was a small rather frail creature, like some fragile bird, and did not like living in Comfort. She did not take comfort in the sea air, the gulls, the wind and surf. Rumors started to swirl around that she took no comfort in James and Megan's friendship. So, as time went on, she became more of a recluse and rarely left the lighthouse. The more James mentored Megan, the more fragile Anna became until Anna virtually disappeared. And that's when the fires started."

"Fires? What do you mean fires?" I gasped.

"Now just wait, I'm coming to that. It started as just small stuff. A trash can one time, a wooden park bench the next. We have iron ones now. Never saw who did it, never anything too serious. Until the night someone tried to set the pier on fire. Did a lousy job, too, mostly just smoke and mess. Still, no one ever saw the person. The next night, I was outside hanging laundry on the line and happened to glance over at the parking lot where you left your car – remember?" I nodded. "And there in the moonlight close to Comfort Point was James and Megan embracing. Well, it was enough to make my blood run cold. He's old enough to be her father and her appearing so young, innocent and pretty. I loudly cleared my throat to let them know they'd been seen. Well, they hugged again, turned and went their separate ways. Well, I went back to my laundry and then inside. Know something? After the lighthouse fire, the night Megan died, I was out one evening just admiring the night and out of the corner of my eye I saw a mist. Fog really. Drifting over the spot where the two had stood. It seemed to hover there and then move down toward the pier and pause in front of Megan's studio. I shook my head, looked again, and it disappeared – like it was never there. Strangest thing I ever saw. Never told a soul about it. Can't for the life of me think what it could have been. Just… oh, I don't know… interesting."

"The lighthouse caught fire? I'm confused. I thought it was made of brick? Or so it looks from here."

"Oh it is. The tower is brick and stands about 60 feet tall with a somewhat functional beacon. We only use it for emergencies. It casts a light twenty or so miles out to sea. But, the house attached is made of old wooden planks taken from the old sea vessel – The Adventure. The house has old dried out wood paneling, floors and doors. A right tinderbox, if you see what I mean. So it started smoking, the firemen were called and it was all hands trying to save the thing. So, everyone was out there in the dark and smoke holding hoses and praying James and Anna were safe. So, no one notices until much later that Megan's art studio out on the pier was on fire. By the time the flames were noticed and another fire truck was sent, the entire studio was gone. Thank God for those fire walls between stores or that whole side of the pier could have been gone. It wasn't until morning that the news came about who had died."

"You mean that Megan was in the studio when the fire was started?" I asked.

"Yes, she was found, or what was left of her, on the floor near the door burnt to a crisp. And the strangest thing was that Anna's wedding ring was found there as well. So, off the police, firemen and men folk went back to the lighthouse. And there was James covered in ashes and soot, soaking wet, sobbing and wandering aimlessly about the place. Kept saying that Anna was burning and that he had to put her fires out. It was much later that the whole story came out. How Anna had started the fire that killed Megan and gutted her art studio. Anna had then rushed home and tried to set the lighthouse on fire. James tried to stop her and as the fire spread, Anna caught fire. In James moment of insanity, he had scooped up his burning bride and rushed her straight into the ocean. The tide stripped her from James' arms and the body was never recovered. James was treated for minor first and second degree burns, spent some time in a health center and a few months ago moved back to live in Comfort."

"What? A freshly burnt body gets dumped into the ocean with no explanation, no nothing? Isn't that a bit weird?" I gulped my tea and leaned forward on my seat.

"Oh yes. It was quite the scandal. Both the police and fire people investigated, ran tests, and found enough to say that burnt skin and bone fragments were found. So, we buried poor Megan in our Comfort Cemetery and James saved us all a scandalous trial by dumping his burning wife in the ocean. Anna must have gone crazy with jealousy and started setting fires until she got good enough to torch Megan's place. Why she set the lighthouse on fire, no one will ever know."

"And James? Surely he must have some answers. Or something?"

"Well, since the fire he has kept busy restoring the lighthouse. He won't let anyone inside until it's complete. But he works on it. He has become a model member of our small community. He spends most of his days in his art gallery selling his lighthouse paintings. I still think he's obsessed with that lighthouse, but then I'm no judge of art or talent. And no fires have been set since that fateful night."

Mabel leaned forward and whispered, "But I still wonder about the mist I saw. Was it a ghost? Was it Anna? Was it just some fog off the ocean? I've never told a soul about that. Couldn't bring myself to. Don't know why."

"What about the lighthouse? Is it still working? Is it finished? Has anyone been inside?"

"No. James has told folks that the repairs are almost complete, but says it will never be opened to the public again because of the tragedy that happened that night. Why it was almost a year ago now. About this time of year, come to think of it. My, how time flies."

Mabel and I sat in silence digesting the cheesecake and remarkable story. We left the deli and returned to the Blue Heron to face a kitchen without a stove and for me to make a phone call to my favorite financial planner and miracle maker.

Tilting my head, I caught what sounded like laughter floating on the breeze. I looked up to see Chloe chasing a misty cloud of white.

"How in the world…?" we said simultaneously. I ran ahead and made a diving catch for Chloe like a short stop chasing a grounder. Chloe squirmed but stayed in my arms.

"How on earth did Chloe get out?" Mabel asked beside me.

"I have no idea. Um, Mabel, did you by chance hear laughter?" I asked, not meeting her eyes.

"I most certainly did and I find this all rather too much. Hearing laughter, Chloe the escape artist out and about chasing a bit of fog, there are strange things happening here, Katy. And I can't make heads or tails of any of it."

"Well, I for one have had a long day. I'm beat. Let me escort you and Houdini here and see if we can find out how she got out." It took a few steps to realize that the side kitchen door was open ajar, but with no evidence of a cat or person to be had.

Mabel and I agreed to be more careful and I headed off to my room with a spooky feeling in my heart and a self-satisfied cat in my arms. We spent the rest of the day in my room playing Kitty soccer, Mousey, and Stringy. I think we wore each other out. I kept glancing at the lighthouse outside my window and thinking about the strange story Mabel told me, the laughter floating on the wind, and Chloe chasing a cloud of fog. I hoped for dreams that would be filled with black paws, laughter, and fresh scones, not ones filled with burnt wood, smoke, and ghostly wisps of white.

CHAPTER 6

The next morning I awoke with a plan of action and a means to go about it. That promptly flew out the window when the screaming started. I was out of bed (Chloe flew under it) and down the stairs before I realized I was wearing an extra large purple T-shirt, fuzzy pink socks, and red undies and nothing else. I raced into the kitchen, grabbed a frying pan and raced out the back door arms swinging. How I missed the delivery man I'll never know. I did smash his driver's side mirror and front head light though, before a pair of arms pulled me off the truck and spun me around.

"What in the world are you doing, Katy? Have you lost what's left of your mind as well as most of your clothes?" Mabel blared about two inches from my face.

"I heard screaming and came to rescue you!" I said, lamely.

"In your underwear?" Mabel asked while adjusting her

stance and gently letting go of my arms.

"Well, it sounded urgent. I didn't pause to grab clothes."

"But you did manage to grab my good skillet and carry out an unprovoked attack on a truck..."

"...Which I will be willing to pay for as long as no one sues me or takes pictures of me in my underwear."

"What if I want to take pictures of you in your underwear?" a deep voice asked.

I whirled around to see a round old man with overalls and a badge with the name Willy printed on it. "And how much are you willing to pay me for my truck? Geez lady, what did my truck ever do to you?" he asked.

"Look," I said, sensing I was about to go down with my ship, but not without a fight and some sense of perceived dignity. "I was sound asleep, heard screaming, got up and came down stairs to defend my innkeeper's honor."

"With my good skillet?" Mabel asked, starting to chuckle.

"Yes, I'll make good on the skillet, too. Now will somebody please tell me what is going on and why there was screaming and why I just gave this poor truck a good beating?" I asked, never wanting to get in the way of logical thinking.

"Well, it seems Willy is here to put in a new stove, one I did not order and one I know nothing about."

"What don't you know about a stove? I've tasted your scones and you seem to know a stove pretty well to my way of tasting," I said.

"Well, it's just that I haven't been to the bank yet, haven't pulled out my Rainy Day money and most certainly haven't ordered any stove. So, can you see why I was yelling," Mabel questioned as her eyes narrowed.

"Why would you yell about a stove?" I asked, not liking the direction this conversation was going.

"Because it's not mine!!!"

"Who says?"

Willy took this opportunity to step up and clear his throat and shuffle his feet. "Well, Miss Mabel, it says here on this here invoice that this here stove is to be delivered to a Miss Mabel Moretti at the Blue Heron and to deliver it at the most earliest of conveniences. Whatever that means. So here I am and here's your stove, so can I keep working? I mean I haven't had my breakfast yet."

Up until then I hadn't noticed that Mabel was in her bathrobe and slippers and that the day was just dawning. By the look on Mabel's face, that's not the only thing that was dawning.

"Miss Katy, may I see you for a moment while Willy attends to the new stove. A word if you please..." as Mabel walked a short distance from the Inn. I trailed after her feeling like a third grader caught ditching class.

"Well, Miss Katy? Do you have an explanation for this morning's unusual activity?"

"Like I said I heard screaming..."

Mabel interrupted, "Yes, I understand you heard me yelling my extreme pleasure and confusion. I DO NOT SCREAM. Imagine a woman my age doing something as silly as that." Mabel continued, drawing herself to her full five feet, "I am curious to know what your thoughts are and I would like to hear them, now!"

"Well, I think someone delivered you a stove and I think you might want to check the invoice to see who sent it. And then, I think we should both go inside to supervise Willy and get more sensible clothes on. I, for one, am not accustomed to parading around in my underwear." And with that, I turned and marched back to the Inn knowing I had dodged the issue for now, but was still under suspicion as if it was high treason on the bounty.

Hurrying into the kitchen, I continued upstairs, pausing to notice that the new stove was moving into place and that Willy and a familiar pair of jeans were putting the final touches on the placement and attachments to the new stove. Still like the legs, I thought as I ran up the stairs.

After showering, dressing in a simple denim skirt, white tank top, and clingy red sweater, I fed and watered Chloe who had decided to emerge from under the bed and greet the new day. Noticing her litter box was clean and level like a Zen sand painting, I vowed to pay Mabel even more than the rate we had already agreed to. So, I gave Chloe a quick hug and kiss and promised to take her for a walk later, providing she behaved herself.

I returned downstairs to find Mabel in a frenzy of new owner bliss. She trotted to and fro polishing one corner of the stainless steel stove and turning knobs, checking gadgets and all the while humming to herself while stroking her owner's manual. Willy and Bo's legs were nowhere in sight. I quietly approached the new stove owner.

"How are things? Have you solved the riddle of who sent it to you? Any clues?"

Mabel stopped humming long enough to give me a sharp glance over her bifocals, "I have every idea who sent this to me, but I just can't prove it."

"Well, who then and why can't you prove it?"

"Because the name on the invoice is some type of accounting firm, and the lovely lady I spoke with said that it was not an error and that all parties were satisfied if I was pleased with the stove. I told her I was. And she said, and I'll quote her here, ahem, 'then all that's left is to choose.'"

"Choose what?" I asked dreading the answer.

"A cat," Mabel said simply as she stood before me waiting for my confession.

"A what?"

"A cat. It seems I am the owner of this stove as long as I agree to become a foster home for a cat. Rather strange isn't it, that after all this time petless, I have a cat as a border and am now being told to foster a second?"

"That is rather odd. Only one cat did the lady say?" I asked wondering why Holly had told me two cats were the price of a new stove.

"Yes, just one. Is there anything you need to say to me?"

"Yes, just one thing. I'm hungry. When are you going to take out ol' Bessie the stove and see what she's got?" I would deal with Holly later and thought to avoid all other subjects entirely.

"Well, if that's how you are going to be, then I have no alternative but to a cook up a huge brunch for us and see what Bessie, the stove, can do. Leave me be and come back in an hour. Better yet, go to Cuppa and pick up some tea for us. I'm running low and think a new flavor is in order to celebrate this wonderful stove. And Katy?"

"Yes, Mabel?"

"I will find out what you are up to and why. But until then…" Mabel's eyes sparkled with tears of gratitude and words unsaid, "… please tell Chloe to keep her chirping to a minimum until I can get brunch made." With the final word, Mabel turned and began pulling food out of cupboards and pantry shelves.

I hurried off to the Cherry's Cuppa Comfort to tell her about Mabel's new stove. I figured Cherry was on the front line of the Comfort Gossip Chain and in no time the news would spread about the new addition to Mabel's kitchen. After purchasing a couple of exotic blends of tea, I paused outside James' Art Gallery to examine his works of art more closely. I stood staring at a myriad of water-colored lighthouses: some in stark sun, some in shade; some with cloudy, wind-tossed days and some with moonless nights. Each was a picture in composition, light, and shading with the same lighthouse as its sole subject. Truly the artist was a master of color, light and harmony. And a bit obsessed indeed, I thought. Returning to the Blue Heron, I found Mabel in a flurry of culinary chaos and activity. Leaving her the teas on the table, I headed back outside to formulate my plan of action - a visit to the lighthouse before brunch and to meet the owner and artist.

As I walked toward the parking lot, I paused to check on my rented car, which seemed like a life time ago. I reached the path that lead to the lighthouse and stopped. I pulled out my cell phone, dialed and waited for the familiar voice.

"Exponential Financial this is Holly. May I help you?"

"What do you mean one cat and not two? What happened?"

"Hemingway and Xavier have found homes with that nice new couple with the twin girls born a few years back. Remember? They started trust and college funds the day the girls came home from the hospital. I'm sure I mentioned them…"

"How did you manage to pawn off two cats on a family with twin girls?"

"Birthday presents. They turned two yesterday and I just had to give them something to enrich and educate their lives. A person is not complete without a cat and a 401K. You know that. Now, why are you calling? Has the stove arrived? Is your friend Mabel pleased? Have her call me when she wants me to send Taffeta."

"Taffeta, darling?"

"Yes, Taffeta, sweetheart. Mabel wanted an older cat, not a kitten, so I chose Taffeta for her. Don't you remember? Taffeta is the pewter colored show Persian that I rescued from that horrid woman whose house was in foreclosure. The one who had the nerve to think a show cat belonged in a crate in the basement without light or sunbeams to sleep in. It served her right when the IRS got a hold of her."

"Holly, how did the IRS... you didn't.... you wouldn't... that's cruel even by your standards. You didn't actually sic the IRS on that awful woman did you?"

"Well, I can't abide a person who has no respect for cats. And a Champion show cat at that. Best of show three years running... Do I have to tell you what that does to me???"

"Okay, Holly. I'm sure she deserved it. God help me if I ever get on your wrong side. You'll have me peeing in a cup and submitting to cavity searches..."

"Just as long as little Chloe is doing well. Has she licked anybody else today?"

"No, just the one leg that one time. She sure seemed to like his leg. Those legs fit mighty nice in his jeans I must say. Okay, thanks for the stove and Taffeta. I look forward to meeting her. And Holly thanks for your quick work. You did wonders."

"I know. But every cat deserves a good home."

"I meant about the stove for Mabel. Thank you for doing that..."

"Oh that. No problem. Your interest bearing accounts are doing nicely. No harm done. Enjoy the stove and Taffeta. Bye for now!" Holly the cat lady hung up. I shuddered to think what the world would be like if Holly was ever made Queen.

I proceeded past the parking lot, patted my rented Jaguar on its hood, and walked on the trail behind the parking lot that was etched in the crags of the rock face. The trail seemed pretty straightforward minus the incline and dirt. It seemed wide enough for a car going one way, but only just. I followed the path until it did an unexpected turn to avoid more rock and continued straight to the door of the lighthouse. I paused to catch my breath and to peer more closely at the lighthouse.

Having not been on any other coast than California, I can only describe this lighthouse as inspiring. The whitewashed house seemed grimy from the elements, textured by crashing waves, sea salt, and fire. The solid red door was flanked on either side by two large windows with waiting, empty red flower boxes. The lighthouse tower was tremendous with the beacon wearing its red roof as a hat. It looked as though someone attempted to whitewash that part and so the gray planks were a sharp and earthy contrast to the whitewash, red door and boxes. It looked picturesque in a perfect setting as a sentinel upon a hunk of rock silently guiding boats in from the sea. The thought made me wonder if it had a foghorn or if it needed one. I would have to ask Mabel or the owner.

I stepped forward to walk to the door when it burst open and a tan and trim man stepped out hastily closing the door behind him. He came forward toward me then in mid stride changed his march to a walk while smoothing his slicked back gray hair. More of a swagger really. Not like a drunk, but like a man who walks with all of his energy and brains in his pants. "Here it comes and bring it on," I thought as he swaggered up to me all smiles, perfectly straight teeth, pressed dark trousers and crisp cotton shirt.

"Hello and welcome," he said as he adjusted the brightness of his smile and extended his hand. "I'm James Reinhold, owner and occupant of this fine lighthouse – the Comfort Lighthouse is the official name – but of course that sounds so obvious. And who might you be?"

"Katy Hawkins, local tourist and current house guest of the Blue Heron."

"Ah Mabel, what a splendid lady, a real asset to our community. She's done a nice job with the Heron, although I'm not much into Victorian, are you?"

"I don't know enough about Victorian or any other style of house other than comfy and cozy and be it ever so humble there's no place like it," I said giving him my brightest smile. Two can play at this game.

"Ah…right. So, what can I do for you, Miss Hawkins?"

"I was just curious if you could show me around the place. I've never been this close to a lighthouse before." Batting my eyes at him had no effect.

"Good heavens, No! I should say not! This lighthouse has been in a state of constant and meticulous refurbishment since the unfortunate business a year ago. It is not open to the public and especially not to tourists."

"Really, what a shame. I was rather thinking of writing a book on West Coast Lighthouses. This one would be prominently featured." Okay, so I lied to him, but he was way too charming for my taste.

"My, what a lovely idea, but I really must insist. I would hate to harm the memory of those involved and to dredge up the past would be of little comfort. I'm sorry."

"Well, thank you for being honest with me… Excuse me, but what is that smell?" I sniffed the air like a hound dog. "Why it smells like smoke… are you…?"

"OH NO! I must run – my God – my – my, uh, toast! Yes, I forgot my toast! Please excuse me – must dash." He fled back to the house, through the door slamming it with a formidable bang.

Well, round one to Mr. Reinhold. But I was not going to be deterred. In all my years as a massage therapist, I always relied on my first impression and intuition. Both of them were saying that he was odd, shifty, way too charming, and hiding something. I would have to formulate a better plan when I met with him again. For now, my tummy was talking and demanding a new stove celebration brunch. So, I hurried back down the path and straight to Mabel's to enjoy a feast fit for a queen – with a new stove.

After finishing off a festive and filling brunch, Mabel and I spent the rest of the day puttering around her kitchen enjoying her new stove. Mabel made casseroles, lasagna, a peach cobbler, and grilled a steak on the stovetop. No knob, burner or accessory was left unturned or unused. I helped out with the chopping, cutting and cleanup. As we cooked, we talked like two old friends. Except one of the old friends kept shooting me looks and occasionally wiping tears from her eyes. Mabel was too proud and too amazed to come right out and say that she knew I was the gift giver. I was too proud and too amazed by how good I felt and how much I had come to care for this woman in such a short time to tell her. She knew I knew and I knew that she knew and that was enough – for now. Chloe was released from our room and was made honorary taste tester. She loves cheese, so she especially enjoyed the Reggiano Parmesan that I grated. She was chirping happily every time a crumb was dropped on the floor. She would scamper over and devour it like a tasty morsel of dead mouse.

After putting all the food away, tasting some in the process, I left Mabel happily reading her owner's manual for Ol' Bessie. Chloe and I retired upstairs to relax and digest. But I felt uneasy. My mind kept returning to the fires and the charred studio of a woman I didn't even know. I wondered about Megan's work and what her art looked like. If it was anything like the pictures hanging in Reinhold's gallery, she was truly talented and had learned much from her mentor. I decided a walk would still my thoughts. So, I grabbed my tennies and made my way into the dusk of an early spring evening leaving Chloe to sleep off her big belly of tasty treats. The air smelled glorious, full of salt and sea mixed with marinara sauce. Checking on the parking lot, I made a mental note to call the rental place to see when they wanted their car back. I did look up at the lighthouse. It just didn't seem as friendly or inviting since meeting its owner. I decided to walk down the path from Mabel's toward the pier thinking some window-shopping would ease the churning in my head. When I reached the Bike Shop and strolled past, I heard a noise. I paused and glanced inside the garage. There at the bench was the same pale skinned man I had seen earlier. He was bent over a small worn bike like none I had ever seen. My mind clicked into place and I realized that it wasn't a bike, but a wheelchair, small like for a child and heavily worn and out of date. As I watched, the man was trying to fix one of the wheels that looked beyond repair. As he worked, the screwdriver in his hand suddenly slipped and cut his other hand at the palm. In one fluid motion he picked up the screwdriver and flung it across the garage to bang on the far wall, landing with a thud on the floor. The next moment the man started cursing and hitting the bench with his bloody hand, until the curses became sobs, sobs from a man who seemed beyond repair himself. I slipped away leaving the man to his private agony, feeling sad and ashamed for having witnessed his private grief.

Heading toward the pier, I stopped at the blackened shop. Staring at it for what seemed like hours, I tried to remember every conversation and every impression from this place called Comfort. Finally I realized that all things were not as comfortable as they appeared. I headed back to the Blue Heron and paused in front to glance at the lighthouse sitting silently on its rocky cliff, staring out to sea. I wondered about the owner. As my hand touched the kitchen door I heard laughter behind me, as light and airy on the ocean breeze. I whirled around just in time to see a mist float around the lighthouse beacon and then disappear as before. Really, my imagination was taking off. First laughter, then a floating mist figure. What next, a fire? I marched into the kitchen and up the stairs mumbling to myself about what too much sea air can do to a person. I never smelled the smoke.

CHAPTER 7

I slept in late the next morning because Chloe woke me twice in the night, both times howling and pawing at the window overlooking the lighthouse. Each time I got out of bed, picked her up and settled her on my lap to be petted. She fell asleep after much kneading of my arm and bathrobe. I finally decided to sleep in the chair, waking a few short hours later with a stiff neck, a slight headache and a seriously negative attitude. Hopping into the shower, I longed for good food and strong coffee hoping that would heal my symptoms. After my morning constitutional, I changed into jeans, sweatshirt, tennies and bright pink cat socks. I smile every time I wear this pair of cat socks, a gift from Holly many years ago. I still believed silly socks were good for conversation starters, to relax the most tentative of clients and ease the mind away from the pain and stress release of a deeper massage. It's a vice I planned on keeping for the foreseeable future. I ran downstairs into the kitchen noticing that the sky had turned from a warm light blue to a dull gray figuring that was the cause for most of my mood. I munched on leftovers from yesterday's brunch after reading Mabel's note telling me that she was shopping in Uptown and would be back later this afternoon with a surprise.

Leaving Chloe playing with her pet fake mice, I went in search of some answers. Hurrying outside I noticed that the air smelled like a mixture of wood smoke and axle grease. Walking past the Bike Shop, I stared straight ahead trying not to picture the scene from last night. A half plan was forming in my mind involving only partially answered questions and suspicions. Heading toward the Mercantile, I barely noticed the blackened trashcan that was still smoldering with soot. Someone must have wanted to burn their trash today, I thought. Quickly walking past and barging through the door into the Mercantile, I tried not to blink at the over-abundance of items bulging off the shelves. It seemed more filled than the time before. Without thinking or questioning my judgment, I purchased a small handheld flashlight, a carpenter's multi-tool, black gloves, candles and matches trying not the listen to the voices in my head. As before, Charley rang up my purchases while Dotty sat behind the counter reading. This time the book was a thick leather bound textbook titled *Weaponry for a New World*. The scary part was that she was reading it intently using a yellow highlighter and silently moving her lips. I bet she's brilliant, I thought, shuddering.

Next, I bustled to the touristy shop I had seen earlier, still laughing at the store name – Comfort Tourist Trappings. This town definitely has a sense of humor. I browsed through the shop taking note of all the knickknacks that most tourists buy and later regret. Surprisingly, amongst the cheap and awful were some lovely coffee table books of the local artists, ocean and neighboring communities. There were no books on the town of Comfort itself. How interesting.... I purchased a large oversized book of local artists complete with biographies to do some light reading and research later. Being a postcard fanatic, a habit from my parents, I also purchased a dozen postcards to send to Dennis, Holly, Patrick, and a few former clients who had become friends. Thought I'd let everyone know Chloe and I were still alive and kicking. The clerk bagged my purchases in a lovely tote bag featuring sea otters, dolphins, and other marine life. Bracing my shoulders, I went next door to the Reinhold Gallery feeling as comfortable as a lamb to the slaughter.

The first thing I noticed about the gallery was that it was open with a fairly good number of people milling about admiring the art work hung with care on the walls. It seemed as if each picture, whether it was oil on canvas, a watercolor on parchment or even a simple pencil sketch, was hung with thought of placement, lighting, and pride. It was hard to reconcile this impression with the glimpse of the man I had encountered at the lighthouse. The man himself was busy behind a small counter, counting out change to a customer with the ever-present smile pasted on his face. I looked into his eyes and noticed not a hint of gratitude or friendliness, but a deep vast empty void of all emotion. There was no kindness to match his smile. How odd for a man who is the seeming pillar of the community and local boy done well, I thought. James must have sensed my stare, because he turned and met my gaze. Recognition flashed thorough his deep gray eyes and he quickly appeared at my side holding out his hand.

"My dear Miss Hawkins, so good of you to come to my gallery. I so wanted to apologize for yesterday and my abrupt departure. My toaster has been the bane of my existence for weeks and I simply cannot leave it unattended. I so hope you will forgive me," he said with the smile lit on his face that never traveled to his eyes.

"My dear Mr. Reinhold, I'm so glad nothing was harmed. Your toaster is forgiven and don't give it another thought. Now, about your gallery, I would love a tour, if you can spare the time," I said matching his oozing charm with mine.

"My dear, please come this way and I'll show you the works. This gallery is separated into three sections. To the right are the watercolors with corresponding prints from inexpensive to collector's additions – you know, something for every taste and every budget. To the left are the sketches I have done over the years – again with corresponding prints in varying prices and presentations. And in the back, my dear..." at which point he grabbed my hand, tucked it in his arm and marched me to the back of the room, "...are the oils. Magnificent works of art on canvas using only the best oils. All a work of art and dedication and the apex of my collection. As you can see, they are truly the jewels in the crown."

And indeed they were. The canvases were large with decorative and ornate frames. They could have been framed in burlap and matted in band-aids and they would still be stunning. There were eight paintings in all representing various seasons and times of day. The last, the centerpiece, was a work not just of the lighthouse, but the town mapped out below and nestled in bright vivid colors of a glorious sunny day. It was as beautiful and as clear as any photograph only with a deeper sense of emotion. Love, pride and passion flowed through each stroke of the brush and with each splash of paint. It was remarkable that these works could come from a man whose eyes were so cold and whose smile appeared so plastic. I stared at each one in turn, speechless, knowing that James was watching me. I managed to tear my eyes away long enough to mutter, "You must be proud of your achievements."

At this statement, James bristled and said far too loudly, "My dear, it is not about achievement, it is about THE WORK itself, the ability to capture beauty and hold it forever on a canvas or parchment or even on a plain piece of paper, that matters. To convey the emotion into a work and have a person feel it is the only goal I hope to achieve. It is the essence of any artist!" He said that last bit at almost a full Handel's *Messiah* volume instantly silencing the entire store. I wasn't sure if I'd just been lectured or if I needed to put a ten spot in the offering basket.

James collected himself, placed the plastic smile back on his perfect teeth and looked down at me. "Miss Katy, you have caused a stir in my soul that I haven't felt in quite some time. I sense a kindred spirit in you, am I right? I look for an opportunity to explore this connection further, but I must attend to my other patrons. Please, may I call on you later this evening? I feel we have much to discuss."

"Ah, sure, Mr. Reinhold," I said hesitantly.

"James, please call me James. I like the way you say it - the way your mouth curves – almost a pout," he purred.

"James, then. I'm staying with Mabel at the Blue Heron. I look forward to seeing you later this evening. Good-bye and thank you for the tour."

I hurried from the gallery and rushed toward the pier before I allowed myself to dissolve into nervous giggles. I knew the guy was full of himself, but never to this extent. You'd have thought he was preaching the cause for ending world hunger or curing cancer, not the plight of a small town famous artist. It made me wonder just how small town he was and how famous. I wanted more information and decided to do some sleuthing on the background and history of Mr. Call-Me-James-While-You-Pout. I also decided that some much-needed fun was in order as well. So I headed to the bookstore I had seen next to Cherry's Cuppa Comfort pausing only briefly to giggle at the sign over the shop. "Spell-Binding Books – books for all occasions and all walks of life." Wow, I'm really beginning to think this town has a serious case of puns. But I happily walked through the door and spent the next three hours browsing shelves filled with murders, mayhem, puzzles, biographies, metaphysics and anything else printable and readable. I left with a Sudoku book and a promise to myself to spend more time there in the future, not ready to accept that my brain was thinking things like future and belonging and community. Clearly, I wasn't ready to leap over that hurdle yet. There was a mystery to solve. Why fires and why Megan? I'd have to think about home and hearth later.

After inhaling a sumptuous roasted veggie sub at the Deli, I headed back to the Blue Heron just in time to see Mabel pull up in her sensible mid-sized blue minivan. She stepped out, waved and motioned for me to join her by her car. Coming up next to her, she indicated to a rather large pet carrier. I really didn't notice the size because I was too interested in the occupant.

"Taffeta, I presume?" I said.

"Yes," Mabel replied. I looked up into her face and saw a humbling look – a moist mixture of joy, sadness, love, devotion and child-like innocence. Her eyes were wet, but her mouth was smiling. Mabel opened the carrier and out jumped the biggest, fluffiest sack of pewter gray fur I had ever seen. If judged by volume, I would say the cat weighed about fifty pounds. But I figured the tonnage was much lower given the fact that Mabel could cradle the cat without her knees buckling. It seemed that

Taffeta and Mabel had already made an acquaintance and both had decided it was love at first sight.

"I haven't had a pet in probably fifty years. And this charming lady is by far the most beautiful creature I have ever seen. No offense to Chloe, but this lady has class," Mabel said.

"No offense taken," I said rather crisply. "After all, beauty is in the eye of the beholder."

"Do you think they will get along alright, Chloe and Taffeta, I mean?"

"I figure on keeping Taffeta in the back parlor with me or in my flat until she gets used to things. Then we'll see where she would like to roost. Until then, Chloe has the run of your suite and the kitchen as long as she wants. Just don't tell the Health Inspectors that." And with that Mabel, cradling Taffeta in her arms, walked into the house and somehow all was right with the world – or at least this corner of it.

I decided to take Chloe for her promised bug hunt after hearing that dinner would be somewhat late. "We're bonding," Mabel had yelled from somewhere in the back of the house. So, I took out Chloe's purple leash and matching halter, suited her up and carried her down the stairs and out the door. She made a beeline for the road leading to the parking lot and proceeded to roll around on the concrete and dirt and turned her ebony coat to a lovely shady gray. We meandered and sniffed our way toward the concrete embankment by Comfort Point and proceeded to head up the path toward the pier with Chloe leaping and jumping at bugs that made the mistake of crossing our path. Chloe stopped as we got close to the Bike Shop. One minute she was sniffing a tricycle and the next she had wound herself around the bikes and a brake pedal. As I stooped to untangle her, I heard a giggle. Glancing up I was startled to see a family coming back from a stroll. The tall pale-faced man I had seen the previous night was pushing the antique wheelchair holding a small child. Yet, he did not have the sad face of before but a cautious one. By the man's side was a strikingly beautiful exotic dark skinned woman who looked like a High Priestess from a movie. Her posture was erect, eyes straight ahead and inquisitive, with facial features similar to those etched on Egyptian tombs. They wheeled toward us and stopped as I finished untangling Chloe. Scooping up Chloe I walked over to meet them halfway.

"Hi! I'm Katy and this mischievous creature is Chloe, my cat."

"Hello. We're the Taylors. I'm Drew, and this in my wife, Margharite, and this is our son, Benji." At last, a name to go with the pale face. Drew was tall and thin with the body of a cyclist. His voice was polite and wary at the same time. His wife was every bit as tall beside him watching me as close as a protective mother would. Benji sat in his wheelchair, his dark curly hair rumpled from the mild ocean breeze. His face was light and full of life, not pale like his dad's.

"Hello, Taylor family! Pleased to meet you. I've been admiring your bikes – even though I know next to nothing about them."

"Well, it's a nice hobby I have when I'm not on the computer as an analyst," Drew said, his eyes assessing Chloe and me.

"And it makes a nice change from mops, brooms and commodes," Margharite added.

I laughed. "Well, I guess that means Drew, you're a computer wizard and Margharite you work at the Mercantile…?"

They both laughed and seemed to relax a bit. "No. No, it means Drew is the Comfort Bank and Trust Manager who tinkers with bikes and such in his spare time. And I clean houses for a living. It pays bills and keeps me close to home, to

Benji," she said.

At that point I looked down at Benji and he was staring at Chloe. I gently squatted down and placed Chloe on his lap. She looked up at him, placed two paws on his chest and licked his chin. The boy's knurled hand softly patted Chloe on her back. She arched her back and started kneading his chest with her paws. Benji smiled and laughed a soft, but heartfelt laugh. We smiled at the scene. Chloe decided that his lap was as good as any, so she quickly curled into a ball and pretended to nap.

"Have you played with a cat before?" I asked Benji.

"No, Miss," he answered shyly.

"Would you like to take Chloe for a walk sometime?"

"I can't. I can't walk. I live in my chair," he said as the laughter drained from his eyes.

"I bet you I can get you to walk her just like I do. Would you like that? I bet you one ice cream cone on it. What do you think?" I didn't look at his parents' faces because I didn't want to know if I had just stepped over some boundary line. I reached out my hand. "Do we have a bet?"

"Yes," Benji said quietly. Then he looked up at his parents. They both smiled a painful smile of past failures and nodded to me, Drew's cautious mask firmly back in place. It seemed they both thought I should learn my lesson in failure, but they were too polite to say so.

"Okay, Benji, it's a deal. I supply you with one ice cream cone of your choosing and you walk my cat. I'll see you tomorrow around mid-morning if your parents approve." I looked up at them to give them my most honest and trustworthy look. They nodded again like I was a fool and we agreed that tomorrow at ten o'clock would work. I mentioned that I was staying at the Blue Heron with Mabel and that they could use her as a character reference if needed. I was sure there would be a phone call from them within the hour. I scooped up a drowsy Chloe and started to walk down to the pier in search of tea and sympathy, turning back to wink at Benji and promising to meet them at the Bike Shop at ten.

CHAPTER 8

Chloe and I scampered along the pier and headed straight for Cuppa Comfort and bright cheery Cherry. I picked up Chloe as I opened the door. Poking my head in, I waved at Cherry who stood behind the counter helping a customer. She smiled looking down at my bundle of black fur in my arm and waved me to the far wall by the picture windows overlooking the ocean. Cherry joined us a few moments later setting down two cups of strong tea with a hints of cinnamon and cloves. She placed a few small kitty crunchies on the seat for Chloe who happily chirped and started munching. Cherry was all smiles.

"I always like to be prepared for my guests," Cherry said. "Especially new ones. I hope Chloe appreciates the extra effort."

"I think Chloe already ate the extra efforts. Thanks for the kitty treats. That was thoughtful of you, considering your preference for birds," I said.

"I love all of God's creatures – every one! I just have a preference for the friends of the feathered kind. But Chloe is so cute and so little. Did you shrink her in the clothes dryer or something?"

"No, she came that way. I always say that her biological mother was not very motherly and so Chloe missed out on some of the basics. I found her in a trash dumpster when she was three weeks old. So, she didn't get much of her mama's nourishment. But hopefully I made up for it by spoiling her rotten and giving her lots of love."

"She sure looks loved to me. So, what brings you up this way – other than my fine tea? Still planning to stick around for a few more days?"

"I'll be sticking around Comfort for a while. I find this place charming, the people friendly though cautious of me as an outsider, and the ocean air just perfect for my soul."

"I'm sure the Taylors will be happy to hear that. They came in a few minutes ago with little Benji. He was so excited about walking your cat. Drew was asking questions about you, you know, your character and if you could be trusted. That man is very protective of his family, especially Benji. But, if you ask me, you're in for trouble."

"Why?"

"Honey, I don't know how to break this to you, but Benji can't walk. He's got Cerebral Palsy and has been in that wheelchair for as long as I can remember."

"I figured there was something going on. But he doesn't necessarily need to walk. I'll just change out Chloe's lead for a long retractable one and have him hold the lead while she bug hunts."

"Eew! Must you bring up bugs? Can't you just say while she plays or explores or something?"

"I thought you loved ALL of God's creatures, Miss Cherry?" I teased.

"I do! I do! But must you bring up some of the more creepy and crawly of creatures?" She wailed.

"Sorry. Thanks for your concerns about Benji, though. I promise to treat him gently and kindly. And, I will approach Drew and his wife with tender steps. I just think Benji could use some Chloe time. However, I did notice that his wheelchair seems somewhat old and small for him."

"Well, God bless those Taylors. They've had their share of problems with that boy. He is God's little prince, sweet and shy. But the insurance company thinks he's demanding and trouble just because he wants a new chair – which they won't cover. Drew had to build the ramp in front of his home by himself; no city or county seemed interested in paying for it. The insurance company won't pay for a new chair until little Benji stops growing. And people are cleaning their own houses these days, so Margharite isn't working as much. Thank God, Drew's employment is steady or those people would be on the street! They are some of the most fine and upstanding folk around here."

All through Cherry's speech her voice had gotten louder to the point she ended her final sentence in a dull but impassioned roar.

"So, I guess from the decibel level, you like the Taylors?" I asked innocently with a smile.

"Well, yes. I'm always the champion for the underdog and downtrodden," Cherry said as she mopped her sweaty forehead with a folded napkin. "My, is it warm in here or is it me? I do work myself up so. I wish I knew someone who could help them. Not that they accept charity, mind you. Oh no, proud as punch and willing to work for the good they get is that family."

Cherry was gearing up for another blow of steam.

So, I quietly changed the subject.

"So, since you seem to know all the fine people of Comfort, what can you tell me about Megan, the artist that died?"

"My heavens! How do you know about all that trouble? Did Mabel tell you?"

"Well, Mabel told me only bits of Megan's story after I asked her about the burnt out studio," I replied.

"Well, that Megan was a truly gentle soul, but she didn't have the sense God gave a goose. She took to that James Reinhold like a substitute father and my, did it go way beyond that. What she saw in that man I can hardly imagine. Once you get past his oozing charm, flashy exterior, and fine-combed hair there's nothing inside – just hollowness. Have you seen his eyes? They're like empty pools of darkness from one of those creatures from the deepest crevices in the ocean, like a squid or eel or something. All black and cold. But what a nice smile. A dentist must have made a fortune on him." Cherry sat back in her chair and looked at me curiously.

"So, have you met the man himself?" she asked.

"As a matter of fact I have." I went on to tell Cherry all about my encounter with James at the lighthouse and the rather weird and charming behavior at his gallery. I mentioned him inviting himself over for drinks to discuss art and artistry with a kindred spirit.

"Kindred spirit, my granny's panties!" Cherry exclaimed. "I bet he's out to schmooze you and turn you into one of his fans. Oh yes, there are a few around town, don't let them kid you. But those of us who knew Megan know better."

"Know what?"

"Know that the story he told on the night of the fires, his wife's death and supposed involvement, and how he's just a grieving widower. That story has more holes than a flow-through tea bag!"

Well, I thought to myself, that's quite a few holes.

"So, what do you think the truth is?" I asked with an interested tone.

"I think he knows more and is saying less. I think he's too scared to leave for fear that someone will finally suspect him. I think he's dumb to stay because he's not really appreciated in this town. His art is one thing – full of vibrancy and passion. But the man is empty and cold as a cast iron tea kettle." And with that proclamation, Cherry sat back and mopped her forehead again. At least the decibel level was less.

"Well, my dear, I must get back and brew my witch's stew. Thanks for the chat and for bringing in Chloe. She is a marvel and welcome here anytime. And stay away from that Reinhold person, he's no good and harm comes to those that get close to him!" Cherry said standing up.

"By the way, Miss Cherry. Do you own Creature Comforts – considering your love of animals, after my visit I figured you might?"

Cherry's laughter peeled off the ceiling before she could reply, "My gracious, no. Wynetta Vane owns the place. She's been my friend since the orphanage years. We've been friends through thick and thin. Now there's someone who would appreciate Chloe's finer points." At which point, Cherry indicated with her head for me to look at my cat. Chloe was busily swatting at the wadded up napkins on top of the table and deftly hitting them off the table onto the floor. When all three napkins had fallen, she looked over the edge of the table and merped. I figured at that point, my usually well-mannered cat had worn out her welcome. We left quickly with Cherry laughing and holding her ample sides, Chloe firmly held in my arm smiling satisfactorily to herself, and me wondering what other trouble we could get ourselves into today.

Chloe and I walked past Comfort Properties, Gavin's place, and I wasn't surprised when he leaped out of his chair and came bustling out to greet us. I had my mind already geared to edit his hissing, hoping it wouldn't be so pronounced.

"So, what brings you back to see us? And who is this yummy creature. My, is she it or what?" Gavin oozed.

"Gavin, this is Chloe, the kitten. Chloe, this is Uncle Gavin, he's a new friend of ours," I said. Chloe seemed somewhat reluctant to make his acquaintance. I didn't blame her.

"Oh do stop!" Gavin shrieked as he giggled. "I can't stand it. I simply can't stand this charming creature. She must come inside. She must. She must!" And Gavin pushed us into his office and strode over to the corner where an ornate and heavily padded pet kennel sat. I dropped Chloe on his desk where she sat eyeing his collection of pens in his pen holder. Gavin peered inside and shook his head. "I'm so sorry. Miss Martha seems to be in a state at the moment and not available for visitors. But I insist you come back and meet her when she is, uh, more presentable."

"Um, Gavin, who is Miss Martha?" I asked, secretly hoping Miss Martha wasn't a Spider monkey he dressed in drag.

"Why Miss Martha is my most significant of others. She is my all, my being, my…" Gavin was cut off from saying more by a small yip that seemed to be coming from the kennel.

"Miss Martha! Have you dressed dear? We have guests." Gavin stooped down lifting the Holy veil and scooped out what looked to be a wrinkled wad of pantyhose.

"Miss Martha Davenport Bijou, may I present Miss Katy Hawkins and her love urchin, Miss Chloe." And with that dramatic pronouncement, Gavin extended the palm of his right hand and there sat the wadded pair of pantyhose. Or so I thought until it barked.

"Um, Gavin, what precisely is… um, what breed is this special…?" I rambled.

"Why Miss Martha is a tea cup Chihuahua, silly. Surely you knew that?"

"Of course, now I see. It's just that, um, I'm not as familiar with dog breeds as with cat, but Miss Martha does seem, um, exotic," I stammered.

"My dear, Miss Martha Davenport is the daughter, the High Priestess, of the Uptown Revue."

"Forgive me for asking, your Highness, but what is the Uptown Revue?" I asked, dreading the answer and fearing it would scar me for life.

"Why it's the all male revue. Cross-dressers, Wannabe's, He/She's, you name it. All singing and dancing and prancing the night away. Miss Martha is part of my act," Gavin proclaimed.

My God, what a vision, I am scarred for life.

"Well, Gavin, that is about the most exciting thing I've heard all day." Talk about a nice recovery. I can suck up with the best of them! "I had no idea this part of California was so cosmopolitan!"

"Why yes, darling, you must come out sometime with us. Miss Martha and I dress alike and we have special choreographed moves. We are THE HIT of the revue. I truly enjoy it, Darling! You and Chloe simply must come see us sometime. You must! You must!" Gavin's eyes sparkled as he spoke. Having come from Denver, where anything is truly possible – lifestyle wise – I am open to lifestyle choices. But it's not every day that you have a lifestyle choice thrust upon you in the shape of a teacup Chihuahua.

"Gee, Gavin and Miss Martha, that's a generous offer. But

Chloe and I have to pass for the time being. Um, I'm not sure how long I'll be staying in Comfort," I stammered.

"Fine, fine, fine, I understand. Now don't get me started on our Halloween extravaganza. Enough! Enough! But just say the word and we'll double date. Won't that be fun, fun, fun?" At that point, Miss Martha yapped and Gavin gasped and hurriedly rushed over to the opulent kennel and deposited Miss Martha back into her boudoir. "Miss Martha needs her rest; she's performing tonight and must be in tip-top shape. She's a real crowd pleaser. Now, what can I do you for?" Gavin asked rubbing his hands together. "Have you decided to move here and want to rent, lease, or buy? I do it all, you know, really, I do." Honestly, I believed him – in every aspect.

"Thanks for the offer, Gavin, but I'm really not in a position to make that decision yet. Though, I was kind of curious about the studio next door. What happened?" I asked almost innocently.

"Now girlfriend, you didn't just come in here to gossip did you? I just love it! I bet we're going to be the best of friends, just the best! No sit down and I'll tell you the tale of sad, sappy Megan."

"Why sad?" I probed.

"Sad because of the person she became, not the person she was. You see, she was a truly dear person. Not very open, if you get what I'm saying. Not like you, you know a kindred spirit," Gavin replied.

What is it with me and kindred spirits? Does everybody think I march to their drum?

"Well, dear, she was very good, artistically speaking, so I hear. Never saw her work. After she connected with that Mr. James, oh dear, did I say connected?" Gavin twittered. "I mean once James got his talons in her, she was a goner. He had her thinking that she was good and talented and therefore everyone hated her and was going to steal her talent. He poured his training and talent, along with his paranoia, into her. So, she took to hiding her work. She was building up to this big gala – her big unveiling."

"Well, how did it go? Was she really as good as everyone claimed?" I was hooked on his story.

"Who knows? She burnt to a crisp a week before the big event. All the time she puttered around next door with James hanging around, telling where to hang what, and lighting, and oh my this, and oh my that. Sickening. And she goes and gets herself scorched by some crazy. That's it, the end of sad, sappy Megan. The artist that almost was."

"So, no one ever got to see her work? Did all of it burn in the fire? No remnants? Nothing?" I asked.

"Not even a speck. And she could do it all. I could smell the paint sometimes when the wind was just right. I would love to have seen what she saw with her artistic green eyes. Just sad..." Gavin sighed.

"Do you really think it was some crazy person? Or could it be someone else. Someone she knew?"

"Oh I know what happened. That crazy wife of James' – that nut Anna did it. Saw them out doing the nasty or something and went mad as a hatter. That Anna was about as frail and as spineless as a washrag with that hang dog expression. You know, I've seen hound dogs with happier expressions. I think old Anna offed Megan, then offed herself and offed the lighthouse in the process. Then, I think poor ol' James covered up his poor wife's doings. Probably found her in the lighthouse burnt like crispy bacon. That's what I think at least." Gavin adjusted his chair and leaned forward. "So, are you looking into things that aren't a girl's business?" He asked. CLUNK! We turned to see Chloe, having knocked his pen holder over, systematically batting his pens on the floor, one by one. When all the pens were gone, she turned and walked toward Gavin. He held out his hand, which she sniffed. Gavin giggled. She licked him and then crawled into his in-box.

"My, my, I think this marvelous creature likes me. Well, thank you Miss Chloe. I like you too! Maybe we can double date sometime, just the four of us, you, me, Miss Chloe and Miss Martha," Gavin said with his eyes bright.

Trying to get my thoughts back on track after the Chloe half time show, I said, "Well, it just seems strange and sad, like you said. She sounds like she was a nice person and something like that shouldn't happen to people like her. So, I'm curious."

"Well, just be careful. People don't always appreciate bringing up the past, especially if it's dead. And you know what killed that cat – curiosity." Gavin leaned back in his chair and laughed the laugh of the truly different.

With Gavin's giggling interrupted by a yip from Miss Martha, I tugged on Chloe's leash pulling her out of his in-box. I hurriedly bade my goodbyes and rushed out with Chloe close on my heels. As an afterthought, I stopped into Comfort Food and ordered a Mint Chip ice cream cone for myself, to sooth my rattled spirit. Chloe and I wandered leisurely back with our minds going in opposite directions. Chloe was thinking about bugs, wads of paper, and a new teacup chew toy. I was alternately licking and thinking about Megan, James, insurance companies who decide whether a wheelchair is a necessity or not, and what Gavin looked like in wadded clumps of pantyhose.

CHAPTER 9

Reaching the back door of the Blue Heron, I quietly went upstairs where Chloe and I napped. My mind wrestled with images and conversations and tried to make sense of it all while I slept. My mind was still whirling when I awoke. So I figured I'd push it aside and concentrate on dinner and some light reading about local artists from the book I had purchased. I was just settling down to read when there was a tap on my door. Mabel stuck her head in and marched in once she saw Chloe and I were awake. I swear Mabel must be equipped with radar – she always knew what we were up to.

"Well, we've got trouble, missy," Mabel exclaimed.

"You mean trouble right here in River City?" I teased.

"Yes, I mean trouble that starts with J and ends with S and aims to be a big pain in the ass," she glared.

"Oh God! I completely forgot that James had invited

himself over to talk with a fellow kindred spirit. Gads, that man makes me nauseous," I moaned with my head in my hands.

"Well, he's in the parlor with Taffeta, at least he was. She took one sniff of him and high tailed it to the kitchen and straight into my fine linens."

"I didn't know she could fit in your fine linens," I replied.

"She can't. It's really not a pretty sight. Her head and shoulders are smashed in the cabinet like sausage into a casing and her hind haunches are sticking out like, well, like a lady with her butt in the air. It's really quite extraordinary."

"I'm sorry to have missed that," I mumbled. "I guess I need to hurry downstairs and entertain our guest."

"Not our guest, my dear. I will not be in the same room with that sleazy man. You get to handle him yourself. I would freshen up a bit first. You look like an unmade bed. And he's all dolled up for you. Tight black silk shirt, white linen pants – with a crease mind you – and bearing a bottle of expensive red wine. Taffeta and I will be in the kitchen if you need reinforcements, but I'm warning you, if you so much as show an ounce of interest in him on any level, we will be having strong words over strong coffee." And with that, Mabel marched out of the room – the battle won in short order.

I quickly freshened up and pulled on tailored, dressy black slacks and crisp white blouse, mentally thanking Mabel for laundering and ironing my clothes, and headed downstairs to face James the sleaze.

Having not set foot in the back parlor, I knew from Mabel's instructions that it was situated in the exact opposite corner from my suite, one floor below. My suite faced north and west, so I headed south and east. I slid open the etched glass partition doors and entered the room. My eyes took in the lovely antiques, fine wallpaper and curtains in accents of mint green, tan and cream. The entire room inspired calm, class and a sense of taste and refinement. No wonder James looked so out of place. He stood with his immaculate hair and plastic smile like a mouse at an elephant party. I stuck my hand out in greeting as I strolled in. James held my hand, cupped it and kissed the palm while his eyes never left my face. I half smiled back.

"My dear, how splendid you look. It must be so hard to pull one's self together with such limited resources while traveling." He took my hand and led to the small sofa while I pondered whether I had just been slighted or complimented. On the coffee table James had taken the liberty of freeing two Austrian crystal goblets from their rightful places in an ornate antique hutch by the window. Uncorking the wine, he patted the space beside him and I sat trying to put as much space between us as I could. He poured the wine while explaining the history and his support of the winery on the label and to explain that it had needed to breathe for precisely five more minutes before it would be deemed perfect for drinking. We lifted our goblets and he proposed a toast "To Art and its Muses!" James exclaimed and then gulped giant mouthfuls of wine like my Uncle Frank used to chug the family's hooch. I sipped, swallowed and thought, for dry red wine, it wasn't bad. For the next ten minutes James droned on about art, the importance of art and the meaning to the world of the art and its artist. I have to admit, I didn't listen too closely. But I was warming up to the wine. Finally, the drone slowed and James poured another goblet full of wine. As I watched him pour, I noticed a small black tail switching back and forth from under the hutch. Chloe! How in the world had she managed to get down here? With one eye on her and one eye on James, I smiled sweetly as James asked about my experiences with art.

"Well, I'm not very worldly when it comes to art – painting, oils, sketches and such. I know what pleases me and I know what I like, but it might not be what someone else would choose," I said.

"My dear, do you mean, you can't possibly be saying, do I hear you correctly? You would like to choose one of my paintings. Oh my dear, what a wise and perceptive decision from someone ignorant in the arts," he exclaimed. I gasped.

"James, what I meant was, that, well, there's much more to know before one makes a decision. Um, chairs and books are one thing, um, but, ah, art, art is forever!" I gasped again. God I sounded pathetic. And at that moment Chloe disappeared.

"Well, then my dear, I will use every means necessary to help you choose one of my works. I will ease your mind and work with you every step. To think when you touch one of my paintings, you'll be touching me… when you are alone with my work, you are alone with me…"

PLUNK!

Chloe had jumped up on the coffee table and deposited a dead mouse into James goblet. I gasped. Chloe let out a piercing howl of feline fierceness. The mouse had plopped in the goblet spraying little droplets of red wine on James white Italian imported pants and thankfully missing my white blouse. James arm flew in the air at Chloe as if to swat her like a fly. Chloe leaped onto his lap and with one swipe of her razor sharp claws had left James' hand with ribbons of blood. Satisfied, Chloe took off like a shot racing up the stairs howling as she went.

The howling caused Mabel to fly in from the kitchen. Taking one look at the situation, she declared, "We've got a floater!" She snatched up the wine glass and stormed from the room saying she would be returning with a "Medical Kit." I took one of the fine linen napkins that I was sure James had liberated from the hutch as well and held it to James' bleeding hand. I couldn't find a word to say. James, to his credit, was speechless as well and tried his best to hide the tears that were welling up in his eyes. Mabel returned and gruffly poured rubbing alcohol on his open wound. James yelped and slumped over onto the sofa in a dead faint. Mabel and I stared at each other with just the faintest of twitches starting to tug at the corners of our mouths. While James lay inert on the sofa, Mabel finished applying antibiotic cream and a large band-aid to his hand. A few moments later, James' eyes fluttered and opened. I calmly explained that Mabel had bandaged his hand, that Chloe was updated with her shots and that it might be best if he sees his physician in case the wound needed stitching. James made a move to reach for the wine bottle, thought better of it, stood up and quietly left the room. I hurried after him, walked him to the official front door, thanked him for a lovely visit, and watched him walk unsteadily toward the pier.

I ran back to the parlor to find that Mabel had produced another wine glass – one without a mouse – and had poured herself a glass, having refreshed my own. She had her feet up on the coffee table and was taking small sips of wine between great bouts of laughter. I kicked off my dressy flat shoes, curled up on the opposite end of the sofa and joined her in wine and merriment.

"Now that's about the best time I've had in this parlor in a long time," Mabel said. "My God, did Chloe really drop that mouse in his wine glass, or was that your doing?" She asked.

"I can't believe she did that. I have no idea how she got out of our room, found said mouse, and killed it." I dissolved into another fit of giggles. "Oh my, and she's made mince meat of his hand. I have no idea what got in to her. Do you think she's okay, Mabel?" I asked a little concerned.

"Okay? Honey, that cat just did what half the people in Comfort has been wanting to do for years: render that man speechless. Oh my, she deserves a Medal of Valor and a yummy kitty treat later." Mabel went back to laughing and sipping. "Good wine, though," she claimed with her eyes twinkling. We spent another hour laughing and smiling and not feeling guilty for any deed done. Actually we didn't feel much. It was really good wine.

I helped Mabel clean up then headed upstairs to have a word or two with Chloe. I found her on the window seat curled up tightly in a ball. At my entrance she raised her head and simply stared at me. She looked calm and serene without a trace of the howling hellion she was earlier. I scooped her up and placed her on my lap on the rocking chair.

"Now Chloe, is there anything you want to tell me?" I said staring into her not so innocent eyes.

"Merp."

"Well, I just don't understand what got into you. You haven't even met him before."

"Yowl!"

"Well, I'm just surprised at you, that's all. I hope to God he doesn't sue us. Wait a minute! What do I care? You're right! The guy is a scumbag and, according to Mabel, deserves to be mauled. But really, Chloe, your behavior is becoming quite odd. First you lick Bo's leg and now you maim a stranger. Oh! And you escaped and chased a laughing fog cloud. What next?" I asked. "Other than I sound crazy just saying this stuff out loud."

I looked down to see that Chloe had rolled over onto her back and was looking like an otter all shiny black, cute and adorable, this being her I'm-Happy-And-Am-Loved look. I scratched her behind her ears until she fell asleep. I continued to rock for awhile while thinking about licks, scratches, and strange impressions. When Chloe woke, we spent the rest of the evening playing stringy and mousey soccer. Mabel and Taffeta came up briefly to deposit a tray of leftovers and get acquainted. Chloe and Taffeta declared a truce and agreed not to take much notice of each other. Mabel still had a smile that kept tugging on her face. I bet her sides ached from all the laughter. We said a cheery good night to each other and turned in early. It had been a most remarkable day.

CHAPTER 10

Promptly at ten o'clock the next morning, Chloe and I deposited ourselves in front of the Bike Shop with Chloe dressed in her purple halter and retractable leash and me in a simple pink sweatshirt, jeans, and tennies. Benji came out of the side door and down the ramp. Margharite was pushing his wheelchair and looking dark and regal in the sunshine. We smiled hellos to each other. I squatted down and asked Benji if he wanted his ice cream cone now or after.

"After," he said, never taking his eyes off Chloe. I placed the leash in Benji's knurled hand and showed him how it operated. "So, let's go ramble over to the grassy area by the Point, okay?"

"Okay. Can you push me a bit?" he asked bravely.

"You bet!" Turning to Margharite and asked, "Do you want to join us? I would love the company."

Margharite smiled, her eyes still somewhat wary, and

nodded. I put Chloe on the ground where she immediately took off to bug hunt, positioned myself behind Benji's chair and proceeded to stroll toward the grassy area. Benji kept a constant eye on Chloe and did a fair job adjusting the leash as necessary. Margharite and I walked in silence. We positioned Benji's chair on the grass and settled down on the iron park bench at Comfort Point. Margharite turned to me and said quietly, "Thank you for this. There aren't many things that Benji can do. But, he seems to be doing this well. Maybe when he's older we can find job for him as cat walker." Her eyes were teasing as she spoke. I smiled back at her enjoying the lilt and deep accent in her voice.

"Well, I did promise him payment in the form of ice cream for taking Chloe on a bug hunt, er, walk," I said. "He seems capable. He sure lights up when he smiles."

Margharite smiled back. "He is such a special boy. He's our only child. His spirit and intelligence outshines his twisted body. But I believe he can do anything. Anything. My husband and I try to involve him in activities. But with money tight and a wheelchair as battered as his body, it's difficult." Margharite said with her back straight and her eyes firm. No self-pity there, I thought.

"I guess I sound like a proud Mama, but he is the brightest spot in my life. And I fight for him every day and for my family! My husband does not warm up to strangers. He is very protective of Benji. So, don't take his coldness personally – it just concern."

"Have people been tough on you and Benji?"

"No, most of the townspeople are generous and kind. We shy away from outsiders. But there have been a few. That man – that art dealer. Now he is a difficult man," Margharite responded.

"What happened? What did he do?" I asked, growing increasingly concerned.

"Oh, it was nothing," Margharite spit out the words. "That's the point isn't it? You see? Benji and I were at the pier, one of his favorite places, and his wheelchair got stuck. One of the spokes broke and the chair would not move. I struggled and tried to move it and it would not move. And HE walks by. He stops and sees me struggle and he just stares. I asked if he could help me and he shivered like he caught cold and says he would not help. Then he hurries away. Did nothing. I had to pick up Benji myself. He is quite heavy now and prop him on the bench while I struggle and finally free that chair. And Drew, clever as he is, cannot keep the chair fixed. It breaks and breaks, it's just not right. We need a new one. Is that too much to ask?" Margharite asked that last question to herself as much as to me. I think she forgot I was sitting there. She looked up and seemed embarrassed by her words.

"Please, don't worry. I may be an outsider, but I've been known to question the Fates and curse my lot. Sometimes it helps just getting it out before you burst inside. Don't you think?"

"Yes, you are right. There have been days I stand and shake my fist at God." She smiled, her angry eyes flashing while her cheeks flushed under her exquisite dark skin.

"Oh, I've been known to shake a fist or two myself. Am I correct is assuming that the man you are referring to is Mr. Reinhold, the owner of the lighthouse?"

"Yes!" She exclaimed. "That man so charming – on the outside – but like a wormy apple inside. Yes, definitely a wormy apple!" she said, seeing my shocked and bemused expression. We burst out laughing. After a few moments, we lapsed into a contented silence as we watched Benji reel in Chloe. He would giggle every time she pounced on a bug or leaf.

From around the corner of the Point, James Reinhold strode purposefully with his head down and his hands in his pockets, although I could see his right hand was still bandaged. He stopped abruptly by our park bench.

"My dear Miss Hawkins! I did not see you there," he exclaimed. From the look on his face, some of the polish had come off his apple. His nearly immaculate hair and clothes were wrinkled and somewhat ordinary today. He made no hint of seeing Margharite beside me.

"My dear Mr. Reinhold, I hope you have recovered from last night's incident and hope your hand is not too painful," I said, testing the waters.

"I am quite well, Miss Hawkins and expect a full recovery. I do hope you keep your cat on a firmer leash and under better care in the future," he said with a sneer.

"Why yes, Mr. Reinhold. I have hired a part-time caretaker for her – as you see." I indicated with my hand where Benji and Chloe were playing. James turned and stared for a moment then turned back to me.

"I was hoping to see you today to invite you, albeit informally, to a small gathering I'm having at my gallery tomorrow night. Nothing fancy, just a few select people, patrons of the arts you know. But I can see that your attention is elsewhere…"

I interrupted, "Why, Mr. Reinhold! Margharite and I would love to attend tomorrow night. But, we have some important business to attend to in town. However, if we get back in time, you can count on both of us to be there. Thank you for such a charming invitation. We are both delighted, aren't we, Margharite?" I asked innocently, while seething inside.

James looked aghast from me to Margharite and, not knowing what to say, simply nodded and walked away – once again with his head down and his hands back in his pockets.

Margharite whirled around to face me and opened her mouth for what I'm sure would have been a flurry of words. But I held up my hand to stop her.

"Please, let me speak first. Mr. Wormy Apple invited himself to the Blue Heron yesterday to ingratiate himself to me. He brought a fine bottle of red wine and proceeded to drone on and on about kindred spirits and all sorts of utter nonsense. That is, until Chloe dumped a dead mouse in his wine glass."

"She did what?" she asked.

"She dumped a dead mouse in his wine glass, splashing wine all over his fine white linen pants. Then she mauled him!" I said.

"She did what?" Margharite asked again.

"She took a swat at him. You saw the bandage on his hand – he's cut to ribbons! He passed out when Mabel tried to bandage his hand and left shortly after that. He really didn't have a good evening."

"Oh, my goodness! I love your Chloe cat! Thank you!" And with that, Margharite burst into tears and laughter while giving my shoulders a quick hug. After several minutes, she calmed herself down.

"You do not know – I did not like that man much. I carry his poison, his rotten apple, inside me. Big is my hate for such a man. You tell me Chloe does this thing. I see that hating that man does me harm here inside. Does my family no good to hate such a man. But Katy, what you mean about you and I have business in town?"

"Oh, I was just so angry that he wouldn't even look at you that he got my goat. So, I made up a story. I do have half a mind to go there. I just don't trust that man and my gut says that something is amiss. And I always listen to my gut. It's never wrong."

"So, what do we do?" she asked the million dollar question.

"Well, I have a plan, but I need a lookout. Can you go with me tomorrow night? Can Drew watch Benji while we party with art patrons and poisoned apples?"

"He will not be happy, me spending time with you. He is very cautious. But, I will explain it is for a good reason – to protect my family and our town. Yes, he will be home tomorrow night. What is this plan and what are you up to?" she asked.

So I told her. Eventually, she agreed to meet me tomorrow night at the park bench by the gallery. We collected Benji and Chloe and headed to the Deli for an early lunch and ice cream.

After lunch, we meandered back to the Bike Shop. I had made a new friend and I think Chloe felt the same about Benji. After hugs and purrs, I headed back to the Heron entering the kitchen to look for Mabel. Chloe immediately went over to see Taffeta. Mabel was baking up a storm with Taffeta on a plush cushioned bed near the stove. I chatted with Mabel getting her caught up on the latest chapter in the Rotten Apple saga. Then I asked slyly, "Does it get busy for you around here, Mabel?"

"Why do you ask, my dear?"

"Well, could you use an extra pair of hands to do some light cleaning or help with the cooking or anything? Didn't you tell me you have a busy next couple of days and that the Heron will be running at almost full capacity?" I asked sweetly.

"What have you got up your sleeve, Katy?" Mabel asked as she put down her towel and came over to the kitchen table where I was perched.

"Well, I just spent a splendid morning with Margharite and Benji and couldn't help but feel the need to do something to help them. They are such good people, Chloe and I feel like we have new friends. I was just wondering…"

"Wondering if you could get Margharite a job here to help me while helping her? Is that what you are thinking? Look at me, Katy!" She demanded.

I looked up at her.

"Katy, what is with you that you want to help people you don't even know or just met? Honey, it's a nice thing; however your job is not to fix everyone on the planet. Is there something you want to tell me? I'm not prying, but you do have some strange ideas and compunctions. Is there…?" she asked again.

"No," I hesitated, "I just want to help and she won't take money and money would be just a band-aid anyways. It doesn't solve everything. So…?" I looked at Mabel and shrugged.

"Well, I'll think it over. Taffeta and I could use some part-time help considering I have a guest who seems to have taken up permanent residence in the Rose Room and another guest who keeps dunking her mice into her water bowl. I could use help just for those people!" Mabel declared with a wink and a smile. She got up and headed back to the counter to continue with her baking. Feeling dismissed, I left the kitchen and headed upstairs, but not before giving Mabel a hug and kiss on the cheek.

Mulling possibilities over in my mind, I decided not too long ago that there were some things I could do to help those who can't help themselves. So, I reached for my cell phone and placed a call.

"Exponential Financial, what do you want!" Holly answered.

"Holly, is that you?"

"Katy? My long, lost friend? Is that you?" Holly mumbled.

"Holly? Are you sick? Is something wrong? What is it?" I asked growing alarmed.

"Oh, nothing. Just nothing. Only Horacio. That's all..." She mumbled.

"What do you mean only Horacio?"

"That's the only furry friend I have. All the other cats are gone. Long gone..."

"What happened? Where are they?"

"Well, given to deserving caregivers, of course. What did you think?" Holly snapped – her voice sounding more like her operatic self.

"Well, I just thought something had happened. Are you okay? Talk to me, girlfriend!"

"I'm fine, really. I just miss the pitter patter of four fuzzy feet. I've never had just one cat in the house. It's rather quiet. And Horacio is a Maine Coon, so he doesn't meow like a normal cat or, heaven forbid, a Siamese. He chirps, but not very often. So, enough about my sad melodrama, what brings you a calling?" Holly sounded much better.

"Well, I need a few favors, and yes, they would be billable."

"Okay, since I have no other pressing paws to hold, I have a pen. What do you need?"

"First, I need a state-of-the-art wheelchair for an eight-year-old boy. A chair with every conceivable gadget to get him from hither to yon and beyond. And no, they have no room for a cat. Second, I need any information you can hunt down on a Mr. James Reinhold and his dead wife, Anna. Up to and including schooling, trouble with the law and how talented of an artist is he. Finally, can you call the car rental company and tell them to come get the Jaguar or buy it for yourself? I don't need it right now and it just sits in the parking lot. I think that's it. Any questions?"

"Just one. Are you going to tell me why, or do I just go blindly doing your bidding? Not that I mind... just curious."

"How much time do you have? It's a rather long and involved story."

"Horacio doesn't eat for another two hours, so I have loads of time. Spill it!"

So, I told Holly the whole story. Every impression, every experience, every person I've met and every conversation I've had. I brought her up to date on my life in Comfort and she listened quietly. After spilling all the beans, she asked only one question.

"Were you serious about me buying the Jaguar?" she asked.

"Yes, I am. I'm thinking of hanging around here for a while. I want to figure out what happened to Megan, if I can. And I want to get to know the Taylor family and Mabel and Cherry and I'm sure a host of other people as well."

"Well, then I will get to work on your projects for you. I'll do Benji's wheelchair first. I'll see about those pesky insurance people as well. And I'll start a massive computer search on Mr. Rotten Apple. And Katy, thank you for the car. I could do with a new car," Holly said quietly.

"Well, then it's settled. And Holly, two more things."

"Yes, dear."

"First, if there is anything else you need, other than a few more cats. Please ask me. Always remember, you were my friend and favorite soprano before you became my go-to gal."

"Thanks, Katy girl, that's nice of you to say..." There was a slight pause and sniff into the phone. "And the second?"

"That I want you to know that I am not running away. I just feel like I can make a difference here. If someone is more comfortable because of me, then I want to do my part. If I ever start sounding like I'm running away from my problems, be the first one to smack me senseless. Deal?"

Another slight sniff. "Deal!" she said. And then I heard it

— a slight meow coming from the phone. Then shuffling and Holly shouted, "Oh my goodness! There are two tuxedo cats at my back door... I must dash... will talk..." Click. I was saved from Holly's melodrama by a pair of black and white cats. I just hoped she would get to business, too. Well, with my main chore for the day done, I curled up with the artist book and began reading. Though James was mentioned, no pictures of his work were shown. Another dead end. Hopefully Holly would turn up something to confirm what my intuition was telling me. Something wasn't right and I was bound and determined to find out what it was.

I was so engrossed in the book, I failed to notice the clouds that were forming off the coast. Chloe began pacing back and forth on the window seat. When I looked up, she was on her back legs pawing at a cloud passing by our window. Except this cloud took form. I rushed to the window just as Chloe growled and made a lunge for the figure. As her little paws hit the glass, the cloud seemed to rotate. I found myself staring at a skeleton formed of fog and mist. Chloe growled again and began hissing. The skeleton's mouth opened and I swear I could hear laughter. And with a sudden burst of wind, it vanished.

Chloe's fur was standing on end and she looked like a fuzzy black Q-tip. Her gold eyes scanned the air looking for the mist, but it was gone like a puff of smoke. I reached to sooth her, but thought better of if after hearing her low growl and watched as she jumped off the bench seat and headed straight under the bed.

I sank down in the rocker and started rocking as furiously as Madame DeFarge's knitting. I pretended to believe that it was all just my imagination, except for Chloe's refusal to come out from under the bed made me change my mind. Deciding to spare Mabel from this latest episode, I spent the remainder of the day in our room. Chloe didn't come out and snuggle with me until long past midnight, her purring mixed with the laughter that still echoed in my head.

CHAPTER I I

The next morning, I delayed my breakfast to wait for the other guests to finish. Hurrying through my morning constitutional, I quickly pulled on a pair of black pants, black shirt, black bra and matching undies out of the small closet in my room. Adding a denim shirt made sense for today's errands, then changing into a lovely hand-knitted lavender sweater later for the party that evening. My plan was to do as much research on James as possible and then meet up with Margharite later. I also added a small dressy purse to store my flashlight, multi-tool and gloves. Hastily adding my American Express gold card and Dad's old Swiss Army knife made the kit complete. I spent the rest of the morning reading the art book again and learning next to nothing about James Reinhold.

As the day wore on, I began to feel antsy and started pacing. Chloe took one look at me and jumped down and hid under the bed. This was not a good sign. Finally I had enough and put a call into Holly. She was up to her armpits in wheelchairs and was speaking with a local manufacturer when I called. She also informed me that her son, Andy, was working on the searches and he should have a full report by tomorrow. If I live that long, I muttered to myself. Andy, Holly's son, is a wiz at computers who does a little bit of questionable research and is the technical genius behind Holly's financial planning business. He is the second of her four boys and is the glue that holds the family together with a mind and intelligence as deep as the ocean. One could only guess what information he would have for me. I asked Holly, as an afterthought, to see if she could find out who owns or holds the lease of Megan's studio. It had occurred to me that her studio had stood empty after all this time. Why wouldn't the owner or someone lease it or buy it and use it. It just didn't make any sense to my business way of thinking. So, puttering away the afternoon, I left to do recon of the area to get a closer look at the layout of the entire pier and James' gallery. I wanted to make sure I had an escape route and that I wouldn't have any surprises.

Walking past the Bike Shop it appeared quiet and locked up. Continuing on to the Deli, I bought a veggie sandwich to tide me over until the party. Pausing for a moment to look around, I turned left and headed past the Deli toward the large Victorian building that announced itself with barks and meows. Between the two buildings is a narrow alley that leads to a small deck that runs the full length of the pier in the back. A row of exit doors stood presumably matching the entrances of each business. So, I thought, a person can come in the back way and open up the shop without going through the front. Logical and practical, I thought, as I nibbled on my sub. What the heck does that mean? Pondering the thought produced a nervous giggle. If I broke into a business, I could leave by the back entrance just as long as nobody saw me. No, this type of thinking will not do, I muttered. Since when do I break into places? I'm not a cat burglar and I have no intention of starting now.

Just then I saw a back door open and Gavin walked out pulling it closed behind him, making sure it was locked. Ducking behind the wall of the Deli and holding my breath, having no clue why I was holding it, I clutched my veggie sub to my chest like a security blanket. Gavin walked right past me without seeing me and continued on toward the bank. I slipped into the alleyway and stared. Another wild thought was forming. I found myself walking quietly up the alley onto the deck, indiscriminately trying doors. The first door, the Deli's, was open and yummy smells escaped from it. I tried Gavin's next, finding it was truly locked. Moving next door, I paused and slowly twisted the knob. It opened under my hand. What the heck? This had to be the door of Megan's studio – what was it doing unlocked? Before I could think twice, I shoved the last bit of my sandwich in the door jamb mortise, essentially blocking the door from locking. I quickly moved on and didn't try any of the other doors until I reached the end of the pier at Cherry's back door. Her door was open as well and I could smell the spicy exotic scents from all those wonderful teas and coffees. I quickly took three deep breaths and tried to clear my head, which was spinning. What had I done? I had just committed sandwich abuse. And I just gave myself an uninvited invitation. Quickly turning around, my eyes searched the deck area. There were no signs of anyone lurking about. Rushing back down the pier, I slowed only slightly as I passed Megan's studio to make sure no spinach was hanging out of the door. It looked locked, but my sandwich and I knew better.

I scurried back toward the Blue Heron and paused by the Point. I decided to sit and think, so I eased onto the park bench Margharite and I had occupied the day before and did some serious thinking. What I was thinking was slightly dangerous, a little bit illegal, and messy. But a part of me didn't seem to care. A part of me wanted answers and wasn't prepared to let a locked door stop me. Let alone an unlocked one filled with a veggie sub. I thought of Dennis, my dear lawyer, and wondered how much he would charge should I get found out. I then wondered, in a place like Comfort, do they even have a jail?

After a bit of deep breathing, I got up and hurried back to my room where I exchanged my shirt for my lavender sweater, grabbed my black purse, gave Chloe a head scratch, and headed off to the party and the rendezvous with Margharite.

We had agreed to meet at the park bench near Cuppa Comfort by James' gallery. I couldn't help but notice that James' side of the street had the same alleyway and deck like Gavin's side. However, this side had a path between the Mercantile and Sharkey's bar leading down to the beach. At the end of the pier, I waved to Margharite who was looking ravishing in slim black pants, gold sandals, and a metallic gold shimmering top.

"Wow!" I said. "You look terrific!"

"Thank you," Margharite gushed. "I do not usually dress up, mostly pants. But this is different, fun. Drew was not happy that I am helping you. He finally agreed to watch Benji. So, what is your plan?" She asked getting down to business. I explained part one of my plan, not wanting to scare her with my new part two. She listened quietly. "So, if you are about to get caught, what do you want as code word?"

"Code word?"

"Yes, code word. I watch many movies to help improve my English. The lookout always has a code word – so the good guy can make a fast getaway. So, code word?"

"Okay, how 'bout something artsy…" I said feeling a small wave of hysteria forming in the pit of my stomach. The picture in my head was of me in a yellow ill-fitting jumpsuit, ankle chains and swinging a pick ax, all because I forgot the blasted code word.

"How about crimson – as in the color red. Say something like the lovely crimson sunset. Or the color of my skin if we get found out?" I asked with the wave of hysteria moving from my stomach to my chest.

"Crimson." Margharite chewed the word like a savory fillet. "Good. Let us go. I told Drew I'll be home soon. It is game night; I do not like to miss out. My Benji is a tough Scrabble player."

"Okay, crimson, let's go." I said more confidently than I actually felt with a picture in my head of Benji visiting me in prison and playing Scrabble with me and the other inmates. What a lovely thought. I squared my shoulders, stuck my chest out, took a deep breath and erased the thoughts of cavity searches and group showers and headed into James' gallery with Margharite close beside me.

My first thought upon entering the gallery was that his lighting system must be on dimmer switches, because the ambiance was definitely darker with more moods and less sunlight. The paintings were still characteristically displayed. The rest of the gallery seemed subdued. Twenty or so people were milling about eating tiny appetizers from small silver trays. Gee, spare no expense, I thought. Margharite immediately fell upon a group of people who greeted her warmly. Probably parents or people she knows from Benji's school. Feeling deserted, I decided to have some appetizers to try and calm the huge nervous beast behind my sternum. As I tried to make my way to the table of munchies, I suddenly felt a presence beside me, and a warm, slightly moist hand on my lower back.

"My dear Miss Hawkins, so lovely to see you again," James purred into my ear.

"My dear Mr. Reinhold, it is a great pleasure to see you again as well. I hope your hand has fully recovered."

"But, my dear that was eons ago, let's be in the moment. And the moment is... I'm with you. Now, let's get you some nourishment and then I'll introduce you to some important people." His hand pushed me like a grocery cart to the bar set up by the register and grabbed a glass of deep red wine for me. Memories of floating dead mice flashed before my eyes suppressing the chortle stuck in my throat.

"Here, my dear, our wine. Let us sip together and think of fine times to come."

"Cheers!" I said taking a swig of the fine wine. It tasted like the same wine as yesterday, good, full bodied and without a mouse in sight. I thought of saying that out loud to him, but figured I didn't want to ruin my welcome quite yet.

The next hour passed quickly with James introducing me to every single person who was of note: the head of the Uptown bank, the mayor of Uptown, and other semi-prominent people of the local area. Margharite kept her distance, but her eyes were on me like a hawk and watching my every move. I finally was able to break away from James' ever-present hand and slowly made my way to the back corner of his gallery by the eight magnificent canvas paintings. They were still there in their glory and looking as extraordinary and powerful as the first time I saw them. I stepped closer and inspected the edges of the painting and noticed James' signature placed at the lower right corner, rather prominently. Well, I'd brag too if I painted those, I thought. Margharite materialized beside me.

"I adore the lovely colors he uses. Especially the crimson."

I smiled and nodded. Slowly making my way to the left of the gallery next to the first painting, I slipped through a dark heavy curtain I had spotted the first time I visited James' gallery. It was a bit disorienting at first, but once I shoved my hand in my purse and clicked on the flashlight, I became illuminated. It appeared this was James' inner office where most of his paperwork business occurred. A small desk fit snuggly on the right side and a file cabinet was opposite on the short left wall. The door marked "exit" was a few feet back, which gave me a sense of relief until I saw the smaller sign that read "Emergency exit only! Alarm will sound if activated." Great, so much for escape plan one. Unfortunately, I didn't have escape plan two. Well, let's get to work. I thought the file cabinet would be locked and it was. So, I set to work on the desk. After working my way through the usual bills, statements and invoices, I spied a sheet of paper lying by the wastebasket on the floor. Picking it up and turning it over, there staring back at me was a pencil sketch of the lighthouse on a clear summer day. Even though it was a rough sketch, the picture looked quite technical and good but had none of the warmth, power or passion as the other works filling the gallery. It must be an early rough draft indeed, I thought.

Then I heard it, Margharite's voice saying, "Use of color is so important, no? The blue, the yellow, red, the crimson..." That was enough for me to stuff the sketch and flashlight into my purse. I flattened myself next to the file cabinet trying to shrink myself eight sizes smaller. The dark curtains parted and Margharite, holding back one of the curtains, sailed right in and exclaimed, "Why, this is not a bathroom," covering me in the dark curtain effectively blocking my exit from view. Quietly untangling myself from the curtain, I meandered slowly finding myself back in the main gallery. Taking a hasty look around, I was relieved to see no one noticed my unique entrance. I made my way to the table of food and started filling a plate. Meanwhile, James had rushed to Margharite's side and exclaimed, "Madam, this is my private office and I will not have the likes of you invading it!" He yanked the curtain from her hand, snapped the curtains shut like the show was over and cupping her elbow he pushed her along toward the front of the gallery depositing her near the bar. Taking his hand off her, he actually wiped his sweaty palms on his creased pants before returning to his inner circle of guests with a fierce backward glare as he went. Moving to her side with an over-piled tiny plate of food, I pushed her out the front door. We walked to the bench by the end of the pier and sat down with a crash.

"Bon Appétit!" I said as I placed the plate of food between us. We nervously ate everything on the plate before we both started to feel relaxed. In between bites, I told her about his office and showed her the pencil sketch.

"How odd," she said. "You think a man with paintings like those on his walls would have rough drafts just as good. You know… genius. Good is always good. I do not think it comes as easy as it looks."

"That's what I thought, too. But I guess I'm no expert. Thanks for bailing me out. Are you up for more tomfoolery or are you heading home?"

"Oh, no, that is all for me, I promised Drew. I had my share of fun for one night. I will go straight home to try and beat my son in Scrabble. I have to be up early tomorrow."

"Really? Why?"

"Do you not know? Mabel has hired me part-time to help her out at the Heron. She says she is busy and needs the help. I thought you put her up to it?" Margharite said looking at me sideways.

"Wow! That's the first I've heard of it," I said truthfully, because Mabel hadn't told me yet. "Congratulations! I think Chloe and I have been keeping her busy, I'm sure she'll be pleased to have you."

"Speaking of Chloe, would it be okay with you if Benji continues his pet sitting with her?"

"Of course! Chloe and I would insist upon it. Except, I'm giving him a raise, from ice cream cones to cold hard cash. Deal?"

"Deal!" she said with a dazzling smile. "I will let Benji know. And Katy?"

"Yes, Miss Crimson?"

"Thank you."

"For what?"

"I was not sure at first – with you being an outsider. But I believe you are the best thing that has happened to this town in long time. Maybe Drew's ice will melt now that you are a friend. Good night, Katy."

"Good night, my friend." And Margharite hurried off toward the Bike Shop to game night. I sat still and quiet on the bench listening to the surf crash on the nearby rocks. I tilted my head up and looked at the night sky with the waning moon up above. It was a beautiful night and I hadn't died or been arrested... yet. The stars were twinkling and the sky was a deep Bible black. Tension began to ease out of my shoulders. I sat for a few moments and contemplated my foray into breaking and entering with a bit of burglary, and thought my new life was getting quite interesting.

CHAPTER 12

Staring at the darkened studio down the pier I let out a deep sigh. Opportunity is not a lengthy visitor, a voice in my head said. Ignoring a myriad of the other voices in my head that were telling me to go home and not push my luck, I stood up and headed back down the pier. Rounding the corner, I crept through the darkened alley slowly and stealthily, inching my way toward Megan's back door, feeling like the Comfort Cat Burglar. Gently, I pushed the door open bracing for the sound of a wailing siren like the threat on James' door. None came. Inching into the room, I silently closed the door. Digging into my purse, I pulled on my black gloves thinking I should have done that before I opened the door. Ah well, circumstantial evidence, I thought. Case dismissed for lack of evidence and plausible motive.

With one quick move, I shoved the flashlight into the

palm of my gloved hand and turned it on. The light was muted enough I could see. The air was still thick with the smell of burnt wood, ash and stale dreams gone up in smoke. I slowly made my way around the studio listening for any noise and watching the front window for any movement. The studio was empty except for pieces of litter strewn across the floor. I made a full circle around the room not knowing why I was here or what I was looking for. It felt almost peaceful to be in Megan's studio. I willed her to talk to me from beyond the ashes and begged her help in solving her puzzle. Why were you killed, Megan? What happened here? Show me, Megan, please. I listened but no voice came. Just whiffs of smoke hanging in the air and clinging to the walls.

With my next step, my foot skidded forward with a rasping sound while almost making me tumble and do the splits. I froze and clicked off my light. It felt like I stood like that for hours with my feet miles apart and every muscle of my legs straining, my ears on red alert for any odd noise other than mine. I cautiously turned the flashlight on. With all the balance of a ballerina on ice, I moved enough to squat down and stare at the floor where my foot had slipped. There was a clean patch in which something had been moved. I moved my foot and picked up a piece of litter my foot had skidded on. Turning it over, I froze. My heart almost stopped, my blood grew cold and my head ached like it had too much ice cream. My head started to shake from side to side. No, no, no. Over and over it went, trying to make sense of what was in my hand. Oh, Megan, what have I done? I asked her in the dark. Thank you for showing me this, but it just might just get me killed.

Clicking off the light, I waited until my eyes adjusted to the dark. Slowly standing up and holding the paper in my hand, I glanced down again at my feet and looked again at the clean spot on the floor. Before I could think of what I was doing, the paper and my purse were clamped between my knees with my arms reaching behind me to unhook my bra. In an instant I had the straps pulled through my sleeves releasing my breasts from their confines into the cool dank air. I knelt down and using my black bra, I scrubbed the floor smearing the ashes into the clean spot, erasing my foot prints. I waddled with my purse and the paper still clamped firmly between my legs. I just made it to the back door when I remembered to wipe my prints off the doorknob. Poking my finger in the door jam, I flicked out the remains of my veggie sandwich and pitched it over the side into the ocean and told myself to make a large contribution to a marine life foundation in the morning. After wiping off the jamb, I put the bra down the front of my pants figuring at this late hour no one would notice a strange bulge and flapping boobs. Carefully, I tucked the paper up the backside of my shirt.

I quietly started back down the deck area to the alleyway. In the distance, the low sound of laughter wafted with the breeze. I tilted my head in the direction of the sound as my eyes caught motion coming from the lighthouse. A mist was circling around the upper tower around the beacon as if it was dancing. Then it suddenly disappeared. I raced through the alleyway, ran right across the lawn, past the Bike Shop into the Blue Heron kitchen, praying I was safe.

Stopping just inside the kitchen, I gasped. There sat Mabel at the kitchen table with Taffeta on her lap. Mabel looked up from her tea and gave me a curious look, cocking her head to one side.

"Do I dare ask why you are dressed all in black and why you smell like the inside of an incinerator?"

"Well, um…" I lifted my eyes skyward looking for

inspiration. "Um, how about no. Don't ask. And don't tell anybody either."

"Well, Katy, I've had about all I can take of this. What are you up to, my girl, and I mean now," Mabel's eyes narrowed at me.

"Mabel, you know I adore you and Taffeta. It's just currently it's not in your best interest to know. If you know, then others might suspect you know and then, you know, things might happen that I do not want to happen. Okay?" I explained, thinking that was a clear explanation.

"Katy, my dear, you do realize that you are making absolutely no sense and now you are starting to smell up my kitchen. Seriously, you smell like burnt toast!"

"Well, I'm sorry, but I've had one busy day. Can I bribe you into taking these smelly clothes off my hands and laundering them? I'll pay you the moon – name your price."

"Okay, Taffeta and I will excuse ourselves and you can strip down to whatever God gave you and leave the stuff right where you stand. I'll put Taffeta in the parlor and then check to make sure the coast is clear so you can streak up to your room. Chloe has been chirping, so you might want to see what she wants," Mabel quipped as she picked up Taffeta. "And I won't even ask why you are braless and have a lopsided bulge in your pants..." I smiled that Mabel got in the last word again and began stripping down to my undies, thanking the underwear god that I hadn't worn a thong. I flew upstairs, not a soul to be seen, with the paper clutched tightly to my chest. It didn't cover nearly enough.

Hurriedly stepping into my room and rushing to the vanity, I hid both papers in a small side drawer under an old Oprah magazine. I looked at Chloe who was on the bed nibbling the tail off of a bright green mouse. I hurried into the shower to wash the latest adventures off my skin and out of my hair. Standing under the shower for a long time trying to clear my mind, I decided to think of better things. After drying myself off, I slipped into a comfy T-shirt, fresh undies and silly elephant socks. Wrapping in a Blue Heron robe, I gathered Chloe into my arms and rocked her to sleep. Things always look better in the darkness if you have something warm and loving in your arms and the sound of purring filling your ears. It was near dawn before my head finally gave up and let me sleep. It was a deep sleep, but troubled.

I awoke to the sound of paws scratching kitty litter. I eased my body out of the rocking chair vowing to never fall asleep there again. My butt was numb, my feet were tingling, and my neck felt like it had a hatchet in it. My first thought of the day was, "God, I need a massage!" Taking another shower, I realized that during the night my mind had formulated a plan of action for the day. It would start at breakfast with Mabel in her safe and happy kitchen coupled with a nice swim up the river Denial. After dressing in light colored denim jeans, a white T-shirt, a deep purple sweater and matching deep purple socks with white paw prints, I filled Chloe's bowls with kitty crunchies and water, making a mental note to buy more food for Chloe and have some clothes sent to me. After last night's adventures, I didn't think I could wear my black bra ever again.

Mabel and I had a quiet breakfast with pancakes, bacon and hash browns. It was quiet with no guests invading the silence. Every time she asked me about last night, I didn't say anything, just smiled. So, she finally gave up. Leaving Mabel looking up at me curiously, I went back upstairs to grab my purse. I decided to continue my delusion by going shopping.

My first stop was to Creature Comforts, which was an assault on all things animal. The shop was remarkably clean and smelled decent for a place that houses all things four legged, furry or feathered. I went straight to the cat toys and spent several minutes looking at all the temptations they had to offer. Chloe would like the pink ball with bright red feathers attached. I tried not to look at the live mice in their cages let alone the dead toy ones in multiple colors. Instead, I chose two cases of Chloe's favorite gourmet wet food and a large bag of her Hairball formula. Approaching the counter on the right side of the entry door, I smiled at the plump woman behind the counter. She smiled back and her face filled with crinkles and lines that could only be made from years of laughter and good living.

"Why, I do declare, you must be that Katy Hawkins the folks around here are a talking about," she said.

"And you must be Wynetta Vane – Cherry's best pal," I said, smiling at her deep and wide southern accent. This gal is a picture. Wynetta had big bleached blond hair, pale blue twinkling eyes, an ample bosom that made mine look like mosquito bites. She was round with dangerous curves and folds of fleshy softness. She wore a bright red checked western style shirt stretched to maximum capacity and tight denim jeans tucked into red western boots. I prayed she wouldn't have to bend over for fear that her pants would explode.

"Why, yes I am! And I am so pleased to make your acquaintance. I heard rumors that you have a beautiful black cat that accompanies you everywhere. Where is she?" Wynetta emphasized the word she.

"Well, Chloe is back at Mabel's no doubt getting under foot. If you'd like, I'll bring her in sometime. Of course, if that's allowed."

"She is more than welcome. I would love to make her acquaintance as well and to get to know her. I'm a personal shopper in my spare time and I love the opportunity to purchase things I know she would just love."

"What a wonderful idea! How creative!" I said, feeling I had landed in the southernmost tip of Texas, sipping mint juleps.

"Well, then it's settled. Now, let's ring up these here purchases." And with that Wynetta got down to business. After paying for everything, I realized I would need a Sherpa to carry the loot back to Mabel's. Wynetta must have read my mind because she offered to deliver it to Mabel's later.

"I've been just a dying to see her new stove. I hear it's something special. And she's got no idea who sent it to her. So, don't you worry about a thing, honey, I'll take care of everything. Also, if you would like to start a regular delivery schedule, I'm more than able to handle that, too. I heard you were planning on staying for awhile. That would be so nice." She smiled like she meant it, too.

"Well, I haven't really decided yet. But I do enjoy the sea and the surf. And most of the people here have been so kind and generous. I'm not in a hurry to leave, that's for sure." It was my hope I didn't say that last line like a parrot mimicking her. But the accent was so thick it was contagious.

"I figured you wouldn't be leaving here until you figure out what happened to Megan," she said.

"What?" My head snapped up and looked her straight in the eye.

"Well, it's a bit obvious that you are looking into her death and why her studio burnt down. You've been asking questions." It didn't sound like an accusation.

"I guess I'm just curious by nature. It is quiet and peaceful here and it just doesn't seem like a place where a tragedy like hers would happen," I explained.

"Well, looks can be deceiving. Cherry and I could tell you

stories of places we've been and people we've been placed with that would turn your hide into quivery jello!" she exclaimed. "And all of them nice enough places and nice looking, nice sounding folks. But, behind a closed door, living and breathing nightmares. Cherry and I have seen the worst and have lived to tell the tale. The funny part is I still believe that most people are just good, decent folks trying to do the right thing as best as they can. Maybe that's why my favorite book is *The Diary of Ann Frank*."

"Why Wynetta, you have a beautiful way of seeing the world, the good and the bad of it. If you and Cherry are like every other person in Comfort…"

"Honey, I don't think Cherry and I are like any other person anywhere…" she interrupted.

"…Then I may have to buy a retirement home here," I said as I laughed.

"Well, my dear, you are more than welcome. Gavin said that he thinks you're just delicious. Which is a nice way of saying he likes you. He must have talked for ten whole minutes about Chloe, your wonder cat, and how lovely she is. You and Chloe have had the locals talking up a storm. Outsiders are mostly tolerated, but you seem to be winning over the hearts of most of them."

"You know, that Gavin is a character, but seems pretty harmless. Everyone I have met here is just friendly and down-to-earth. What you see is what you get," I said.

Wynetta grew still. "If that is true, then one of us is sneaky as a fox in a chicken coop," she practically whispered.

"What do you mean?"

"Well, Megan died. But no one knows why. That tells me that someone around here must have done it or knows more than anyone is saying. That doesn't sound friendly or down-to-earth to me. That sounds sneaky. Like someone trying to get away with something. I must confess I'm not sure I like that thought." Wynetta was dead serious now.

"Wynetta, what do you really think? I have asked people and I would like to know your opinions. Do you think James' wife Anna started the fires and killed Megan?" I asked earnestly.

"Katy, do you ever feel things? Like when something bad is going to happen? I've had those feelings all my life. Got that odd feeling and couldn't explain it, and boom! Something happens that confirms my feeling. Impending doom, they call it. I've had that feeling since Megan died. Like it's not over… like something is missing. It's hard to explain…" Wynetta said, deep in thought.

"I've had feelings like that myself," I said to her. "I was born intuitive and it's only increased with age and experience. Always trust my gut and I'm never wrong. I guess that's why Megan's story bothers me. It feels wrong. Gavin said that she was killed because of passion, that people in desperate situations only operate from a place of passion."

"Oh, I don't know if I agree. I think passion for life and the life you have chosen is one thing. But passion that is fueled by fear is completely different. What we fear and what makes us afraid are two strong motivators as well." Wynetta's brow was furrowed like four rows of corn as she sought to explain her thinking.

"If you have been living a charmed life… having the life you have dreamed of and a secret is found out, what would happen? Would that person fear losing what they fought so hard to have? Would they be afraid to be found out? What would their passion lead them to do? That's what I keep thinking. All of my dear friends and neighbors here are living good lives that they chose and worked hard for. What would make them fearful enough to kill?" She stopped talking and looked at me like we had both seen the sudden change. Like a shaft of light altering the sunlight. We both stared at each other and knew we had just reached the why. Why kill Megan? Because there was something to fear and there was something to lose. I thought of the two pieces of paper in my possession and knew that some of the pieces of the puzzle had just fit into place. I hoped Wynetta hadn't seen the giant light bulb hanging over my head.

"Katy, I'm starting to like you. I know Cherry thinks fondly of you, too. Please, please, please be careful, honey. Don't do something without thinking it through – all the way through. You're dealing with people's lives, their secrets and their passions. Folks get rather protective about such things." With a nod, Wynetta handed me the toy I bought for Chloe, squeezed my hands like they were dishrags, and looked deep into my eyes. At that moment I felt I could not hide from her, she had seen inside me and was too polite for a gentle southern woman to say so, for which, I was truly grateful.

CHAPTER 13

I hurried from Creature Comforts and walked absentmindedly back to the Blue Heron. A sudden movement by Mabel's side door caused me to look up, stop suddenly and stare. The next moment I was running and flinging myself into pair of strong and hairy arms.

"Andy!" I said to Holly's son.

"Hey good looking! What's cooking?" We hugged like lost shipmates. I smiled at Andy's dark tousled hair, warm brown skin and warmer brown eyes. Handsome comes in extra large packaging. He looked a bit heavier since I had seen him at Christmas. Life must be treating him well, I thought. Looking at Andy, I am always reminded of what a truly unique person and mother my friend, Holly, is.

"What in the world are you doing here?" I asked, still shocked to see him.

"I came to deliver that info you asked Mom about. She said you needed it immediately and you never look at your laptop... so, here I am," he grinned.

"You're right!" I laughed. My laptop was still in the bottom of my duffel bag and likely to remain there. I wasn't too thrilled with modern technology and I figured my fancy new cell phone was as technical as I would ever get.

"Can you stay for lunch? Are you hungry?" I asked, suddenly realizing I was starving.

"You know me... I can always eat. I never turn down a meal especially if I'm not cooking."

"Well then, let's eat! I'm starving and could chew someone's arm off," I said.

"Whose arm?" a voice asked from behind me.

"EEK!" I yelped, spinning around to stare at Mabel who was smiling into the sunshine.

"Mabel, gads, you might have given me a heart attack!"

"Well, you deserve it for the stunts you've been pulling," she said, smiling broadly.

"Now what did I do?" I whined, though not convincingly.

"Why is there a month's supply of cat food in my kitchen?" she asked.

"Oops, I forgot to mention that Wynetta would be dropping it by for Chloe," I said, relieved she was not implying about my bit of burglary last night.

"And who is this handsome man? Do you know him?" she asked almost innocently.

"Oh gads... Mabel, this is Andy, my best friend Holly's second oldest son. Andy, this is Mabel the innkeeper and my new friend. I was just about to take Andy to lunch. Would you like to join us? We'd love the company..." I knew Andy never met a stranger, only new friends.

"I would love to. I'll bet Andy can tell me stories about you that I would love to hear. And I can tell him about the truck you attacked with my best skillet," Mabel said with a grin.

"Why did you attack a truck, Katy?" Andy asked, playing into Mabel's hand.

"Don't start or I'll tell Mabel how and why you are named Andy. I need food before you two gang up on me," I grumbled.

"Why are you named Andy, and what's wrong with such a fine Christian name as that?"

"Now you've done it, Katy!" Andy smiled, turned his head and gave me a wink.

"So, do you get to tell her or me?" I asked winking back.

"Food! Then singing," Andy bellowed putting arms around Mabel and me. He guided us off toward the pier to the Deli, with Mabel pointing out the points of interest to Andy while he made polite and sincere conversation. We passed the next two hours catching up and getting acquainted. I only had to kick Andy under the table once, when he was about to say what Holly truly does for a living. With Holly being my chief financial person and keeper of my lotto secret, I didn't want that getting out yet. So, a swift kick silenced him and redirected his thoughts to other subjects. Before we left, Mabel brought up the subject of Andy's name again. I was hoping food would distract Mabel, but she persisted. Andy smiled sheepishly and motioned for me to tell the story.

"It seems many, many years ago in a land far, far away..." I began.

"Oh cut that out! You know I was born in San Bernardino," Andy said. "Get to the story!"

"Okay, well anyway, as we all know, Holly was born on Christmas Day."

"She was?" Mabel asked, clearly delighted.

"Yep!" I said. "And as you can already imagine she gave birth to some rather interesting boys as well. Take Andy here for example. Andy was born on Easter morning."

"Late morning, heck, it was practically afternoon," Andy said with a grin.

"Yes, but it makes a better story how I tell it," I continued. "So, it's Easter Sunday and Holly is ten months pregnant and fatter than the Christmas turkey she had in the oven for dinner. She is out in her back yard garden tending to her vast assortment of flowers and plants, when all of a sudden she starts humming the hymn the choir sang at her church that morning. Right when she gets to the chorus – WOOSH! – her water breaks," I make a wide sweeping gesture with my hand.

"So, there is Holly, standing in her garden, water is a flowing, singing for all of heaven to hear…" Clearing my voice, I start to sing, "And He walks with me, and He talks with me…" At this point, Andy joins in and we both continue singing, "And He tells me I am his own… And the joy we share as we tarry there…" We lean our heads together and harmonize "None other has ever known…" Andy and I finish and burst into a fit of giggles while Mabel shakes her head, not quite sure what to make of it, but chuckling to herself.

After thinking about it for a few moments in silence, Mabel says, "Now wait one darn minute! I happen to know that hymn by Mr. C. Austin Miles. It's one of my favorite hymns – called "In the Garden" – and I've sung that more Sundays than you two have been alive. And nowhere does it mention a person named Andy."

"Oh yes it does!" Andy and I chime together.

"Oh no it does not!" Mabel says louder.

"Oh yes it does – I bet you lunch on it!" I say with another wink to Andy.

"You've got yourself a deal. So explain yourselves," Mabel said with rightful indignation.

Eyeing Andy, I said "One more time – from the chorus! Andy… walks with me… Andy talks with me…" We both peer at Mabel. Mabel just blinks.

"Andy…. tells me I am his own…" We stop singing.

"Are you trying to tell me Andy is 'And He'?" Mabel asked, staring incredulously from Andy to me.

"Yes," we say together as we start giggling again and poking each other like five year-olds.

"Oh for pity's sake, that is the most ridiculous story I have ever heard!" And with that Mabel bursts out laughing and tries to sing bits of the hymn between spasms of giggles.

We spent a few more minutes laughing and singing. Mabel paid the bill, grousing while she did so, and we left the Deli. Mabel headed over to the Mercantile for a bit of "light shopping."

"I don't think it's possible to do light shopping there," I called out to her. Andy and I wandered around a bit before heading back to the car. He pulled out a file he had tucked into the back of his shirt, handing it over with a smile.

"Here is the information you asked Mom to gather for you. Actually, I did most of the searches. She was busy with wheelchair stuff and insurance companies. It should make for some interesting reading. What are you hoping to find?" Andy asked.

"I have no idea. But I'm just curious at this point."

"Well, maybe the info will help. I also have…" Andy paused as he fished in his front pocket, pulling out a gold colored key, "… a skeleton key. Mom had a feeling you would be up to no good – her words, not mine, so don't get all testy. So, this key should open any door. And, this key…" Andy pulled out a smaller silver key from his pocket, "… should open anything else you have in mind. Practice with it, it takes some work to get used to it." Andy placed both keys in my hand.

I was stunned. Holly knew me far better than I thought, and I guess that meant Andy knew me far better as well.

"Andy, thank you. I don't know what to say."

"Just be careful. Mom still needs you to update your will and select a custodian for Chloe should you meet an unnatural end. She really is beginning to like her job and is thrilled to be busting the chops of some insurance company. When I left she said something about doing to the insurance company what Sherman did as he marched to the sea. And then she started singing the "Battle Hymn of the Republic." That's never a good sign, you know. So, just be careful," Andy warned with a grin.

Having known Andy for a number of years, I knew he was fully aware of all the trouble he caused for himself and his mother. I think some of the boy still lives beneath that manly exterior. I just wasn't fool enough to tell him.

"So, now what? Are you hanging around? Do you need a place to stay?" I asked.

"Nope. I'm going to grab the Jaguar and drive back," he beamed.

"Drive? You're taking the Jaguar all the way back to Colorado? Are you nuts?" I yelped.

"Why not? Mom said she wanted the car; the car company was more than happy to sell it to her. It's bought and paid for. I have the title in my back pocket. So, give me the keys, woman, and I'll be on my horse and ride. Or in this case, in my Jag, purring." Andy was glowing with newfound appreciation for the finer things. Oh dear, I wondered, what have I created?

"Right, let me dash in and grab the keys," I said as I ran through the side door into Mabel's kitchen. I reached for the keys that were hanging on her key rack and raced back outside.

"Here you go, Andy my boy. Please be careful driving. If you wreck the car or yourself, I'll never hear the end of it. You know your mother – she'd be singing Wagner for weeks!"

"I do. And yes, I'll be careful. She would scream if anything happened, or worse. She might even start singing Carmina Burana." Andy gave me a quick hug, loped to the car, turned the key in the ignition and revved the engine to hear it purr. With a wave and a big smile, he drove off. I smiled back as I stood watching him go, another happy soul on this planet. Andy was one of my favorites. He brought joy wherever he went. And I vowed to never tell Mabel that Andy and I won more free lunches with our "In the Garden" routine than a senior on blue plate special day.

As I headed back to my room, I realized it was starting to feel like home and I wasn't sure of what to make of those feelings. With a murder to solve and not wanting to end up dead myself, I'd think about how long I'd stay in Comfort later.

Chloe greeted me with a chirp and eyed the kitty toy I had in my hand. Flinging the file folder on my bed, I spent the next hour playing with Chloe and her new toy. By the time we were done, she was exhausted and snoozing on her window seat and I was on my hands and knees picking up bits of feathers. Would I ever learn? Some toys are not made user friendly.

Settling down on the bed with the file folder, the rough draft liberated from James' gallery, and the piece of paper found on Megan's studio floor, I immersed myself in all that had been collected. It painted a more complete picture of James and Anna, but nothing that would knock my or anyone else's socks off. James excelled as an art student – had potential, one piece of paper indicated that one of his professors said that he had excellent skill and technique, but needed to broaden his scope.

A suggestion was made to go to Paris to study light, color, and depth. Interesting, I thought. A note was made that James had spent five years in Paris and came back to Comfort married to Anna, a fellow art student whom he had met while in Paris. There were fewer details on Anna, other than she was an only child of older parents and they had passed on shortly after she left for Paris. Sad, but nothing sinister.

I read the rest of the folder and found nothing interesting or noteworthy. I did notice that Andy had managed to look into James' financial history and he seemed well off and was still listed on the title of the lighthouse, though he had not paid off the mortgage. Nothing to show that he was a murderer. Nothing to show what his secrets could be, what his passion was other than his obsession with his lighthouse. Then I looked at the rough sketch of the lighthouse, no big surprise there. But the lines were odd. Gone was the depth from the other paintings I had seen. Since it was a simple pencil sketch, I couldn't judge the color. But something was lacking in that sketch, not just color. It was life, beauty, and passion – all the elements that turn simple drawings into works of art.

Reaching for the piece of paper I had stumbled on at Megan's studio, I smoothed it out and stared at it. It, too, was a simple pencil sketch of the lighthouse. But this one simple drawing was magnificent, with depth and feeling drawn from a few pencil lines. Peering closer I gasped, realizing that the sketch was an exact copy of one of the "crown jewel" paintings currently hanging in James' gallery. My mind was still too stunned to add one plus one and get two. As I saw it, I had three ideas. The first idea is that James' rough sketch was just that – a rough sketch done by an artist in its early stages of being. The second was that the sketch found at Megan's was James', which meant we could place him at the scene shortly before the fire. How shortly before the fire, I couldn't guess and wasn't sure on how to find out. Lastly, the sketch found at Megan's was Megan's, which meant that all of the works hanging in James' gallery were done by Megan, not James. And that thought made me tense and my blood clog like a stopped up drain. My body definitely did not like idea number three.

So, I went over all the information and looked at the two sketches again. I tucked both of the sketches into the file and resolved to take the folder to the Bank and Trust tomorrow for safekeeping. As I closed the folder I saw a note that Holly had written on the back. It read that she was having trouble finding out who owned Megan's studio because it was cloaked in multiple layers of red tape. She added that it would take her some time to figure it out and trace it back to the rightful person. Until then, I'll keep this folder and the two sketches hidden while I try to find out which idea was right.

I spent the rest of the evening doing Sudoku puzzles and trying not to think. I never made it to dinner because my healthy appetite had gone when the Reinhold information came in. Chloe was content to have me around and played happily at my feet. My mind kept asking me one question over and over. If pushed into a corner, what would I do? Would I come out and fight or would I curl up and give up? These thoughts led me to think of my parents and what they had fought for over the years for family and honor and doing what's right not just because it's the right thing to do. Sometimes the right thing to do hurts and doesn't feel good. And sometimes doing the unexpected can hurt as well. Chloe had long since fallen asleep and was snoring before I went to bed. But my mind had answered its own questions. Tomorrow, I fight. But in my own way!

CHAPTER 14

I awoke early the next morning feeling centered and ready for what lay ahead. After showering, I put on black pants and a multi-colored sweater with a white camisole peeking through. There was enough time to change Chloe's litter box, feed and water her, and make sure she was ready for her bug hunt with Benji. I skipped down the stairs and ate breakfast with four other guests, which was nice because Mabel couldn't ask any probing questions about murders and my personal funeral arrangements. Shortly after breakfast with folder in hand, I headed over to the Bank and Trust. Within minutes I had my own personal safety deposit box with the folder safely tucked inside. I took a moment to have a word with Drew Taylor and the bank president, Mr. McAdams, who was about ninety years old and exhibited a proper sense of privacy and decorum. He looked like he belonged as head of the Bank of England, not in a small seaside village. Mr. McAdams vowed he would be tortured before he would reveal the contents of my box. During the conversation, I had a mental picture of him at the Tower of London facing the guillotine and shouting, "God for Harry, England and Chloe!" right before the ax fell. I smiled inwardly and hoped it wouldn't come to that. I mentioned to Mr. McAdams that should anything happen to me, please deliver the information to Holly, my financial planner. This grabbed his attention and we were able to connect him to Holly should the need arise. I left feeling better, humming "Rule Britannia" and craving Earl Grey tea.

Leaving the Bank, it was very hard to miss the delivery van pulling away from the front of the Bike Shop. The whole Taylor family was out front. Looking in my direction, they waved me over like stranded souls flagging down a rescue plane. I hurried over and came to an abrupt stop when I saw what the fuss was about. The wheelchair had arrived. A thing of beauty it was. It was sleek and black with thick tires that had knobs protruding for better gripping. It was streamlined with pouches for whatever Benji would want. And most importantly, it fit his small bent frame with room to spare. This was something he could grow into. Drew was studying the literature that had accompanied the chair while Margharite just stood and silently wept into her clasped, upturned hands. She spied me looking at her and rushed over to engulf me in a big bear hug. I was getting teary myself. Benji was bobbing up and down and wanting to go zooming over the entire west coast. Who could blame him? The only thing the wheelchair didn't have was a turbo prop or a steam engine. Holly had outdone herself. I was completely blown away and couldn't wait to tell her the news of their reaction.

Margharite was trying to say something to me between her

sobs that I couldn't make out. Finally I was able to figure out what she was saying.

"The insurance company called last night to apologize for the foul up. Their foul up. Not our foul up. They say a more suitable wheelchair on its way. At no charge to us, and the paperwork had finally gone through with the added provisions. They said all of Benji's medical and health care would be covered now until he is twenty one. After which, they switch him to a special policy for disabled adults. We cried and danced last night after the phone call." Margharite stopped, drew a breath, and proceeded to start a fresh round of sobs. Drew looked at his wife and continued their story.

"This morning, a lady from some financial institution called to let us know that provisions had been made for Benji to be sent to a school specifically designed for disabled kids, in Uptown of all places, where he would get special schooling and where he could meet other kids like himself – with special needs. And that he was awarded a scholarship for full tuition payment until he graduates from high school. And that a private party had agreed to fund his college education once he decides on a major and what area he would like to study. Can you believe it? After all this time, our prayers came true!" And with that Drew grabbed Margharite around the waist and started dancing with Benji and me clapping and singing. I'm sure we made quite a sight, but it didn't matter. Benji promised to walk Chloe, but said he might be a bit late, as he had to learn his new wheels. I said anytime was fine. I hugged Margharite and promised to stop in later to check if the Easter Bunny was going to make an appearance. Drew gave me a hardy hand and a smile and I left with the sound of their laughter in my ears, a big grin on my face, and with the thought that Drew's ice toward me was definitely melting.

I skipped and danced my way back to Mabel's, who was in the kitchen making brownies, as if she would be anyplace else. I grabbed her around the waist and danced her around the kitchen singing and laughing while secretly hoping this little minnow would not be swallowed by a big fish. But, until that big fish appeared, I was going to celebrate. Mabel danced along with me and laughed not knowing why. She sure is getting used to me. Once I calmed down where I could make sense, I told her about Benji and his new wheelchair. Mabel smiled. At that moment I knew I could tell her my big secret. So, I let go of her waist and guided her to the kitchen table.

"Mabel, I have something to tell you and it may come as a bit of a shock," I began.

"Are you going to tell me what you are doing and why you are doing it?"

"Partly. First, I have a confession to make – I'm the one who gave you the new stove," I confessed.

"I know that, Katy. I just don't know why."

"Well, because I can. Because I like you and you needed it and I didn't want you to use your rainy day money for it. So, I decided to give back to someone who has been kind and generous to Chloe and me."

"Okay, but that really isn't the deepest reason for the why. But I shall not pry further. Anything else?" she asked.

"Well, I am also the person who bought Benji his new wheelchair."

"What? You? But how… this is different. This is… unbelievable. Katy…"

"What? You think Benji is different in his need. A wheelchair and a stove are the same thing. Both allow a person more freedom to do what they love. With you it was easy. Ask a few pointed questions about likes and preferences and presto, new stove! But, with Benji, I had help from a friend to make sure he has the best one available. Now he can go be who he is supposed to be without anyone or anything telling him no." I pleaded with my heart for her to understand.

"But, Katy, love, why? Why do this? Why get involved? Why?" Mabel was searching my face for clues.

"Because I inherited more money than... well, a lot. And, I have known hardship and struggle and sacrifice. I do not like being told what I can and cannot do. So I meet you, see a need. Hearing about Benji and watching him struggle, well, than why not step in to help. If I have learned one thing in this life, it's that one person can make a difference. So, do you understand? Even just a little? Because money does not matter if you don't have joy or a purpose in life. And the money I inherited has led me to a purpose: to better people's lives. And honestly, I think it's that simple. I can make a difference and actually see it happen." I looked into Mabel's eyes as she slowly realized my sincerity and vision.

"Okay, just how much did you inherit? I thought you said your parents were simple middle class folk and left you comfortable when they passed. Just how comfortable are you, dear?"

"Let's just say I could buy you a new stove every day for about fifty years and still have money left over for food."

"My dear, I am completely speechless. And that takes a lot of doing. Why here and why now?" Mabel asked.

"Because my parents passed away, I inherited the money, and Chloe and I needed a vacation. And maybe because I was running away from my past as well. So, we hopped a plane and drove Highway 1 until Chloe saw the sign that simply said 'Comfort', and here we are." I waited a moment, and then went on. "Do you have any other questions for me, Mabel? I will not hold any secrets from you, because I have other tales to tell you, if you want to hear them."

"Just one. Are you going to continue pursuing what happened to Megan?" Mabel asked.

"Yes."

"Well, since I may be cooking for your funeral, you might want to tell me what you have been up to. Who knows? Maybe I can help in some small way," Mabel smiled slyly.

"Okay, first, I'm not planning on dying for Megan. But, I do have more questions and fewer answers." I proceeded to tell Mabel everything I knew, including every conversation and detail, ending with my minor breaking and entering and why I came home braless and smoky. For the most part, she took the news really well.

"So, it's either James or someone we don't know enough about yet. Am I correct?"

"Yes. That's my thought, too. So, I plan to start talking to more people and asking more questions tomorrow. But I must ask you, Mabel, actually I'll beg if I have to, please don't speak of this to anyone. I've come to care for you and Taffeta too much and Chloe has become quite attached to you. Please just let me stumble my way through this. If I get to a place where I get scared and feel completely out of my league, I'll stop and tell the Uptown police. But I have no proof and no evidence, so nothing to show for my thoughts. So, I'll keep going until Megan tells me to stop. Okay?" I pleaded.

"Okay. Fair enough. But you have to give me daily reports, and if I don't see you every few hours, I'll call the National Guard down here so fast no one will know what hit them. Are you hungry?" Mabel asked, deciding she had enough surprises for one day.

"Starving as usual."

"Good. Dinner is at six, just the two of us. Veal Parmesan, salad, garlic bread and ice cream pie for dessert. Does that sound to your liking?" Mabel asked, getting up from the table to finish making brownies.

"Perfect. But what are the brownies for?"

"The Deli. They are trying to expand their business and the boys just love my brownies. So, I promised to make them two dozen every day until we see how their business does. You didn't have anything to do with that, too, did you?" Mabel asked, eyeing me with her truth detector.

"Absolutely none," I said honestly. However, it does give me some great ideas, I thought, as I waved and went upstairs. I spent the rest of the afternoon calling Holly and catching her up on the Taylors and Benji's new wheelchair. She sounded happier than a Siamese cat clawing drapes. Benji came by and he and Chloe went off for their bug hunt. He seemed taller and wider in just a few short hours. I spent the afternoon before dinner reading but not retaining as I readied my plans and line of questioning. At precisely six o'clock, I rambled down to a lovely candlelit meal with Mabel. It still amazes me how much I care for her and how important she has become in such a short time. After dinner, I helped Mabel clean up, brushed Chloe after her dusty and satisfying bug hunt and waited until dark. Changing into my cat burglar outfit, I quietly left the B&B by the side kitchen entrance.

It was relatively easy to creep down to the Point and cut through the alleyway between it and the Mercantile. At this time of night, the town was quiet and looked deserted. I tried the doorknobs of the Mercantile, the flower shop, and the Tourist Trappings. They were all locked. I stopped suddenly as I sensed movement came from Bo's Nuts and Bolts shop. I gently poked my head around the corner of the doorway to get a better look.

Bo, or at least a person wearing the same Wranglers, was seated at the front desk doing paperwork. Again, I couldn't see his face and most of his upper body was in shadow. Darn it all, I thought. At this rate I'll never see what he looks like and will never know why Chloe likes him so much that she licked him.

Slowly I made my way past his door and stopped at the back entrance of James' gallery. I carefully tried the doorknob, hoping his alarm wouldn't sound. It was locked. I fingered the skeleton key Andy had given me, which was now burning a hole in my pocket. It felt almost too risky to try it. I didn't want the alarm to sound – if there was an alarm. And, I didn't want to be caught by Bo, or anyone for that matter. So, I inched along until I was in front of the gallery. All seemed quiet. I watched as the light went out in Bo's shop. Luckily, I heard the back door open and close and footsteps lead away from my hiding place. Whew, I thought, that was close. I lingered a few more minutes just to get the feel of the place and decided that my Plan B could wait another day. Just as I was rounding the corner to walk down the pier, a waft of smoke hit me full in the face. Flames were shooting up from the direction of the Blue Heron.

Like a demon possessed, I ran screaming Mabel's name as loud as I could. The fire seemed to be coming from outside the kitchen door and working its way toward the back of the house. I ran the perimeter of the house until I found the coiled up hose that I was sure had to be there. Grabbing the faucet and giving it a few twists to start the water flowing, I pulled the coil and ran to the flames licking at the kitchen door. All the time I kept yelling Mabel's name. And then it hit me. CHLOE. As I sprayed water at the slowly dying flames, I could hear voices coming from across the way. Instantly, Drew Taylor was by my side and grabbed the hose to take over. I was just about to make a mad dash through the kitchen door when I saw Mabel through the haze and smoke. She was sitting huddled on the ground holding a large towel. I ran to her screaming, "Where's Chloe?" Mabel lifted her head and opened enough of the towel for me to see that Chloe was safe in Mabel's arms. Mabel's eyes told me another story. "Where's Taffeta?" I yelled. Mabel just shook her head and looked down at Chloe, tears slowly running down her cheeks. I whirled around and ran toward the kitchen door.

The fire was mostly out and sodden ash and burnt wood filled the air. Drew motioned to me and I walked over to him as he was scuffing the ground, spraying water on any potential hot spots.

"Drew, Taffeta, Mabel's cat, is still in there. Can I get through?" I asked anxiously.

"I wouldn't until things settle a bit. She's a smart cat and probably went into hiding. We'll find her, don't worry. You need to focus on Mabel. She looks beaten down, like no wind in her sails. Go to her. Be with her. We'll find Taffeta and let you know."

Returning to Mabel, I knelt down until one arm was wrapped around Mabel and the other was gently stroking a bundled up Chloe. Chloe looked unhurt and unfazed. She moved closer to Mabel and me as we sat and watched neighbors and friends stomping out the rest of the fire, assessing the B&B for damage and looking for Taffeta. It was almost dawn before Mabel, Chloe and I were allowed back into the kitchen. After some cleaning, I settled Mabel in her chair in the kitchen with Chloe still wrapped up in a towel on her lap. I hurriedly made tea and grabbed a plate of brownies.

"Mabel, drink your tea and eat a brownie. You've had quite a shock tonight," I said gently.

"I'll have you know that these are the brownies I was to give to the boys at the Deli tomorrow," she said, trying to get some vim into her vigor.

"I'm sure the boys will understand. Now sip and eat. I'm sure Drew has a few things to tell us, don't you Drew?" I asked, seeing him come in. He helped himself to a cup of tea and made his way toward the table.

"Well, I do have a few things to say. First, the fire is out and it looks like it was more smoke than damage. You'll probably want to repair and repaint around the kitchen door area and maybe get a new kitchen door to boot. Most of the damage was to the yard, clothesline, bushes and ground around the side yard. Lucky you were out walking when you were, Katy. The damage could have gotten out of control and who knows what might have happened. I sent for the Uptown Fire Marshall just to have a quick look. As I'm head of the Comfort Volunteer Fire Brigade, I have that right. I think it was definitely arson. My guess is that they used something easy and accessible like plain old gasoline or turpentine to start it. But I want the Fire Marshall to confirm it for me. So, he should be by and will let me know what his findings are." Getting up and gulping the rest of his tea, Drew placed his cup in the sink and headed toward the door.

"Oh, one other thing. We couldn't find Taffeta. She is not here at all. So, I bet she got out and is hiding somewhere nearby and will come out when the sun is up or when she gets hungry. Margharite and I will keep an eye out. She may be in the Bike Shop for all I know. Well, good night, huh, or should I say morning. Most of the neighbors have gone, so it should be more peaceful for you both. Call me if you need anything." And he left.

"Peaceful?" Mabel said, staring down at Chloe in her towel.

"How can it be peaceful when someone just tried to burn my house down?" Mabel asked gathering steam.

"Mabel, it's my fault…" I started to say.

"Now I will have none of that!" Mabel bellowed. I sensed that her steam had been gathered.

"We are both responsible adults and as I see it, it was an attack on us, not just you or me. So, that means you are getting close, Katy."

"Yeah, but I just wish I knew what question got somebody rattled."

"Miss Katy, I have made a decision. I am going to get Bo out here first thing and have him make any repairs that are necessary. I am going to make more brownies and get this place cleaned up. And you, my dear, are going to keep going. This isn't just about Megan anymore. Someone just made it personal and I'll be damned if I will let anyone or anything frighten me or scare me off. Have you got that, missy?" Mabel declared.

"Yes, ma'am," I answered, not sure if I should salute.

"Okay, then you get Chloe settled and open up all the windows upstairs, and let's get this placed aired out. Thank goodness we didn't have guests last night. Can you imagine what a mess we would have been in? Now move!" Mabel had spoken. I scooped up Chloe in her towel and headed out of the kitchen toward the stairs.

"And Katy?" Mabel said her voice quivering just a bit. "If you see or hear Taffeta, please let me know…" She swallowed and went to her kitchen sink. I nodded to the back of her and headed up the stairs. I went straight to our room first and deposited Chloe on our bed. Searching her little black frame for any hint of bruises, cuts or burns, all I found were claws. She was not in the mood to play doctor. As soon as I completed my exam and found her healthy and full of herself, she scampered off the bed and over to her litter box. Ah well, I thought, what a good idea.

CHAPTER 15

I headed to my bathroom to do the same and opened up the small window for some fresh air. Glancing at myself standing in front of the large mirror, I nearly leapt out of my skin. I looked ghastly. Smoke, ash and bits of singed plant debris clung to my hair and on my clothes. And I smelled like the floor of a burnt out taxicab. After hastily stripping in the bathroom, I scrubbed and rinsed every inch of my body until my normally olive skin was as pink as a pig's belly. The smoke remained in my lungs and I vowed that Chloe and I would take a trip to the pier later to breathe in the salty air. Dressing quickly in my jeans, white T-shirt and lavender sweater, and putting my hair into a pony tail, I tidied up our room, opening windows, and then moved on to the other three guest rooms. With windows open, I scurried around cleaning and sprucing up the place that was usually in tip top shape anyways. I left Chloe to her sunbeam and a long sunbath after feeding her, watering her, and refreshing her used litter box. She seemed no worse for the wear. In my sprucing up of the other guest rooms, I searched high and low for Taffeta. It seemed strange not to find her body let alone any sign of her. Heading downstairs with my bundle of black cat burglar clothes and Chloe's towel, I found that Mabel had opened the windows in the front parlor, formal dining area, and back parlor. She had thoroughly cleaned the place as well, including the small guest bathroom off the dining room.

I headed toward the kitchen, stopping to drop off my smelly clothes in Mabel's laundry area. I stopped and cocked my head; well, where did Mabel sleep? Does she even live here? I never gave it much thought. So, I marched into the kitchen to ask.

But Mabel was nowhere in sight. I headed out the kitchen door, noticing that the kitchen looked spruced up as well. But, no brownies. Not paying attention, stepping out the door, I walked straight under a ladder. Looking up and squinting into the sun, I spied the now familiar legs wrapped in the same pair of jeans.

"Hi, Bo," I said, smiling to myself that I knew his pants by sight now.

"Hey, Katy, is that you? Are you and Chloe okay? Anybody hurt?"

"Nope, Chloe's fine. I examined her completely and she's fit as a fiddle, well, a fiddle with teeth and claws."

"Huh, sounds like she doesn't like this business anymore that the rest of us. Are you okay?" he asked again.

"Fine, thanks. I'm just tired. Didn't get much sleep last night. Have you seen Mabel?" I asked, staring again at his fly.

"Yes, she's at my office making a phone call. It seems

whoever burnt the place cut the phone lines as well."

"Why?"

"Don't ask me, ask your arsonist. I don't know who cut the lines, but I have a feeling I know who might have."

"Who do you think it is?" I asked.

"James. He was around for the last round of fires and it looks like this fire fits the pattern of the others. There's just something about him that strikes me as odd. Like he knows something, or is hiding something, or both."

"Great. But why would he set a fire at Mabel's?"

"Have no idea. Have a question for you though," he said, readjusting his stance on the ladder.

"Yes, I'm listening."

"Why were you out last night on the pier jiggling doorknobs?" he asked, climbing a step higher on the ladder.

"WHAT? You saw me?"

"Hard to miss. You walked right past my door. I heard you try James' door, then move to the front. Just figured you were either crazy, up to something, or both. So, I turned off my light, locked up and left to go meet you, but I smelled smoke and ran to check that out instead. Got Mabel and Chloe out before things got out of hand. And you?"

"And me what?" I asked.

"Are you crazy or just up to something?" I swear I could hear a smile in his voice.

"How about both?" I was getting tired of talking to his pant legs. "Are you coming down any time soon?" I asked his inseam.

"Not until I make sure this roof is sound and that there's no damage. Why?"

"I'm tired of talking to a ladder."

"Ha!" he barked a laugh. "I'll be down later. And Katy, be

careful. Whether you're crazy or up to no good, somebody is watching and is worried enough to set a fire. Okay?"

"I already promised Mabel I would try to behave myself. Yes, I'll be careful." I started to walk off and had a thought. "Hey, Bo?"

"Yeah?" he yelled back.

"What were you doing at your shop so late?"

"Doing middle of the month invoicing," he said. "Hey, Katy?"

"Yeah?"

"What were you doing at James' gallery last night?" he countered.

"Poking my nose in where it doesn't belong. Crazy, huh?" I said. "See you later," I called over my shoulder as I headed toward the pier. I swear I heard Bo laughing as I walked away. Well, maybe I made up for my rotten first impression. Or maybe he still thinks I'm crazy. But at least he's thinking... I smiled to myself as I headed toward the pier.

It appeared that all of the inhabitants of Comfort were out. Passing the Point, I spied several hands waving a "Good Morning" greeting. I waved back. Looks like the townsfolk are warming up to me. Over at Sharkey's Bar it looked like the barflies were out in full force as well. The wraparound deck held a few people sipping their beers and chewing the fat. When I arrived at the pier by the Mercantile, the place was busy with people shopping, talking and bustling about like bees in a hive. I guess the fire at Mabel's was making the rounds of the gossip chain. I waved at Charley, who was in front of the Mercantile sweeping his sidewalk.

"How are you, Katy?" he asked. "Feeling okay? Chloe unharmed, I hope?"

"We're both fine, Charley, thanks for asking. Are you

having a fine day?"

"Just fine. If you need anything, you just let Dotty and me know. And you tell Chloe she needs to come visit us sometime. Dotty would love to meet her," he smiled.

"I'll let her Highness know. She was bathing in a sunbeam when I left, but I'll try to take her for a bug hunt later." I waved and moved on. Charley smiled and waved back.

The flower shop was so crowded I couldn't make out a single person I knew. I kept going, thinking that I had only met a handful of people in this town and it seemed the handful had multiplied by a fistful. Smiling wickedly, I went back into the flower shop, maneuvered my way to the salesperson at the counter and told her my impulsive idea. She laughed as I wrote out a check to four decimal places and left with a spring in my step and a sneaky grin on my face, knowing Mabel was going to blow a gasket when she found out what I did. Strolling by The Tourist Trap resulted in waves from the owner and shoppers inside. Nuts and Bolts was closed, as I expected, since I had left Bo's Wranglers standing on top of a ladder by Mabel's roof. Pausing at James' gallery door, I just couldn't make myself go in. Peering closer, the gallery was dark with no one inside. The door was locked and no sign hung on the door. Interesting. Heading over to Cherry's, I bumped into Mabel as she was just leaving.

"Hey Mabel! How are you?" I asked, and gave her a warm hug.

"I'm fine, my dear. It seems the whole town knows about our little inconvenience last night and is in quite an uproar," she replied with a smile.

"I noticed. Bo said that you were making phone calls. Are you planning a quick getaway to Maui or one of the other islands?" I asked innocently.

"Ha, you wish. No, I was calling the couple that is scheduled to come this weekend, and made arrangements for them to stay at another beach house up the road. I want some time to myself and to finish any repairs that need to be made. I do not want to risk any injuries or further mishaps. So, they've been moved," Mabel stated without a hint of annoyance.

"Mabel, are you okay doing that? Is there anything I can do? Are you truly okay?" I asked, watching her face.

"Yes, there is. You are to be back by dinner – we're having vegetarian lasagna, antipasto salad, and garlic bread," Mabel said.

"Anything else, Mabel?"

"Just one other thing. Catch this person, Katy," Mabel grabbed my arm as she said it. "Do what you have to do to get them. I'm angry and I don't like to be angry. And people don't like it when I'm angry. I rumble like a western thunderstorm and it's feeling pretty stormy." Mabel gave my arm a firm squeeze, gave me a quick kiss on the cheek and marched off toward home. Mabel looked like Patton addressing the troops and I vowed not to let her down.

I poked my head into Cherry's place and could barely see her red hair over the customers swarming in her store. Her place, too, was packed. I did manage to see a wave and heard her say over the drone of chatter, "I'll catch you later, lady." I strolled past the bookstore, which was also crowded, and into Suds & Wicks. I spent a lovely hour chatting with the nice teenager who was running the place. Purchasing some lovely smelling guest soaps for Mabel made me smile. Maybe the scent of lavender, vanilla, sandalwood, and lilac would ease the smell of the burnt B&B. At least I hoped.

Moving on to the quilt shop, I assembled the largest gift basket they had of assorted quilting projects, all with cat themes, for Holly. After asking the owner to express mail it, I gave her a healthy tip to wrap it up in brightly colored tissue paper. I knew Holly would be surprised. A new Jaguar and a gift basket all in the same week; she'll be so thrilled! I smiled to myself as I left.

Passing Gavin's office, I noticed that it was dark and closed up as well. Well that's odd. I continued past the Deli, waved and got waves and shouts of greetings in return. The place was packed to overflowing with hungry hoards hunkering over hummus. Boy, this town sure loves a good tragedy. It brings all the mice out of the woodwork. I rounded the corner, heading towards Creature Comforts, when a thought struck me. My mind flashed to last night when I realized that, as I was rushing toward the flames at Mabel's, I remembered a glimmer of light shining through Gavin's window. So, both he and Bo were working late that night and both of them could have seen me. Lord knows Bo had. Great, I thought. Either one could have seen me, and either one could have had the opportunity to start the fire as well. Oh goody, more suspects, and two of my prime suspects are not in their offices and one is up a ladder at Mabel's. I smiled thinking of Bo and his laughter, trying not to notice my heart skip a beat.

CHAPTER 16

Sighing, I squared my shoulders and walked into Creature Comforts for some animal therapy – except I never got past the front door. People were milling about and animals were yipping, meowing, chirping, and scurrying. I half expected to hear a moo. Everyone could see Wynetta's head of blond bigness as she bustled around behind the counter. It was suddenly obvious that my day for visiting my new friends was going to be a total loss. So, I quickly closed the door hoping that nothing four legged or scaly would escape and headed back to Mabel's, still shaking my head in amazement at the sheer volume of people milling about. Strolling past the Bike Shop, I heard a voice call my name. Turning around I saw Margharite standing by their front door, motioning me to join her with a finger to her lips. I tiptoed over to her and up the ramp to the front door.

"I have little problem, Katy," Margharite whispered.

"What? Are you okay?" I whispered back.

"Yes, I'm fine. But there is a small problem," Margharite said again.

"Well, then tell me and I'll try to help," I whispered back.

"Katy, my new friend, I do not know how to say this. Maybe if you come see…" She trailed off in her still whispered voice.

"Margharite, tell me!" I shouted in a whisper.

"Look, promise you will not be upset and not jump to conclusions until I tell you. Now promise!" Margharite grabbed my shoulders and looked deep into my eyes, searching for something as yet unknown to me.

"Well, considering I don't even understand a word you are saying, I promise. But why are we whispering and what is the trouble?" I asked a little louder.

"Shh. Come, I show. You will see." And with that Margharite pulled me into her house, motioning me to be silent and walk tiptoe. We tiptoed into the front room, which I guessed was their living room with sofa, two stuffed chairs, and a small television. Lying on the sofa was Benji with his new wheelchair parked next to him. Benji was curled up asleep and covered in a thick gray rug. At least I thought it was a gray rug until it lifted its head and meowed softly.

"Taffeta!"

"Shh. Quiet!" Margharite whispered urgently. She motioned for me to step back out to the front door where she pulled the door closed behind us.

"There, now you see the problem," Margharite said.

"What problem? You found Taffeta. Mabel has been so worried and we have looked everywhere… expecting the worst," I said, relieved.

"But, that is the thing. Taffeta is Mabel's. And there is Benji. He found her last night curled up on his old chair in the shop – how he got her out, I do not know. How she got in there, I do not know. Now she will not leave his side. She stayed with him all day – like a guard dog. What am I suppose to do? Mabel will be crushed if her cat stays with Benji. And Benji will be crushed if the cat leaves and go home to Mabel. What am I to do?" Margharite was searching my eyes again, looking for answers.

"Well, my friend, I think there is only one thing to do." I smiled, gently patting her hand. "I'll be right back. Don't move a muscle." I ran off the porch and over to the Blue Heron, skidding to a stop in the kitchen. Mabel was by her stove buttering bread with a pungent garlic mixture.

"Mabel, I need your help. Can you come with me right now?" I asked. Without a word, Mabel put down her knife, wiped her hands on her apron and was out the door with me in four strides. I hurried with her to Margharite's where we stopped at her door. Margharite quietly opened the door.

"Any change?" I whispered.

"No, no change," Margharite whispered back with a wary eye at Mabel.

"Okay, Mabel, you need to see this, but quietly." I tugged on her arm as Margharite opened the door for us to pass into the living room. There was Benji, still asleep, covered in his Taffeta blanket, which was now softly purring. I bet we looked like the Three Stooges more than the Three Graces. Glancing back at Mabel, she was smiling and hugging Margharite. Turning around again, we all crept back out the front door and down the steps, this time so we could talk with our outside voices.

"Oh, my!" Mabel exclaimed. "I have never seen such a match made in heaven, or in this case," with a sideways glance at me, "from the fiery depths of hell." And with that, Mabel let out the biggest bellow of a laugh to be heard by all within the same area code. Margharite and I could not help but join her. I felt the knots of tension from last night escape as we laughed and hugged and dabbed our noses on our sleeves.

"I was so worried that something had happened to her that I never thought to ask my neighbors. I am so sorry, Margharite," Mabel said.

"What are you sorry for?" Margharite asked. "I am the one who stole your cat!"

"Now, nobody stole the cat!" I interrupted before Mabel could get the wrong idea. I explained on Margharite's behalf what happened with Mabel just beaming beside me. When I finished, Mabel gave a nod of her head.

"It seems to me that Taffeta has made her choice as to who belongs to her. Cats choose their people. And if the truth be told, I was getting a bit tired of her shedding all over the parlor. I have enough to do with Princess Chloe and her demands," Mabel said with a smile.

"What demands? You spoil her at every turn and she's even taken to curling up in your fresh laundry," I said.

"Don't I know it? You're off solving mysteries and I'm left minding that fuzzy black charmer. She has me so bamboozled that I've even taken to feeding her on the good china!" Mabel declared with a grin.

"Oh God! We've created a pint-sized monster. What am I going to do?" I wailed half seriously.

"Absolutely nothing!" Mabel declared. "Chloe is to stay just as she is for as long as she's my guest, and she can do whatever she wants for as long as she wants. Done!" Mabel said, and turning to Margharite, she added, "Truly, Margharite, I believe Taffeta will have a much better home with Benji, you and

Drew. I am delighted for you all. Tell Benji he is one lucky boy. And now, back to my garlic bread!" Mabel quickly turned, a little lighter in her step, and headed back to the Blue Heron.

"Well, are you okay with this, Margharite?" I asked.

"Yes. Benji will be so joyful. He played with Chloe and liked her. Was making sounds of wanting a cat of his own. Seems like the problem is solved. I do not think Mabel is one who uses words she does not mean," Margharite said.

"I agree. And I think Chloe has had a good influence on both Mabel and Benji. She can be a six pound handful, I should know. Look, I should go help Mabel with dinner. I'm truly happy for you, Benji and Taffeta. If Benji wants to resign as official cat walker, I'll understand." I hugged Margharite and headed to Mabel and the garlic bread.

Mabel was in the kitchen busily buttering the garlic bread. Walking up behind her, I hugged her around her waist.

"Are you truly okay with this Mabel?" I whispered in her ear, "or are you the most generous person I have ever met?"

"I am truly okay that Taffeta has found a place in Benji's heart." Mabel turned around and faced me with her eyebrows knitted.

"Who am I to stand in the way of love? Katy, Taffeta was a great gift and I am grateful. But, Benji has a need much greater than mine for unconditional love and long gray fur. That boy's life has been one continuous struggle to be whole, to be loved, to be accepted..." Mabel looked earnestly into my eyes. "I will not stand in that boy's way. And I have something more precious than Miss Taffeta; I have you and Chloe for as long as you need. My dear, that is more than enough." Mabel looked up at me with the biggest grin. "Why are you so worried about an old woman like me?"

"Because I care for you, old woman. I don't ever want

anyone to hurt you or cause you pain," I said feeling a lump in my throat.

"And I you, Katy. You give me courage to face the unknown and the strength to love and let go. Thank you for your friendship – and Chloe's. Now…" Mabel stood up straight as a fence post, "We, yes, WE, are having company tonight. So, go upstairs, tame that beast you call a cat, shower, dress in something calm and soothing and be down here by six with that cat of yours. No arguments. Now go!" Mabel pushed me from her and I saluted her, which drew a chuckle, and marched upstairs like a soldier being summoned to the Ready Room.

Once upstairs, I quickly undressed and showered with one of the new soaps. Just before coming upstairs, I had sneakily placed the other soaps in Mabel's laundry room knowing she would see them later. I changed into my favorite pair of dark gray yoga pants, gray socks with black cats on them and topped the whole ensemble with my white camisole and pale pink hoodie. Mabel said comfortable and soothing, so there. I went over to Chloe who jumped into my arms for some much needed loving. As anyone who knows Chloe will tell you, brushing is not something you do to her unless you have a very low deductible on your health insurance. Chloe looked well groomed and I didn't feel it necessary to bleed profusely before dinner. So, I was sure her fine short fur coat would be perfect for this dinner party.

I headed downstairs promptly at six o'clock, holding Chloe. Walking into the large dining room, all I could do was stare. There sat the Comfort equivalent of the Spanish Inquisition. Gathered around the table, munching veggies from a large tray nestled in the middle of the dining table, were Cherry, Wynetta, Margharite, and Dotty, whom I had never seen without her eyes in a book. Dotty's light brown eyes were peering at me now and I felt like I had been catalogued, profiled and put in a folder to be researched later. Oh, boy, what have I done now?

"Hi, guys! Last time I saw you all it was like an Easter Parade down at the pier, but minus the hats," I said.

A bunch of "Hi, Katy's" filled the air. Mabel came trotting from the kitchen holding a steaming pan of lasagna. She placed it on the table along with the garlic bread, salad, a condiment tray, and the veggie tray that were already set around the entire length of the dining table. All conversation seemed to cease as we looked at the food. Mabel made her way to the head of the table and indicated with a nod that I was to sit opposite her at the foot of the table. When I place Chloe on the floor, she scampered over to Mabel and chirped. Mabel pulled up an ottoman with a small china dish on it. Chloe jumped up, eyed the dish, and began devouring the heaps of wet kitty food. This is new, but I dare not say a word to Mabel. The other ladies were helping themselves to the feast at the table, politely shoveling in forkfuls of lasagna and salad and tearing off hunks of garlic bread. I helped myself and instantly had a plate heaping with warm lasagna, garlic bread, green salad, olives, cocktail onions, marinated mushrooms, and different veggies. A bowl of extra marinara sauce was passed as well, along with a bowl of freshly grated Reggiano Parmesan, from Italy no doubt. A glass filled with red wine appeared before me. The ladies only stopped talking when they were busily chewing their dinner. I followed suit.

After several helpings, many glasses of good Chianti, many "Please pass the…" and bits of garlic bread being used to mop up the excess tomato sauce, Mabel set down her fork.

She genteelly cleared her throat and said, "The first meeting of the Black Cat Society will now come to order!" And she banged her empty wine glass to prove it.

CHAPTER 17

"I beg your pardon?" I said.

"Merp!" Chloe said.

The ladies all stopped their mopping, drinking, and munching and stared at Mabel.

"All right. Now that I have your attention, I have something to say." Mabel cleared her throat again, looked at her empty wine glass like she wished it were full and gave each of us a look in turn.

"I have lived in Comfort most of my life and I have never, until this very moment, felt the need to stick my nose where it doesn't belong. Nor have I felt the need to interfere in other people's lives. And, I have never felt there was need to protect the good people of Comfort. UNTIL NOW!" Mabel slammed her still empty wine glass on the table.

"I have stood by and watched a good person, Megan

Harris, get swept up by a man who is nothing more than a snake oil salesman with a fragile wisp of a wife. I have said and done nothing. I have stood by and looked at the ashes of Megan's studio, her burial ground, as it were, and said and done nothing. I have watched my neighbors, my friends, and those that I have lived with, worked with and shared with for more than fifty years, say and do nothing. Well, my dear ladies, it ends here, now, tonight. I will no longer stand by and do nothing. It took a stranger to remind us how to be a friend, how to help one another, how to love one another. It is time to act and act now. Cherry, pour me some wine!" Mabel ordered.

"Yes, Madame!" Cherry obliged as she poured Mabel another glass.

"So, first I would like to say thank you. Thank you, Katy, for lighting a fire under an old lady. Not that type of fire, you goofball!" Mabel snapped at Wynetta as she was about to speak.

"Katy no more than set my fire than Jimmy Hoffa. What I am saying," Mabel said slowly to prove her point, "is that Katy has lit that spark in me to act and not shy away any more. And I am asking you, my dearest of friends, to join me. Join us." Mabel looked at me with true meaning and adoration in her eyes.

"Katy and I need your help to find out what happened to Megan and what we can do about it. Given the fire last night, I can't help but think that the person is someone we know here in town. I for one want to know who that is, why they killed Megan – and oh yes, she was killed and we all know it! Most of all, I want to find out why someone would take a life that was so young and full of promise. So, are you with me, my friends?" Mabel looked around the room and then directly at the chair next to her.

"I'm in," Cherry said simply.

"Me, too," Wynetta said, sitting next to Cherry.

"I guess I'm in, since I seem to have started the whole thing," I said, looking at Margharite.

"I'm in. I played a small part already," she said, turning to Dotty.

"I'm in and I've brought intel," Dotty said, reaching into her purse by her chair and pulling out a manila folder.

"Intel?" I said.

"Yes, intelligence. Information. Facts and data gathered that will perhaps point us in the direction we need to go," Dotty explained patiently.

"Um, before we, um, get down to business, I really must ask you one question, Mabel," I said.

"What's that?"

"The Black Cat Society? Who thought that up and when?" I asked.

"Chloe and I discussed it while we watched my home and business burn last night. We discussed it further this morning over lunch, which you missed! Chloe seems to be the catalyst that gets people to do the darnedest things. So, there you have it! Any questions? Any objections?" Mabel asked, steeling herself for a fight.

"Nope, not me. I always try to do what Chloe asks. Have you seen her claws? They're lethal." My small joke must have broken the tension because the room was filled with gentle laughter. Cherry refilled our glasses while Wynetta, Margharite, Mabel and I cleared dishes. Dotty wiped down the table and got out her reading glasses and an empty tablet "for notes," she said. We all settled back into our chairs with a large plate of brownies in front of us.

"My first question, before I begin, is to you, Katy. I need to ask you something and I would like a well thought out and honest answer. Will you do that?" Dotty asked.

"Yes," I said.

"Okay, first, why are you so interested in Megan? You have said to everyone that you are new to this area, just passing through, and that you have no known acquaintance with Megan Harris. Is that true? Did you know Megan?" Dotty inquired further.

"No, I have never met her, did not know that she existed on this earth until Chloe and I showed up here."

"Okay, I believe you. Then second, my original question, why are you so interested in Megan? I would really like to know..." Dotty asked leaning forward and looking intently into my face.

"Well, this may not be as easy to explain. So, I'll start small and you can ask me more questions if you wish. I don't know Megan, never met her. But I feel her." I took a deep breath and began to tell these ladies one of my deepest secrets of all.

"Ever since I was a little girl I've felt things, known things. I knew my Grandfather was going to die before he did. I knew when something bad was going to happen, stuff like that. I always told my mom – she told me to always tell her. And then it happened." I took a deep breath, cautious about going on.

"What, Katy, what happened?" Dotty asked gently.

"I saw him, my grandfather I mean, after he died. He was sitting on the piano bench in the living room just looking around like he hadn't seen the place in awhile. I mentioned it to my mother. I remember her holding me to her as she sank into the sofa staring at the piano bench. I told her that Grandpa said he was okay and that we would be too. It made Mom cry. I remember telling her I was sorry I made her cry and she hugged me so hard and said, "Baby, I'm not crying because I'm sad. I'm crying because Papa stopped by to say good-bye. He's okay and so are we." She must have hugged me for hours. After that Mom and Dad would look at me strange sometimes. But they stopped believing I was making stuff up. They believed." I stopped talking and lifted my head up to see their faces. Everyone at the table looked shocked and frozen by my answer.

"Did you see Megan?" Dotty asked.

"No, I've felt heaviness here, but I haven't seen her. I did feel a presence when I was in her studio." Oops, I thought.

"You've been in the studio? How did this happen? Are you crazy?" Cherry shouted from the other end of the table.

"Now hold on people. Let me debrief her, okay?" Turning to me, Dotty continued with the interrogation, "Are you crazy? What were you thinking? You could have been seen – when did this happen?"

"Good one, Dotty, I couldn't have said it better myself!" Cherry quipped.

"Thank you," Dotty replied, turning to me. "Answer the question, Katy. What did you do?"

"Well, the other night, I broke into her studio, and I'm not going to say how, but once I was in there I felt her. Felt Megan. She seemed sad, disappointed, like she was stuck somewhere. I let her know she was safe with me and that I wanted to help. I told her to help me find who hurt her. Show me the way, I kept saying to her over and over in my head."

"What happened? Did she show you?" Dotty asked, urging me on.

"Yes, she showed me," I stopped and looked at Mabel. Communication passed between us without words. I got up from the table raced upstairs to grab the two sketches and skidded to a halt when I remembered that I had them in a safety deposit box at the Bank. I raced back downstairs and leaped back into my chair like I never left. The ladies all stared at me like I had finally lost my mind.

"Okay, so my two key pieces of evidence are sitting in a safety deposit box at the bank. I forgot I had a moment of clarity the other day and decided to safeguard them so as not to endanger myself, Chloe or Mabel," I said to the group.

"Humph, I'm third," Mabel said while placing a hand on Chloe, who was asleep on the ottoman, her food dish having mysteriously disappeared.

"Explain the two pieces of evidence," Dotty said, clearly trying to find a thread of logic in what I was saying.

"Okay, one – when Margharite and I crashed James' gallery party…" I began.

"We did not crash. He invited us," Margharite clarified.

"Anyway, I stumbled on a rough sketch in his trash can and I took it. It doesn't look like anything hanging on James' walls, even for a rough sketch. So, who knows what that could mean?"

"And the second?" Dotty asked.

"The second I found at Megan's studio the night I broke in."

"The thing that Megan showed you?" Dotty asked, finally finding my thread of logic.

"Yes. I literally tripped, or rather skidded, over another piece of artwork. This time it was part of a painting, done in pencil, which looks like an exact copy of one of the oils hanging in the back of James' gallery." I let that bomb drop and sat back and listened to the silence following my verbal detonation.

"You mean to tell me that either James dropped a piece of his artwork done in pencil…" Wynetta began.

"… In Megan's studio…" Cherry continued.

"…or Megan's artwork is… oh god…. no, it couldn't be…"

Mabel stammered.

"Yes, Megan's artwork could be hanging in James' gallery," Margharite ended. They all sat back looking stunned.

Dotty cleared her throat to regain her focus. "Okay, calm down people. Let's focus on one thing at a time. Katy, I have one more question for you before we go forward. Again, I would like a straight and honest answer. Okay?" she asked more firmly. I nodded.

"Why Megan? You could have walked away at any point up until now. You could have left this morning at first light following the fire, but you didn't. Why, Katy? Why Megan and why didn't you walk away?" Dotty asked gently.

"Because she's alone," I said with my head down, staring at the table. "I felt her and felt the depths of her aloneness. She wasn't lonely. She was alone. She doesn't have anyone else. She lived alone and died alone and I felt her and I knew... because I know..." I started to sob.

"What do you know, honey?" Dotty asked gently.

"What it's like to be alone, to feel abandoned," I sobbed. "I'm alone now. When I felt Megan, I felt me. Alone in a world with no one to turn to... No one to call home to... I felt her and I felt me..." I stopped, all cried out, tired and spent. Chloe jumped from her perch on the ottoman, hopped on top of the dining table and scampered toward me and jumped into my arms. She placed her front paws on each side of my neck and rubbed her head under my chin. We sat that way for some time while I heard throats being cleared, noses being blown and sniffs. After some time, I said into Chloe's soft fur, "I feel Megan is not at rest. I sense a presence – something I feel, but cannot see. She wants to go on in her journey. I think I need to help her." I looked up, "I think we need to help her – we need to solve this and let her spirit carry on." I looked deeply into the faces of my new friends and surprisingly found acceptance and belief in their eyes.

"Okay honey, now that we know that you know… that you see… things, what's our plan of action?" Cherry asked, looking at me then at the rest of the group.

"I've come up with a brief plan, if you are willing to hear it," Dotty offered, opening her manila folder.

"We are all ears, Dotty," Mabel said, sitting up at attention.

"First, I think we need to do a bit of recon work. As I see it we have suspects. Who do you think they are, Katy?" Dotty asked.

"I have three, wish it were only two," I said with a crooked smile.

"Their names?" Dotty asked, pen poised over her paper.

"James, because he was Megan's mentor and was fooling around with her. Gavin, because he's odd, is hiding something – other than the obvious – and because his office light was on when the fire started. And last, Bo, because he was at his office that night as well."

"Bo!" Cherry shouted. "Why that man would not hurt a feather on Fran or Ollie! I don't believe it."

"Well, he could have motives we don't even know. Even though I don't want to, I do think he is a possible distant third."

"Okay, James, Gavin and Bo. I think we need to have eyes watching these men for the next couple of days. In my experience, once the suspect starts something, he usually starts to worry about getting found out. So, Cherry and Wynetta you keep tabs on Gavin. Make a list of his comings and goings and who he talks to. Anything you think is relevant. Margharite and I will be keeping an eye on James. Can you do that Margharite?" Dotty asked.

"I will tell Drew and Benji to work around me. I'll help,

too," Margharite said.

"And Mabel, you and Katy keep tabs on Bo. From the way Katy blushes, I think she will find a way to keep his attention," Dotty said as she peered over her bifocals.

"Now what is that supposed to mean?" I bellowed. "I've only met the man twice and both times I was stuck talking to his pants. I haven't even seen his face!"

"Well, then that will give you a good place to start," Dotty said, smiling. "We will report back here in two days time to go over our results and finalize a course of action. Anything else we need to cover?" Dotty asked, turning to the group.

"Yes," I said. "If you see anything suspicious or weird or out of the ordinary, let me know. I'm planning on spending most of the day tomorrow at the pier shopping and talking to people, so look for me if you need anything. And dear ladies, be careful. He could very well know we are watching – tread softly like cat's feet," I warned.

"Right!" Mabel hiccupped. "Right again! Then the first meeting of the…hic…Black Cat Society is adjourned…hic… and now will someone kindly help me find my legs so I can go to my room…hic?" Mabel said with glassy eyes.

"Right!" Cherry said as she stood up and helped Mabel from the table and gently eased her out of the room toward the back of the house. I knew Mabel lived behind the parlor, but I hadn't had the inclination to snoop around the bed and breakfast yet. I'd save that for another day. I got up from the table making sure that all was clean and tidy and took the empty brownie plate to the kitchen. After making sure the kitchen was spotless and ready for tomorrow, Cherry, Wynetta, Margharite and I bid each other hugs and goodbyes. The ladies headed out into the darkness and two of them were walking on tiptoe and peering around bushes. I turned to go back in and nearly jumped out of my skin as Dotty stepped through the door.

"Yikes, Dotty, I thought you had left!"

"No, I was checking on Mabel, who is snoring enough to rattle the rafters," Dotty said.

"Thank you, Dotty, for everything."

"It is I who should be thanking you. You are truly a catalyst, Katy. I think your Mom and Dad would be proud of the woman you have become," Dotty said as she looked into my eyes. "And I thank you for your courage and strength. I haven't felt this alive since being on the boat off the coast of Cuba!" And with that, Dotty gave me a kiss on each cheek and faded into the darkness. I noticed she did not walk on tiptoe, but I could hear no sound of her footfalls. I went back into the kitchen and locked the door. I went around the downstairs checking windows, locking doors and peering through laced curtains. The fort felt secure, I thought. Chloe tugged on my pant leg to let me know she was awake, even if it was temporary, and we both climbed the stairs to our room. I smiled as I thought of it as our room. We quickly got ready for bed, and as our heads hit the pillows we were out in no time.

CHAPTER 18

Sometime during the night, the dream began. The vivid dream hadn't visited me since I came to the town of Comfort. It always started the same with my Mom and Dad packing for a trip in their old white Volvo that they owned when I was a child. I watch as they load their suitcases, leaf through their litany of well-creased old maps, and make sure that the Coleman cooler can be reached from the front seat. I already knew its contents. Diet Pepsi, standing like frozen soldiers along one side, packages of cheese and crackers on top of the mounds of ice like discarded parkas, four baloney and cheese sandwiches and a pack of Fig Newton cookies stashed and ready to be eaten. This is the survival food my parents always took on any adventure. They never called it vacation. "Vacation is what folks call it who have no lives and are bored and in a rut," my Dad would say. Mom would always stop whatever activity she was doing and look at him and smile. "We don't vacate, we adventure," she'd proclaim and go back to her business.

The dream played out the same way every time. I would watch as they packed up the last of their books to read along the way – usually a combination of old Westerns and Agatha Christie. Next, I would watch helplessly as Dad opened the car door for Mom, helped her in, and making sure she was buckled, shut the door. He would make his way around the front of the car and usually stop midway by the hood to do a jig or a dance or run around in a complete circle. Either would always make Mom laugh. He would walk to the driver's door, open it, and look around like he's saying a mental goodbye, then leap in and have himself buckled at the same time the engine would roar to life. He would always lean out the window and yell, "Wagon, Ho!" before pressing his foot on the gas, shooting the car forward and out of sight. I would always be left at the curb yelling, "Wait for me, wait… come back!" But they never did.

There I lay in my beautiful cherry wood bed in a tangle of dusty rose sheets while the familiar nightmare unfolded. Except this time it was different. I heard a voice. It kept repeating the same phrase over and over as the scene unfolded in my dreams.

"Your Mom and Dad would be very proud of you, Katy," the voice said over and over in an endless loop. The voice droned louder as the end of the dream crept nearer, "…proud of you, Katy…the woman you have become… you're a catalyst, Katy…" Until Dad's door slams, his heartfelt "Wagon, Ho" and off they roar away from me. Wait, I yell at them, wait, wait, WAIT!

I sat up with my arm outstretched trying to pull them back to me. Trying to bring back the parents I had lost. Trying to hold on to their memory like wisps of smoke. My other hand clutched my chest as heaving sobs broke from the dam built in my heart. Tears of sadness poured from my heart, heavy with loss, blackened by sadness, and pierced by love. I let all the emotions wash over me like the surf outside my window. I cried for parents lost, but sweet childhood memories found; of parents taken away too soon, and of the remarkable life I was given. I cried until I was empty as a vase of flowers with its contents spilled on the floor, lying on its side, bare of its beauty and color.

I slowly massaged my chest and worked my hands up to my neck and shoulders. My practiced hands eased the tension in my body as I rubbed the taut muscles. Breathing deeply from my belly, I was able to blow the tension out like a candle, allowing my body to release all the toxic mixture of tension, sadness, fear and loneliness. In my mind, I inhaled the sound of cheese cracker wrappers, the warmth of a dusty wind on my face through a car window, and the cool taste of a soda in a Styrofoam cup.

Gently, I untangled the twisted sheets from my feet, trying not to wake up Chloe who was curled up in a ball at the foot of the bed. I padded to the bathroom in my stocking feet and splashed water on my face, blew my nose and avoided looking in the medicine cabinet mirror. I knew I wouldn't like what I saw. Grabbing an antique quilt hanging on the back of the rocking chair, I wrapped it around me intending to curl up on the window seat and watch the surf and the sunrise. Instead I found myself staring at a dance of mist and fog obscuring the view of anything but a few feet in front of my window.

Fog had crept into the town of Comfort like a thief in the night. Its white wispy arms had circled around the small town and smothered any signs of life, blurring anything recognizable. Some of the fog just hung like wallflowers while the rest of the fog waltzed and danced in a rhythm of its own using the spring breeze as its orchestra. I smiled at the fog and thought how fitting its arrival was to my nightmare. I cocked my head to the side, squinted at the misty white cotton, and shook my head clearing the fog in my brain. No, not a nightmare anymore, I thought. A memory, just a cherished memory. A dream to remind me of better days, nothing more. The blanket of fog deadened any sound. I leaned into the quiet and drank in the calm of white. God, what I wouldn't give for a massage.

I got up from the window seat and did a few light stretches. Wrapping the quilt around me I padded to my door, down the stairs and into Mabel's kitchen. I wonder if Bo is a massage therapist. If he can fix anything, I wonder how he would fix a pair of sore shoulder muscles. I smiled wickedly to myself, then shook my head and firmly closed that door to any romantic, dreamy thoughts. Nope, not ready for that type of thinking. Squaring my shoulders, I glanced around the kitchen for any signs of life from Mabel. A napkin was placed on the little kitchen table.

Katy –

Don't ever let an old woman drink that much wine! You're on your own for breakfast, I'm having tea and toast. You're on your own for lunch, too. Leftovers are in the fridge. I'm too hung over to even think about dinner – check with me later.

Mabel

P.S. Tell Chloe to keep to herself today – I'm not fit for company.

I laughed and replaced the napkin. The aroma of freshly made coffee filled the kitchen. Not letting go of the quilt, I poured myself a mug with plenty of fresh cream and sugar. My head was beginning to ache as well. I toasted two pieces of sourdough bread and spread fresh strawberry jam on them. Placing them on Mabel's napkin, I took the lot back upstairs with a special treat for Chloe. So much for detective work today. I can't see my hand in front of my face let alone a pyromaniac. I perched on the window seat munching on the toast and sipping the scalding hot coffee. I was starting to feel more like myself. Less maudlin and melodramatic, more light and calm with just a tug of sadness. And that felt okay to me. I stared at the fog as it danced its way past my window. I don't think this show is going to end anytime soon. So, I decided to get cleaned up and see what trouble I could get into.

Chloe had done her morning constitutional. I cleaned out her litter box, dried off the blue mouse that was floating in her water dish, refilled her crunchies and water and fed her a can of wet gourmet food from Cherry's. After attending to Chloe's needs, I showered and dressed in my most comfy outfit – black leggings, black camisole, thick black cat socks with green eyes and a periwinkle blue fleece shirt. Definitely not high fashion, but warm and cozy. Chloe had taken over my perch on the window seat, gotten bored with looking at a mass of white nothing and had curled up in the quilt for her first morning nap. I covered her with an edge of the quilt and she rumbled a purr of gratitude. I left and went back to the kitchen, leaving my suite door open a crack in case Chloe got lonely. Through the kitchen door I peered out. The fog looked like a thick blanket and a soft mist was falling from its folds. It looked like it was going to be a gloomy day. I tried to picture myself walking out into the drizzle and fog, but couldn't see the point of what I could accomplish. Just then I remembered my escape, a new Sudoku book upstairs, and decided that would be a good place to start my day. I was just running upstairs when I heard Mabel's phone ring. Dashing back to the kitchen I picked it up by the second ring, hoping the caller hadn't woken Mabel who, I had heard earlier, was snoring.

"Hello and thank you for calling the Blue Heron Bed and Breakfast. This is Katy, how can I help you?"

"Katy? You sound like you run the place. This is Cherry."

"Hey, Cherry! How are you this dreary morning?"

"Hung over to beat hell. Thank you very much. Thought I'd have to stuff Fran and Ollie for Thanksgiving, the racket they were making this morning. How are things?"

"Do you mean am I hung over too? Not so much. Had coffee and toast this morning. Mabel left a note on the table saying she was taking to her bed today because she was hung over. Even accused me of making her drink so much!" I laughed into the phone.

"Gads, Katy, don't make me laugh – it hurts! Poor Mabel. I'm glad you are there to keep an eye on her. Chloe okay?"

"Yep! Fit as a fiddle. She's eaten and is already on her first nap of the day. She loves weather like this. Gives her a reason to do nothing – which is what I'm going to do today. No sense in standing in the rain watching people who probably have sense enough not to be out there in the first place. You?"

"I had that same thought. Wynetta and I are here at our stores. But, we'll probably close early, no one around. Place looks deserted. Just called to say that I think our spying plans need to be put on hold until the weather clears. I heard the news say that a storm is right behind the fog, so it's going to be wet for the next couple of days. So, I guess I'll just pop a couple of aspirin, have a fourth cup of double espresso, and restock shelves. Wynetta said she'd come over and help if I needed her. She'll put a sign on her door if someone needs her to check with me here. You and Chloe? Any plans?" she asked.

"I think I'll just kick back, read a good book, do some Sudoku puzzles, play stringy with Chloe between her naps, and maybe shave my legs."

"Ha, you are funny. Why shave your legs? Is Bo coming over?" she teased.

"Ha, yourself. I have no idea if he's coming over here to work on Mabel's roof. I don't think he could see much. No, I'm shaving my legs because I'm tired of walking around here sounding like a cricket when my legs rub together." Cherry could be heard laughing loudly into the phone with bits of "Oh, no, my, oh my," thrown in.

"Girl, you've got yourself one hell of a sense of humor. And don't you give Bo such a brush off, he may be a suspect, but he sure is a cute one!"

"Gads, Cherry. My mind isn't ready for even entertaining the possibilities."

"You mean there's more than one possibility?" She teased.

"Now that's enough!" I said. "I need to go. My new Louise Penny mystery waits."

"Okay. Call if you need anything," Cherry said, and then gave me her number, Wynetta's number, Dotty's number, and Margharite's number – just in case. I wrote them all down judiciously and gave her my cell phone number in return, which she promised to pass on to the Black Cat Society ladies.

"I'll pass it along to Bo, too, if he asks," she said.

"Goodbye, Cherry, you're a nut."

"Goodbye, Katy. No, I'm not a nut; I'm a topping for a hot fudge sundae!" She said as she hung up. That woman appears to be a little bit off her considerable rocker. I raced back upstairs feeling invigorated from Cherry's phone call. I wondered if four double espressos can be contagious over the phone. Just as I was gathering a pen, pencil, eraser and puzzle book, my cell phone beeped to indicate that I had a message. I dug inside my purse to unearth my cell phone. Pressing the message key, I waited for the message.

"Hi Katy, it's the nut. Just making sure that your cell phone is on and that it works. Wynetta reports that all the doors on our side of the pier are locked and it looks like no one is around except for the Deli guys. They want to know if you and Mabel need lunch or dinner. Call me and I'll let them know. They're in the back playing poker and do not want to be disturbed. But, you're a great tipper, so they'll make an exception. Ta-ta!" Cherry said as her message ended. I pushed seven to erase her message and dialed her number.

"Hi Katy!" Cherry's cheery voice said.

"How did you know it was me?"

"Who else would call me here?" she countered.

"Oh, okay. Tell the Deli boys that Mabel and I have plenty of food and that we'll be fine. No need to bust up a poker game for us."

"I'll tell them. Wynetta and I will be joining them shortly. I've passed your number to the Society girls as well as the Deli guys; just so they can keep an eye on you..."

"Gee, Cherry. Is there anybody you haven't given my number to?" I asked somewhat exasperated.

"Just Bo, haven't seen him all morning. Wynetta says hi... oh wait... hold on... here, talk to Wyn," she stammered.

"Hey Katy, its Wynetta."

"Hey, girlfriend. Are you and Cherry bored or something?"

"Why do you ask?"

"You and Cherry sound like you haven't talked to me in

ages. Are you bored or is it the four espressos?" I said teasingly.

"Well, we have been chugging that stuff like Gatorade. I feel like I could plow a cotton field by myself – with bare hands," she said rapidly.

"I shudder to think what you two are like and I am so glad I am fogged in here. Take care, have fun and put a twenty on a hand for me – preferably a winning one," I laughed.

"Oh boy! Thanks Katy, we'll do that… gotta go… I feel lucky." Wynetta hung up as she sang "Luck be a Lady Tonight."

"Chloe, your Aunt Cherry and Aunt Wynetta are about as nutty as two pecan pies." I looked up and all that looked at me was a pair of ears and one eye staring at me from the quilt she had wrapped herself up in. "You're a cutie! Yes, you are!" I said trying to speak to the ears and eye. Chloe stretched out her paw and tucked her head down inside the quilt and sighed. "You look like Pucsatawny Phil," I said. And I figured in this weather, she did not see her shadow and she didn't care.

CHAPTER 19

I had just completed my first puzzle when my cell phone rang again. Gads! I thought as I reached for my phone.

"Hello?"

"Katy, it's Dotty. How are things?"

"Fine. Mabel is staying in bed today minding her hang…" I began.

"I know all about that. That's old news. What's happening now? Any progress?"

"Well, Chloe has eaten a whole bowl of crunchies and wet food, I've just finished my first puzzle and Wynetta and Cherry have called me, but I suspect you know that too."

"Well, yes, they wisely gave me your number so we can speak privately. I'm in the back storeroom where no one can see me or hear me."

"Is Charley there?" I asked.

"Yes. Why?"

"Don't you trust him?"

"Of course I trust him. I hold him in the highest regard and in the strictest confidence," she sternly replied.

"So, why aren't you talking in front of him?" I asked really confused.

"Because you obviously have no sense of decorum when it comes to covert operations. Now, do you want to hear the latest intel or not?"

"Absolutely, just the facts, Ma'am," I said warming to this cloak and dagger stuff.

"Okay, smart mouth, here's what I have learned. Per Wynetta, all is secure on their side of the pier – hereafter to be referred to as the South Side. I have established a perimeter on our side – here forward to be known as the North Side. Are you with me?" Dotty asked urgently.

"With open ears," I said with a grin.

"Whose ears are open?" Dotty asked seriously.

"Um, well, mine and Chloe's."

"You're confusing the issue. Now, we have established a perimeter on the pier and Charley and I will be making periodic rounds to assure there is no breech. Would you like us to report to you after every round?"

"God no, Dotty. I mean, no, thank you. I think that would look like we are up to something – in case someone is listening. Just let me know if something is amiss. Good plan?"

"Good call. Good thinking. We will give you a report before we head home. We have a Weapons Safety Seminar tonight and I like to get there early."

"Nice! Are you teaching or are you attending?"

"I instruct in the proper use of semi-autos. Charley handles the flame throwers, rocket launchers, and other specialty weapons. I used to teach the flame thrower series, but one small mishap resulting in singed eyebrows and a short stay at the burn unit, and he won't let me near them. So, I'll call to report back. Take care and be careful out there." And she was gone. Lord, I prayed, I thought she was the normal one in the bunch. Returning to my puzzle book, I filled in half of the numbers when the phone rang a third time.

"Hello, Margharite," I said.

"Margaritas? You're having Margaritas? At this hour?"

"Holly?"

"Katy?"

"Holly, what on earth are you doing?"

"Calling my friend and client who seems to have fallen off the planet? Are you drinking? Do I need to send Andy back out to do an intervention?" Holly asked with motherly concern.

"No, I'm not drinking. I thought Margharite was calling me."

"Margharite? The Mayan Priestess woman you met?"

"Yes, we had the first meeting of the Black Cat Society and …" I sputtered.

"Good Lord, Katy! Have you joined a cult?" Holly yelped.

"NO!" I bellowed. "I've made friends with a few of the ladies here and we had a big lasagna dinner last night and Mabel dubbed us the Black Cat Society. She and Chloe agreed on the name." I explained.

"She talks to Chloe? And does Chloe talk back?"

"I have no idea. So, Miss Holly, what can I do for you on this foggy spring morning?"

"Morning? I'll have you know I've had lunch and am in the process of printing out reports for the new clients I've acquired. Just called to say thank you."

"Thank you? For what?"

"For the gorgeous new car and the giant gift basket that arrived this morning. I love them both, Katy."

"So, Andy got back safe and sound with a few dead bugs on the windshield?" I smiled.

"Andy had that car cleaned to a squeaky polish before he drove it into the driveway. It's just lovely and still smells like a new car. Mixed with a little sea air and salt, I might add."

"I'm glad you like it. You deserve it, my friend. And as for the gift basket, you've been saying that you wanted to make a cat quilt, so I thought I'd help you along."

"I love the colors, the fabrics and all the different cat patterns. I can't wait to make a baby quilt for the kittens."

"Kittens? Are you telling me you have new additions to the household?"

"Yes, some rat-bastard dropped a soaking wet cardboard box filled with three black kittens in the drainage hole near the beauty shop where I go. The kittens were soaked and shivering. No newspaper, no blanket, no note or explanation of any kind. The RAT-BASTARD!" Holly roared into the phone.

"Calm down, Holly. Are the kittens okay? Black ones, did you say? Do they look like miniature Chloe's?"

"Yes, they are like mini-Chloe's. But they are so small and sick. They have to stay at the vet for a few more days. The vet said it's serious, but that they should pull through."

"Have you named them?" I asked, gently trying to calm Holly's considerable wrath.

"Ashes, Cinders, and Smokey."

"Nice ones. Did you pick those out yourself or did you just think of me in a fiery blaze and the names just popped in your head?" I asked somewhat sarcastically.

"What blaze? What are you talking about? Katy, what happened? Why don't you ever tell me things when they happen? Why do you always wait until I'm the last to find out?" Holly wailed.

With an eye roll toward heaven and a deep sigh, I told her. I told her about the fire, about Taffeta going missing and being found draped on Benji, and about my suspicions about James, Gavin and finally Bo. I brought her up to date about the Black Cat Society and our plan of action that was suspended until the fog lifted. Holly was always a good listener and didn't utter a word unless in clarification.

"Well, my dear Katy, it sounds like you have found yourself smack dab in the middle of a mystery. Andy said you had that gleam in your eye that you get when you have a trail to pursue. I have no idea why we get along so well. You're more of a blood hound than a cat," she moaned.

"Well, curiosity is a cat like quality. But, I don't want to be killed for it. And if the truth be told, I could ferret out a rat as good as any mouser. Besides, you love me. That's what friends do."

"Yes, that's true. Well, to use Dotty's words, I have intel for you – if you are interested. And I must say it's interesting," Holly began.

"Lay it on me. I'm curious to hear what you've come up with."

"Let's talk about Megan's lease. It seems after about five hundred miles of red tape and false trails, I've discovered who owns the studio. Can you guess?"

"James?"

"Nope. Try again."

"Who? I have no idea?"

"Gavin Davis, your hissing gay realtor," Holly said triumphantly.

"NO! How in the world…?" I sputtered.

"It seems Gavin had some legal trouble way back when, which led to financial trouble as it often will. He purchased his office and the one next door a short time before he moved from Uptown to Comfort. About a year ago, he was set to sell it outright, but at the last minute, he leased it to Megan. So, he owns both offices. The more interesting fact is he paid cash for both. So, he appears trouble free. Not that it matters now because his business seems to be booming and he's gotten himself out of debt, his credit scores are pretty good, and the IRS has given him a clean bill of tax health, so to speak."

"WOW! Way to go Holly! I'm absolutely astounded, but have no idea what this means. Megan's studio is still blackened with ash and smoke. I wonder why he hasn't restored it or rented it out or subleased it or something."

"That, my dear, is a question that only you can answer. I would say, ask the guy directly. You have a good sense of people, Katy. You'll know if he feeds you a line," Holly offered.

"Good idea. As soon as the weather lifts, I'll make an appointment."

"Good. Now, anything else you need me to do for you?"

"Yes, I do." I hesitated, paused, and then said. "Pull a wad of cash from one of my investments – no arguments, Holly, just do it. Then drive to Dr. Sylvester's office and give him the bundle. DO NOT INTERRUPT! The rest of the bundle is to be placed in a fund for the black kitties. We will call them the new members of the Black Cat Society. And I'll see what I can do about getting them adopted once they are old enough and strong enough. Any questions?" I asked into the sniffling phone. What a softy I am.

"No. Now Katy, that wasn't what I was thinking and you know it. I'm sure Dr. Sylvester will be grateful," she sniffed.

"Does the good doctor still look like Sylvester the cartoon

cat with his black hair, white mustache and slight lisp?" I asked secretly wondering if he had a Tweety-like sidekick.

"Yes he does. He's a good veterinarian and has been doing good work for the kitties for a long time. I'll tell him you and Chloe said hello. Now, is there anything else you want me to do?" Holly asked trying to get back to business.

"Yes. I'm still confused about the two drafts I found. Is there a way for you to look into James', Anna's, and Megan's records and history at the Uptown School of Artistry and find me samples of their work, their history, teacher's opinions, that type of thing? I feel there is a connection and I'm just too obtuse to see it."

"Right. I'm on it. I'll call you when I know something. It would help if I could talk to someone who might have an angle to get me on the inside – know what I mean?"

"I hear you. I'll see if Wynetta and Cherry have any thoughts. And I can ask Dotty – she probably has my phone bugged and heard this whole conversation anyway."

"That lady sounds like a soldier in a petticoat. I would love to meet her one day. Share ideas."

"She scares me. I can't tell if she's that brilliant or has watched the movie "Patton" one too many times. And I'm too scared to ask her!" I joked.

"Anything else, my dear?" Holly asked.

"Yes, now that you mention it, do you know any good massage therapists?" I whined.

"Yes, as a matter of fact, I do."

"Really? Who?"

"You, that's who," Holly said with a snort of laughter.

"Very funny! I don't think my body is designed for luxury. My back is tight, my neck is sore and my..."

"...Had another one of your nightmares, didn't you?"

Holly asked gently.

"Yes... how did you know?"

"I can always tell. You get like this. You start focusing on the aches and pains that your body is telling you and I bet you haven't done one stretch or had a long walk. Am I right?"

"You're right. I've been living the lazy life of lavishness in between small bouts of terror. I need to get back to my stretching routine and my daily walks. Taking Chloe for bug hunts does not necessarily constitute a high calorie burn," I said as I rubbed the right side of my neck.

"Well, then start on yourself and I'll see if I can find you a massage therapist that has hands as good as you do."

"Thanks, Holly. If I think of anything else, I'll let you know." We said our goodbyes and hung up. Only then did I realize that I had just made a sideways promise to find foster parents for three black kittens. I groaned and rubbed my neck and vowed not to think about Ashes, Cinders, and Smokey.

CHAPTER 20

After the phone call, I spent the rest of the afternoon with Chloe playing stringy, cuddling and doing puzzles. Margharite, like I figured, called me briefly to say that she, Drew, and Benji were home together today enjoying their new cat and playing board games. Shortly afterwards, I called Wynetta and left a message instructing her to purchase any cat accessories she thought necessary for Taffeta, as well as a month's supply of food, and have it delivered to the Taylor's house. I asked her to bill it to my account and to keep a steady supply of food for Taffeta and Chloe for the time being. As before, I'd pay her and would include a very generous tip for services rendered and that hopefully covered any losses she suffered at the poker game.

As it grew dark, my stomach began to growl to the point it woke up Chloe. I decided to go check on Mabel and forage for dinner. Making my way downstairs and into the kitchen I found Mabel sitting in the chair closest to the stove sipping tea.

"Hey Mabel, how's your head?" I asked quietly.

"You should be ashamed of yourself!" she barked.

"Why? What did I do now?"

"You should never have let me have that third glass of wine," Mabel growled.

"I humbly apologize for that, Mabel. But what about the fourth and fifth glasses?" I asked ever so sweetly.

"Humph. Never mind about that. Are you hungry?"

"Yes, starving, actually. I was going to check on you and maybe heat up some leftovers. Do you want anything?" I peered into the refrigerator and noticed that we had leftover quiche from a few nights ago.

"How about quiche, some leftover salad, and orange juice?"

"You aren't really a gourmet, are you Katy?"

"Nope, Lord knows my mother tried. I'm completely hopeless in the food category. I know what tastes good, but have no idea how to fix it. I'm utterly hopeless. But I can microwave with the best of them," I said proudly.

"Then let's have the leftover quiche, skip the salad – doesn't sound good anyway, same goes for the orange juice, and how about some English muffins with lemon curd. Does that sound to your liking?" Mabel grumbled.

"Yes, perfect. Now you sit there and I'll take care of everything. I'm pretty fair at toasting things, too." I bustled around the kitchen preparing our meal. After, bringing our plates to the table, then adding napkins, utensils, and glasses of unsweetened tea, we ate in companionable silence. After eating every bite, I took our plates, rinsed them and put them in the dishwasher and went back to the table to quietly finish sipping my tea.

"Are you okay, Mabel?"

"Yes, I'm just grumpy because my head was about to explode this morning and I feel like we could have been a step closer in finding the suspect if the lousy weather hadn't set in. It makes my joints hurt," she said, rubbing her hands and fingers.

"Well, I did do a bit of sleuthing by phone today," I said, and brought her up to speed on Holly's and my conversation.

"So, Gavin owns the studio. I had no idea! Why hasn't he done anything to restore it? I have half a mind to go down there and give him what for for keeping the place an eyesore," Mabel barked again.

"Now hold on, Mabel. I have plans to talk to him as soon as the weather clears. I'm going to make an appointment and go see him face to face."

"With a lookout at the very least," Mabel commanded.

"Okay, with a lookout. But until then, we sit tight. I've had phone calls from the other Black Cat ladies today and they are keeping a weathered eye, pardon the pun, on our three suspects. Dotty will be calling later with a final report. So, is there anything else I can do for you tonight?"

"No, just let me rest and I promise to be back to my chipper self by morning. Chloe and you tucked in for the night?" she asked.

"Yes, I have no plans but to finish the puzzle I started and do some reading. It will be quiet," I hoped.

"Good, then off to bed with you and I'll tend to things down here. I'll see you in the morning for breakfast. I'm thinking we are going to need fuel for our day," Mabel said as she got up from the table and started wiping down the counters. I trotted off to my room and settled in for a satisfying bit of mystery reading. Dotty called a few chapters later to report that all was well at the pier, that Wynetta and Cherry were heading home, and that the Deli guys had lost their shirts. I was hoping she was referring to the poker game and not some new mystery for me to solve. Dotty hung up after a promise to establish contact again in the morning and we were to resume our plan once the weather cleared. I wished her and Charley well at their weapons training, secretly wishing I could tag along. The rest of the evening was quiet, filled with gratitude and the warmth of new friends. I was at peace and at home.

The next morning brought a renewed sense of purpose that the rain splattering on the picture window did not dash. The fog had drifted away and left in its place a steady drizzle and cloudy gray skies. I could see the pier from my window, which was a vast improvement from yesterday. It would be wet work today, but I knew I wouldn't melt. I jumped out of bed and started my day. As I showered and dressed, I was startled to realize that I was thinking of Comfort as my new home. Maybe somewhere in yesterday's fog I had found a commitment to this place. I felt comfortable here and I was growing fond of Mabel and the other friends I had made. I guess commitments aren't that hard to make. It seems I made this one in my sleep. I put my hair in a pony tail figuring that the rain wouldn't make for a good hair day and dressed in layers so I wouldn't freeze or get too hot from popping in and out of stores. I pulled on my polar fleece shirt over a black T-shirt, threw on my denim jeans, warm socks and started downstairs with Chloe close on my heels.

Mabel was in the kitchen heaping a plate with Vanilla French Toast, eggs, and crispy hash browns. Orange juice and a steaming mug of coffee were already on the table. A place was set on the far end of the counter with a small porcelain dish and matching bowl. Chloe trotted straight to it, jumped up and proceeded to clean her plate of her morning's ration. Well this is new, too, I thought. I joined Mabel, who was already making inroads into her breakfast, at the table.

In between bites I said, "So, I noticed a couple of things over the last few days…"

"Really? Like what?" Mabel asked innocently.

"Exhibit one, Chloe eating on the ottoman during our dinner party the other night."

Mabel stared down at her plate and continued chewing.

"Exhibit two, Chloe rushing down to breakfast here in the kitchen and having her own place setting on the counter. When did that happen?"

Mabel put her fork down on her plate, folded her hands in her lap, and looked up at me with her beautiful blue eyes twinkling. "I've decided that a few changes needed to happen to make my life easier. One, Chloe has every right to eat with us as she is a paying guest here same as you. Two, it is much easier for me to manage her feeding if all her food and bowls are in one general place. And three, Chloe seems to like the arrangement. Any questions?" Mabel said firmly.

"Well, if it is easier for you and Chloe, who am I to stand in the way of progress?" I said. "Speaking of paying, I hope you found the envelope I left on the table. I hope the amount covers Chloe's and my room and board and any extra labor and cost associated with litter removal, extra food – human and feline, and extra laundering of clothing – vacation as well as burglary. And an added bonus for wanting to hold on to the room," I replied equally firmly.

"Frankly, I thought the sum rather outrageous in its generosity, but seeing as how you have gotten under my skin and into my heart, I don't know what else to do. And Chloe is a love who has gotten into my heart, too – as well as my laundry basket." Mabel said peering into her laundry room at the black tail swishing in it.

"Okay, so we are square for now?"

"Yes. I know you well enough not to argue with you or demand a lesser sum. But really, Katy, it is too much," Mabel said earnestly.

"Well, not to my way of thinking. So then you will be happy to know I have made a few more decisions today. I would like to rent out the Rose Room for the next year or so – for Chloe and me. I would like to pay a lump sum. So, I will ask you to come up with a sensible agreement between the two of us and basically name your price. If you insult me by giving me a price that is ridiculously low, I will be forced to multiply that amount by my bust size. And as you can see, that is a rather healthy figure. Any questions?"

"Well, I have never heard of such a thing in all my days," Mabel said through a laugh. "I have half a mind to do just that, not that I really want to know your chest size. Oh my, what have I done to deserve a friend such as you, Katy dear?" Mabel smiled.

"Think of it as purgatory, except with better benefits. You aren't Catholic are you?"

"Devout," Mabel responded with a smile.

"Oops, then think of it as lemonade. You know, when life gives you a lemon…"

"Ha! I will think you are as crazy as a loon… and an unexpected blessing. In all seriousness, is this really what you want to do? Stay here? Why, Katy?"

"Well, I feel at home here, it's comfortable and I love you, Mabel. You remind me of the Grandmother I never knew. And this town is charming and peaceful and…"

"… Has a murderer running around loose, setting fires," Mabel interrupted.

"Well, that would be one of the drawbacks, but that is only temporary until we solve it. Then life goes back to tranquility."

"I frankly have to ask, is life ever tranquil when you are around?" Mabel asked with a glint in her eye.

"Not so as you'd notice. But I'll try to be better," I grinned.

"How about if you try to get me a list of any other services I can provide you other than meals, laundry, companionship, and the use of my best suite," Mabel said.

"That sounds great for starters. I will make that list for you and you give me a number preferably not divisible by my boob size. And we'll have dinner at the Deli guys tonight and hash out all the details. God, I love hashing with you, Mabel! I feel like I've just bartered with an Oriental rug maker from Pakistan!"

"Is Pakistan in the Orient?" Mabel asked laughing.

"I have no idea. My talents usually revolve around mystery authors and good music. Geography is not my strong suit. In fact, I don't even own a suit!" I explained and then burst into a fit of giggles induced by too much coffee and maple syrup.

"Okay, now you're just being silly," Mabel said, wiping her eyes and forcing her smile into a straight line. "You need some air or I'll never get any work done. Keep your door open so Princess Chloe can come and go. She's good company in the kitchen. And let me know if you have any thoughts about her litter box."

"Litter box?" I asked bewildered.

"Yes. Do you want it upstairs with you or would you rather have it moved down here out of sight somewhere?"

"Wow, you do keep a tight ship. Let me think on that. I don't want the health inspector closing you down just because Chloe ate tuna."

"Good point. Keep me posted on your thoughts. Now go.

Your craziness is omitting fumes." Mabel waved her hands at me and shooed me out of her kitchen. I ran upstairs with a wicked smile on my face. Now that went just like I planned. I had a feeling Mabel was thinking the same thing herself.

I grabbed Mabel's rain slicker and was about to dash out the kitchen door when Mabel called from the parlor. Coming toward me she had a wicked smile on her face and was wiping her hands on her apron, looking like she was up to something.

CHAPTER 21

"Just wanted you to know the latest. Dotty called and said to wait to bring Chloe on a day that Noah is not out building an ark," she smirked.

"Very wise. Anything else?" I asked, unaware I had just opened a can of worms.

"Why yes, two small things. The first, Comfort Floral just called and asked when I would like to schedule the new landscaping for the burnt out areas outside," Mabel began.

Can open, worms everywhere.

"They were hoping, like Dotty, that I would wait until after the rain stopped." Mabel continued, "I said that would be lovely and what in the NAME OF TOM GREEN THUMB ARE YOU TALKING ABOUT? She kindly explained that the fire had caused damage to my residence and a concerned citizen saw fit to fund any and all landscaping including labor, materials, and any additional soil amendments, plants, flowers, and sprinkler upgrades I would need. So my question would be… do you know anything about this?" Mabel squinted at me.

"Let's just say I am a concerned citizen and in no way did I want that fire to inhibit your business. Is that a good enough answer?" I asked, feeling like I had only one leg to stand on.

"That's as good of an answer as I will probably get from you anyways. Which brings me to small thing number two…" Mabel squared her shoulders and looked at me with piercing eyes.

"Good news, I hope?" I asked, dreading the answer.

"Why yes, I also received a phone call from the Deli guys informing me that along with the brownies, they would like to place daily orders for cookies and my famous date nut bread."

There goes my other leg, I thought. Not a leg to stand on.

"Gee, Mabel that's great news. If your date nut bread is so famous, why haven't I had any?"

"Because you are too busy sticking your nose into everybody's business!" Mabel barked.

"Are you upset about your blooming catering business?" I asked with sugar coating.

"The only thing blooming is the idiot standing before me!" Mabel growled. "Do I look like a homeless person, like a pauper, like a character out of a Dickens's novel?" Mabel said evenly.

"Uh, no, Mabel. You look like a lady with intelligence, wit, style and a flair for food. I bet you have more recipes…"

"… Than you have sense!" Mabel interrupted. "I happen to be doing well financially, not like a Fortune 500 company, but making it okay. Then you come along and I'm in high demand. What would you have me do, Katy?" Mabel asked, clearly annoyed.

"Say no. If you would rather not be a part-time caterer, tell them no. If you would rather me not board here for the next year, tell me no. If you do not want the side yard fixed up, call the floral people back and say no. I'll use the money to fund a garden or something. It's your life Mabel, your choices. I'm just giving you more things to choose from. I leave the decisions up to you." I flipped the hood of the rain slicker up and strode out into the rain. Well, that did not go at all well, I thought. I splashed through the puddles wondering if I had done too much and what the hell was I doing.

I headed straight to Cherry's for a cup of steaming hot coffee and a friendly chat. I breezed through the door, pushing my hood back off my head, and breathed in the smell of exotic blends of coffee mixed with the earthy spices of her tea blends. With each breath, I could feel the knot in my stomach begin to loosen.

"Just the person I was looking for – HAVE YOU LOST YOUR MIND?" The voice bellowed.

Oh God, now what, I thought as my tummy formed a pretzel.

"Miss Katy, what have you done?" Cherry asked me as she came hurrying forward with her fists clinched. That's not a good sign either, I thought, sighing.

"Do you know what has happened?" she blared.

"I cannot imagine," I whimpered.

"The Deli guys offered to have me cater their coffees and tea for them each morning. They think it's time they went in a new direction and want to focus on their food, broaden their dinner selections, and leave their beverages in the hands of the brew master. Their words, not mine! Imagine! I can set up a small selection of two or three different coffees and have the crossover business here. I've been dying to pick up more coffee drinkers here and turn this place into a specialized coffee house," Cherry said with her hands on her hips.

"That is great news, Cherry. Congratulations. Um, why do you sound so angry?" I asked, praying they had my blood type at the local hospital.

"Because this town is in an uproar and it's all because of you!" Cherry declared.

"Okay, you might want to explain that?" I said, trying not to pick a fight.

"This town was quiet, calm, Comfort, for Mercy's sake, and you come along and turn this place on its ear," she blared.

"Really, I thought this town was home to a murderer with a flair for fire and a bunch of townsfolk who rose up as one and did nothing. I would not call that calm or comfortable. I would call it sad… pathetic. Comfort is not a place where I would want to spend my last moments on earth!" I yelled. I stormed back out into the rain and ran toward the benches by the Point. At least that way, no one will be around to yell at me too, I thought. I collapsed on the bench and drew ragged breaths, forcing the emotions to stay in my gut and not rise up into sobs of anger and frustration. I wiped my cheek with my hand hoping that is was rain and not tears.

I don't know how long I sat on the park bench, but knew it was long enough for the seat of my pants to soak through to the skin. I tried to make sense of what happened and couldn't come up with a thread of a sense. I was fully responsible for Mabel and her landscaping. I had given the Deli guys a hint that Mabel's brownies were a thing to behold and eaten in the finest church socials. I really had no idea they were going to take that hint and run with it. And I did mention that Cherry's coffee was fit for the finest palaces in Europe. Who knew they would run with that, too. Deli Guys, two touchdowns. Katy, scoreless and, from the sound of things, clueless.

I just couldn't understand the anger. Had I done something so wrong as to care and try to help and make suggestions? My thoughts just made me bitter and confused. I settled back into the park bench and thought wet and gloomy thoughts. I heard shoes splashing toward me and was too heartsick to look up. Mabel's sensible shoes stopped in front of my soaked sneakers. I looked up at Mabel covered in a long sweater, a shawl, and a pink plastic rain slicker, holding a matching pink umbrella. She looked like a bottle of Pepto-Bismol.

"Is there room for two?"

"Yes," I said as Mabel sat down beside me and covered us both with her umbrella.

"I have some thoughts I'd like to share with you, if you have a moment," Mabel said quietly.

"I have a moment."

"I appreciate the landscaping Katy, I really do. Especially given the amount I wrote to the Insurance Company for the balance they did not cover. Truly that was a most thoughtful gift and I thank you. As for the baking and catering business, it was such a shock. Baking is something I enjoy. Treats to share with friends and my guests. I never thought of it as a career. It seems like so much work. I couldn't get my mind around how to supply desserts and run a B&B and have a life. Then I realized something."

"What did you realize, Mabel?"

"That I have no life."

"What? You have a life; you have great friends, lovely townspeople, guests…"

"No, what I have is illusion. I have a few good close friends. I have known Dotty for many years and Cherry has become a dear. I visit with the folks in this town, but do I really know them? Do I help out and lend a hand? Megan would have an answer for those questions – one I would not like to hear. And my guests are, quite honestly, few and far between. And some days its more trouble than it's worth."

"So, what are you saying Mabel? I'm listening…"

"That I have dreams, Katy. Things I've laid aside like an old newspaper. So, I'm going to suspend the B&B portion of my business for now and concentrate on the catering business. I'll keep the Blue Heron as a Boardinghouse for now and see what happens. And I am going to continue boarding one black cat and one lovely woman who has opened my eyes to new ideas and opened my heart to dreams, something I haven't done in a long, long time." She reached across and took my hand.

"I'm sorry for this morning, Katy. This old woman spent most of her life living in fear. Fear of change and fear of doing anything not included in her daily rut. Can you forgive an old woman?" Mabel asked, squeezing my hand.

"Yes, if you can forgive a new friend for being overly zealous and somewhat argumentative," I said, squeezing her hand back. We looked at each other as our smiles bridged the chasm that had been between us earlier.

"Can anybody join this pity party?" Cherry said as she flopped down beside me. She, too, was wearing a plastic rain slicker. Except Cherry's was yellow, making her look like a giant rubber duck. Cherry sat down on the other side of me.

"I feel like a hamburger between two buns."

"More like a couple of bun heads!" Cherry said, breaking the tension. "Katy, girl, I am sorry. I owe you a big apology. I just was kidding you back there. Really! I had no idea you and Mabel had words or I never would have given you such a teasing. This town being in an uproar is good. You…" taking my other hand and squeezing it, "… you are a good thing – for this town and for me." Cherry squeezed my hand harder until I lost all feeling. "I had a dream for a long time about a supreme coffeehouse. And now it's going to come true – thanks to you!"

"I didn't do anything, Cherry." I moaned, letting some of my frustration seep into my voice.

"Yes, you did. You spotted Wynetta a twenty for the poker game," Cherry said.

"Dear God in Heaven, doesn't anyone make sense anymore?" I yelled.

"Now just simmer down and listen. Settle. Now, Wynetta came over yesterday to help me restock at the coffee shop. We had a marvelous time. She is so efficient and full of energy, the time passed so quickly. So, we finished early and wandered over to the poker game with the Deli guys. We played for hours and as the hands got better and better, the wine flowed and stuff just poured out!" she declared, making absolutely no sense.

"Um, Cherry, what poured?"

"Ideas, dreams, things we'd do if we won big in Vegas. Next thing I know the card game is forgotten, temporarily, I might add, since Wynetta was winning. And lo and behold, we came up with new dreams to build. So, I'm going to turn Cuppa Comfort into Comfort Coffee House. Wynetta is over at Dotty and Charley's asking them to take over the pet accessory part of her business."

"What? Why? I thought she was doing well."

"She is, but there are only so many pets one can have in a small town like Comfort – Chloe being a welcome addition. But, she was getting so tired of the constant noise – and there are her allergies – and the overall smell."

"In other words, shit happens, it stinks and can be noisy too?" I said succinctly.

"Ha! You said it. She's wanted to sell out for years and finally got the right buyer who is starting a whole web business. So, then Wynetta will come work with me," Cherry concluded.

"Then what will happen to her store?" Mabel asked.

"I'm sure something will turn up – it always does." Cherry said, looking like a cat that swallowed a lizard. I could tell she knew something and wasn't spilling the beans, coffee or otherwise. I'd have to find another source to find out her secret. We were all too stunned to say a word. In just a few sentences, a small amount of Comfort was about to change. For the better, I thought.

"That must have been one hell of a poker game!" I finally said. Mabel, Cherry and I leaned back and laughed until our sides hurt. "Thank you, Cherry, for setting the record straight and keeping Mabel and me in the loop. I feel exhausted just with the sheer volume of changes coming to this place."

"Not changes, dreams," Cherry said quietly. "It's time this town dusted off their forgotten dreams and brought them out into the open. Mabel told me about her closing the B&B. I think it's time she did. Now Mabel, don't get upset, but it hasn't been a winner for a while and you don't look happy anymore when all those strangers show up."

"Especially ones with black cats," I teased.

"Now don't start. What I'm saying is that if you aren't happy doing one thing, switch and do something else. My favorite line from a movie is 'Life is what you make of it, Friend. If it doesn't fit, make alterations.' I watched Silverado a lot when I was growing up in the orphanage and took the tape each time I moved to a new foster home." Cherry explained with a squint in her eye. "Have it on DVD in Blue-Ray now."

"Hey Mabel, we may have to institute a movie night at the Boardinghouse and I want to nominate that for the first viewing." I quipped.

"We'll just see about that," Mabel said. She leaned past me and looked at Cherry. "Should we tell her now or let this all sink in until later?" Mabel asked, her eyes twinkling like candles.

"Oh God, there's more? Tell me now and then take me home. I feel like a wet washrag."

"Cherry and I will be going into business together, as well – catering of course." Mabel proudly announced.

"Now that is an outstanding idea – share the work, share the fun, and share the wealth." I reached around them both and hugged them closer to me.

"And thanks to you, we've even come up with a name…" Mabel added with a giggle.

"Why do you both insist on blaming me for everything? I haven't done near as much as you two give me credit for. So, what's the name? Please don't tell me you're calling it Black Cat Catering. Only pagans, horoscope believers and cat people will hire you," I laughed.

"Nope, but not a bad guess. Nope, we came up with something more apropos. Ready… how about… Blooming Idiots Catering!" Mabel declared and burst into another bout of laughter, with Cherry and me joining in. We must have looked crazy sitting out in the rain laughing ourselves silly – one rubber ducky, one wet washrag, and one bottle of Pepto-Bismol.

"Okay, I'm done in. My mind is a busy signal and if I don't get out of these clothes, I'm going to drown. So, let's hug and then get out of this rain!" I stood up, turned and pulled up Cherry and Mabel. We hugged and smiled while ducking under Mabel's umbrella. Cherry made a beeline for her store while Mable and I hightailed it for the Blue Heron – late

B&B – soon to be Boardinghouse. Mabel and I headed for the side kitchen door and walked into the warmth and welcome that only a kitchen can provide. Mabel left her umbrella in the vestibule and marched to a pile of freshly laundered towels and tossed me one while taking another for herself. We blotted ourselves the best we could.

"Strip! Leave your pile of things on the floor." Mabel tossed me a fresh dry towel and said, "Wrap yourself in this one and go soak in that tub of yours until you look like a California raisin. I've got a pot of Clam Chowder going and it should be ready by the time you come down."

"What about you? You look like you went through a car wash and forgot your car…"

"Very funny. I will be having a soak of my own in my flat – now move!" And with that, I turned around so Mabel wouldn't be too shocked by what she saw, but knowing full well she'd seen naked bodies before. I peeled off my clothes, gathering the towel around me, and flew up the stairs through the door and straight into the bathroom to draw a steamy hot bath. I eased the door closed keeping all the heat in and slowly sank into the enormous tub. I could feel myself beginning to thaw like a lamb chop. It didn't take long for the bathroom door to open. Chloe, who never saw a door she couldn't push open, padded into the bathroom. She curled up on the bathmat and purred. Not one to miss an opportunity to be extra warm.

CHAPTER 22

As I soaked, I thought of the new events and the changes taking place in this small town and was excited to be part of it. The town was drawing me in like a moth to a flame, but I didn't think I'd get burned. I just felt grateful and made a promise to myself to help my friends with their new endeavors in any way I could. Boy, would I have a ton to tell Holly!

I gently got up and dried myself off, displacing Chloe, who chirped and jumped up on the counter by the sink to watch. She seemed content and happy in her world. I looked around the bathroom and noticed that her litter box had moved to the far corner on a large utility rug – to discourage the spread of litter, no doubt. It fit perfectly and I could tell that Chloe had used it recently. I cleaned her box, dried myself off and went in search of warm clothing.

After changing into my gray sweat shirt, black stretch

pants and thick red socks with black paw prints, I picked up Chloe and headed downstairs following the tempting scent of fresh clam chowder and freshly baked bread. Mabel placed the steaming mugs on the table with slices of fresh sourdough bread. We sat in our usual places with Chloe happily munching on the counter.

"I'm a dipper," Mabel said. I grinned back at her because I knew exactly what she meant.

"I'm a dipper, too," I said as we both dipped our bread into the chowder. We spent several minutes in quiet companionship as we dipped and slurped our soup. We watched Chloe finish her dinner, wash her face and then jump down and head for the laundry area. She jumped into the laundry basket and disappeared.

"Is that her morning ritual?" I asked.

"Yes. She seems to enjoy having her first nap on my clean clothes. I don't mind really. Black goes with everything," Mabel said with a smile.

"You are one understanding lady, lady. Thank you for your indulgence and nice job with the new location of Chloe's pooper," I said as Mabel choked on her last bit of bread.

"Ahem," Mabel began, clearing her throat. "So what is your plan for tomorrow since this day has walked away from us?"

"I was thinking of talking to Dotty tomorrow – might bring Chloe along so they can meet. And I want to talk to Gavin – I have questions for him and I think, if I am open and honest with him, he might just answer me," I reasoned.

"Unless he's a raving loon, it which case he'll…" Mabel began.

"Don't even say it!" I interrupted. "I am going to hope for the best, but I'll bring someone as a lookout, just in case."

"Thank you, my dear. Try not to go off and get yourself

whacked or something…" Mabel said sweetly.

"I try not to make a habit of getting whacked. I'm trying to work up an enthusiasm to talk to James. He feels evil and creepy and I just can't stomach the thought of getting to know him to find out if he's the bad guy. So, I'll save him for after I talk to Gavin."

"Sounds like a good plan. Don't wait too long on James, though. If he's the killer, he's watching and waiting and getting more desperate… just a thought." Mabel added the last part as she saw my nose wrinkle in disgust.

"Message received loud and clear, Mabel. I'll be careful, I promise." We finished our meal and washed up. I then headed back upstairs leaving Chloe to her snooze in the laundry basket. I spent the remainder of the day planning questions to ask Gavin and figuring out a way to lure James out of his hole. I opened up the bay window for some fresh air and gazed at the lazy blue ocean. The air smelled of burnt toast and smoldering cinders. I didn't notice the smoke wafting from the lighthouse.

The next morning, the sun was backlighting the sky in pale blue painted with fluffy white clouds. The ground was still damp from all the rain, but at least I wouldn't drown. I bounded out of bed and nearly broke a foot when I landed on one of Chloe's fake mice. Staring around the room I noticed that someone had a good time last night. Fake mice were strewn all over the floor like players at a rugby tournament. I quickly picked up the wayward mice, piling them under the rocking chair. I showered, changed into my typical jeans, lavender sweater, silly socks and dried out sneakers. Feeling hungry, I headed down for a quick breakfast of leftover French toast and hash browns. Mabel had left a note saying she was over talking business with Cherry and would see me later. After rinsing my dishes, I headed back upstairs to grab Chloe and put her in her harness. Unlike most cats, Chloe actually doesn't mind going for walks or bug hunts.

We headed off toward the Mercantile with me carrying her so as to not get her little black feet wet. Each time I stroll into the Mercantile, my heart flutters at the vast quantity of goodies – from boots to digital cameras to milk and oranges, and in a corner toward the front, a vast array of cat foods, cat collars, and cat beds sitting beside dog accessories and other pet needs. I was too overwhelmed to take it in. After placing Chloe on the counter, Dotty held out her hand for a sniff. Chloe took a tentative step forward, sniffed and then licked her index finger. Dotty smiled.

"You can place her back here if you'd like," Charley said. "Or she's fine where she's at..." he added with a grin and a tilt of his head as Chloe walked to the end of the counter, hopped into a light blue denim colored cat bed and curled up to observe her surroundings.

"So, what brings you by?" Dotty asked.

"First and foremost I wanted to introduce Chloe to her Aunt Dotty and her Uncle Charley. And my other ulterior motive is, I have a new plan and I need your help. I want to ask Bo straight up if he had anything to do with Megan's death, but he is never around and I only ever see his pants and..."

"Whoa, now hold a minute... This is girl talk and I need no part of it. I'll be in the back while you girls chat – call me if it gets busy." Charley said as he headed toward the back room.

"So, what do you need me to do – tell you his inseam?" Dotty teased.

"No, now don't start! What I need is for you to ask him, because I just can't possibly... not gonna do it... can't make me..." I continued, "If you do that today, I can run over and talk to Gavin who I noticed has returned from the great beyond and is in his office right now. If you and or Charley can watch Chloe while I talk to him, then she won't eat Miss Martha."

"Okay, let me get this straight. Charley is to watch Chloe as she destroys our store, while I ask Bo if he killed someone lately, while you talk to Gavin and have Miss Martha as a new chew toy for Chloe. Is that right?"

"Sounds perfectly logical when you say it – are you in?" I asked.

"Yep, let me get Charley and you head on over to Gavin's. I'll watch from here in case he turns out to be a pyro-murderer, and then we can come rescue you. Now go… you're wasting time," Dotty said as she shoved me out the door. Turning back, I waved at Chloe, but she was having a bath and did not want to be disturbed. I marched purposefully into Gavin's office and caught him literally filing his nails. Miss Martha was perched on a gold throne with bright red piping around the corners of the gold pillow upon which her tea cup butt sat. She yipped once to announce my presence like an assistant would buzz her boss's intercom. Gavin sprang from his chair squealing and ran around his desk to give me a big girlfriend hug.

"Oh my dear Katy, girl, I am so glad to see you. I have news – great news. You must sit, sit, sit. Miss Martha and I have so much to tell you!" he said.

"Yip, yip," Miss Martha replied.

"You are quite right my dear, where are my manners? How is Miss Chloe Divine? Is she well?" he asked me.

"She's terrific – Charley and Dotty are baby-sitting her today. She likes her new Aunt and Uncle," I said, inwardly groaning – he's infectious.

"I am so jealous! But tell her I understand. When one is beautiful and famous one must be available. So, what brings you in? Buying, renting, leasing?" Gavin twittered.

"Possibly, but first I have a few questions – if you and Miss Martha can spare the time."

"Anything for you, girlfriend... what can I possibly do for you...?" Gavin gushed.

That thought struck me as so odd, I couldn't help but mutter a tiny giggle. Must be his ever present cologne, the fumes are making me tipsy.

"I would love to know who owns the burnt out office next door – I'm thinking of leasing it or renting it or maybe buying..." I said. Gavin pulled out his hot pink handkerchief that matched his blazing hot pink tie and burst into tears. Waves of sloppy sobs splashed into his hanky. Gavin was trying to speak, but the sobbing was making him sound like a warped record. I reached over and patted his arm and hoped he wouldn't swoon or get the vapors. Miss Martha began racing up and down the desk – trotting on her tiny legs – barking wildly. The sobs and yips were giving me a headache and my eyelid started to twitch.

"Gavin, honey, what is it? I'm sorry. What did I say to upset you?" I pleaded as his sobs became snotty hiccups.

"Oh my dear, that is such a sore subject... you have no idea the pain... the humiliation... the expense... Oh, God, Miss Martha, now that is quite enough!" And with that, Gavin stood up and snatched Miss Martha in midstride and slam-dunked her in her tiny doggy shrine-like kennel and closed the curtain. Show's over, please proceed to the nearest exit, I thought. Gavin came back and flopped into his chair with none of his usual grace and swagger.

"What happened, Gavin? You can tell me. Maybe I can help. I'm your friend, remember?" I said quietly.

"Oh, it happened over a year ago. What does it matter now?" Gavin wailed, sweeping his arm into the air and dropping it dramatically on his forehead.

"It matters to me because it matters to you… what happened?" I asked again.

"It all started when I started working at the Revue – the Uptown Revue – remember I told you about it. I'm Nancy Sinatra. I have the boots, the short pants, and the whole ensemble. It was just me then, that is, until Martin," he tried to say.

"Um, who's Martin?" I asked, clearly not following his train of thought.

"Martin was my Frank. He showed up one night and sang "My Way" and I just melted. I knew we were meant to be together. Imagine a Nancy Sinatra meeting her father at the Uptown Revue of all places – you're following me, aren't you?" Gavin asked, seeing my drawn eyebrows.

"You were Nancy Sinatra with your boots that are made for walking and Martin was Frank Sinatra and you were hoping he was going – um, your way?" I said uneasily.

Gavin clapped his hands together like a schoolgirl and giggled. "Hee-hee, you see it too, you see we were meant to be together. We became an instant hit. Overnight sensation. And of course, one thing leads to another. A few weeks later we are picking out paint colors for his dance studio and he comes in one day with a bulge in his trousers." Gavin said with a sigh in his voice.

"Gavin, please, I don't need to know the details…" I pleaded, squeezing my eyes shut.

"No, silly, it wasn't that. It was Miss Martha," he said.

"I beg your pardon?"

"Miss Martha. Martin had gone to Creature Comforts, seen Miss Martha and knew she was meant for us. So he bought her, stuffed her in his trousers, sadly there was room, and brought her home to his mama. Me!" He shrieked.

"Okay..." I began while rubbing my eyelid, "Martin buys Miss Martha, stuffs her down his pants, comes over here and presents her – Mother of God, please don't tell me how – and now you and Martin and Miss Martha make three?" I asked.

"Yes! We were so happy, just the three of us. Then right when he's going to sign the lease, he calls it off – the whole thing. The dance studio, us, breaks up our whole family!" He wailed.

"Why?"

"Because Martin was allergic to Miss Martha and had to take allergy shots – it made him nauseous. Imagine being allergic to something so small," he whined.

"Hard to imagine, really." I said, staring at her tiny throne.

"So, he breaks up with me and Miss Martha and a month later, you know what? That bastard, that low down, dirty, stinking rat marries a... a... a... WOMAN!" The hanky was out again and Gavin was back to sobbing and swooning.

"Why, that low life... that scum, that scoundrel – the cad!" I said, warming to the name calling.

"Now don't you talk bad about Miss Martha's daddy. After all, it's the only one she has right now," Gavin barked.

"So sorry. Um, Gavin, what is Martin's last name?"

"Davenport. Why, silly, do you know him?"

"No, I'm just confused. Miss Martha's last name is..."

"Bijou. Yes, that's her stage name. Everyone has a stage name. Her full name is Miss Martha Davenport – named after her daddy – Bijou – as in seeing a movie at the. Got it?" Gavin asked my pulsating eyelid.

"Yes, I think I do. Well then what happened next after Martin backed out on the lease and left you holding two offices right next door to each other?" I asked, drawing some conclusions of my own.

"Well, that silly Megan Harris shows up all aglow about being a famous artist and so I turn around and leased it to her."

"But that was months ago, why haven't you cleaned it up – it's still burned and filthy and smells... um, never mind, answer the question!" I urged.

"Because nobody wants it and I don't know what to do with it. Do you want an office that houses a dead person? It may be haunted – you never know..." Gavin complained.

"Now you know that's not true; stop being so dramatic!" I snipped.

"Now THAT is not in my nature!" Gavin said with a flourish and burst into a fit of giggles. Really, somebody needs to get him some hormones or he's going to injure his synapses, I thought.

"Do you feel better?" I asked after he calmed down.

"Yes, thank you. I am quite composed now, forgive my small lapse." Gavin said, back to his flamboyant self.

"Good, now let's get down to business. I would like to lease that shell of an office – but I will only do so under two conditions. Agreed?" I said, leaning forward with my breasts plopping on his desk.

"Name them. I'm all ears," he said with his eyes elsewhere than my face.

"First, I will not do business with a murderer – so if you killed Megan, I'm walking on the deal," I wagered.

"WHAT? Me kill that silly girl, hardly. Megan was a chameleon, one of those people who blends into any crowd and becomes the person next to her. That is not me – most certainly. And besides, no offense to those luscious mounds of curvy loveliness heaving on my desk, but I don't do women – kill them or otherwise. So, I'm not a murderer. And the second?" Gavin countered, leaning toward me for the kill.

"I will not pay full price and I will be paying in cash. And I want it now!" I lowered the boom.

"Deal!" Gavin reached across the desk and we shook on it. "Not that I won't find out anyway, but girlfriend to girlfriend, what are you planning to do with it?"

"There is only one thing missing from this town and I intend to provide it – one way or another. Figure it out yet?" I asked sweetly.

"I have no idea…tell me!" Gavin whispered.

"Can you keep a secret – girlfriend to girlfriend?" I whispered back.

"Yes!" He giggled back. So, I told him. He leaned back in his chair and started laughing and rubbing his hands together. "Oh Goody! I get to be first, I get to be first!" Gavin clapped and twirled around in his chair.

"Keep it quiet! No one is to know until I've made arrangements. Speaking of arrangements, here is the number of my Finance Manager – her name is Holly. You and she will get on splendidly – she is a cat person, I should warn you. And if you asked her to sing for you, you'll probably fall in love." I handed Gavin her card and gave him further instructions.

"So, I guess this means you're staying for awhile…" He looked at me with the eyes of a five year old basset hound.

"Yes. I'm staying until you throw me out. And, until I catch who killed Megan. So, Gavin, if you had anything to do with her death and I find out…" I said as I leaned forward until I was inches from his nose. "I swear I'll make you wear a green plaid polyester suit from the 70's with a red paisley tie – all off the rack!" Not waiting for a response, I flounced out of his office with Gavin's hysterical laughter following me as I trotted back to the Mercantile.

CHAPTER 23

Dotty was stocking shelves as I entered their store. Charley was at the counter dangling a piece of twine in front of Chloe, who was still in her blue cat bed – looking like she had no intention of leaving it. Charley had a wide grin planted on his face and every time Chloe swatted at the string, Charley would let out a hoot of laughter. She's better than cable television, I thought. Dotty rushed over to me and dragged me by the arm to the back of the store.

"Okay, tell me what happened," she said in a hushed voice. I told her word for word everything Gavin had said, except editing out the part about what I would be putting into the studio I was leasing.

"Well, you've eliminated one suspect and I've eliminated a second," Dotty responded as she continued to tell me about her and Bo's conversation. After I left and headed to Gavin's, she marched over to Bo's shop. She walked straight up to him and asked if he had anything to do with Megan and her demise.

"Dotty, I'm not sure if that's proper interrogating procedure!"

"Listen, Katy. I've known Bo since he moved here five years ago. I know he was a suspect on your list, but he wasn't on mine. So, I asked him."

"So, what did he say?" I pleaded.

"He asked if you were the one really asking the question," Dotty said with a gleam in her eye. "I said yes."

"Dotty, you know that's not true!" I exclaimed.

"Oh yes it is. You never once asked how the others – and I for that matter – felt about you accusing Bo. So, you have that to think about," Dotty scolded.

"Yes, ma'am!" I said, thoroughly chastised.

"Don't be so downhearted. He took it well. Besides, I think he likes you."

"Oh good grief, how is that possible? I've never even seen his face or his eyes. I keep having conversations with his pants."

"I beg your pardon? Never mind, we need to get down to business. Bo told me that he really didn't have much to do with Megan – she only had eyes for James and her painting. He did say that he thought James stored some of her paintings in his studio while Megan painted and readied all the lighting for her grand unveiling."

"Really? That's seems important. I need to think about this. Our next stop should be for me to talk to James…"

"Well, don't look now but he's just passed our door…" Dotty said. I patted her arm and ran out of the store and hurried as cautiously as up to James as I could without looking too obvious.

"Mr. Reinhold, James… do you have a moment…?" I

asked him, touching his arm.

"Why Miss Hawkins, what a pleasure. I had hoped you hadn't left our simple community just yet," he oozed.

"No, I'm really enjoying my stay here. I was wondering… do you have plans for the evening? I would love to talk with you more about your artwork, if you could spare the time."

"My dear, what a lovely idea. I have so much to say on that subject. What did you have in mind?" he asked, smiling.

"How about drinks at Sharkey's bar around eight? I haven't been in there yet, and it looks like a good place where we can be alone…" I softly whispered.

"Perfect. I'll meet you there. Um, Miss Hawkins, you aren't thinking of bringing your cat, are you?" he asked timidly.

"No, she'll be with Mabel for the evening. It will be just us." I wrinkled my nose and smiled and said, "James."

He beamed and leaned close to my ear and whispered. "I look forward to it… until tonight…" And with that he gave me a kiss on my cheek, turned and walked away. I stood flat-footed staring after him.

YUCK! He kissed me. I hurried back to Dotty. I rushed in the door wiping my hand on my cheek trying to get the cooties off me. Dotty was leaning against the counter laughing.

"I suppose you saw the whole thing?" I asked, disgusted.

"Yes, you sure know how to play him. He took your bait easily. So, what did you offer him or shouldn't you say in front of Chloe?" Dotty teased.

"Very funny. We are having drinks at Sharkey's bar. We will be meeting at eight o'clock. This gets me thinking. Dotty, I have another plan."

"Oh, dear. I don't like the way your mouth is forming that crooked evil smile of yours – the one you get when you are about to do something illegal," Dotty frowned.

"Well, we have eliminated two suspects and we only have one left. So, now is the time. Okay, let me think..." I started pacing the store and stopped in front of the key chains. I stared at them with Dotty watching me closely. I started nodding my head and a plan formed. I grabbed six key chains with mini flashlights on them and headed to the counter.

"Okay, here's the plan," I said as I handed Charley the money for the key chains and clipped one to my belt loop.

"Tonight, before I meet James at the bar, I'm going to break into his studio. I have a hunch and if I'm right, we will know that he did it. So, here's what I need. Dotty, I need you to round up all the members of the Black Cat Society. Give everyone a key chain. Cherry is to be posted inside her shop to be a lookout for me because I will be across the way breaking and entering. Wynetta is to be in the passage between her shop and the Deli making sure the coast is clear and James does not, for any reason, approach from the south side of the pier. Margharite is to be on the front porch of her house watching Wynetta and Cherry and making sure the coast is clear from her vantage point. I will tell Mabel that I want her at Comfort Point to watch him when he comes down from the lighthouse to the bar. She'll follow him and stay by the bar to make sure I'm safe. Dotty, I want you watching from the back door of your shop making sure I don't get trapped by James or anyone else while I'm doing my feat of daring-do. And Charley," I stole a look at him and he was staring at me with a look of astonishment on his face, "I want you to go have a drink at the bar. Keep James talking or at least keep an eye on him because I might be late and I don't want him going to the studio. Got it?" I asked, looking at both of them.

"Were you a Marine?" Charley asked, pulling his wits together.

"No, just don't want to get caught. If James killed Megan, he did it for a reason – a reason he is willing to kill for, to keep a secret. So, any questions? Did I miss anything?"

"Signals and code words?" Dotty asked flippantly.

"Signals, right. Have Margarite as the focal point. Two flashes from the flashlight mean he's been sighted. One flash means message received. Code word... how about 'Chloe swallowed a mouse'. Meaning if things go wrong, deliver that message. If I look like I'm in trouble, come get me and say she swallowed a mouse and needs me. That will get me out of there. If all is well, then say 'nice moon tonight'. Got it?" I asked searching their faces for courage.

"Roger that!" Charley saluted.

"I'm on it," Dotty nodded, turning to Charley. "Good work, we couldn't have planned that better, eh, Charley?" Dotty said, grinning ear to ear. Charley smiled back exchanging one of those secret messages that only happen between people who have known each other for years.

"Okay, I'm off to tell Mabel. Dotty, can you tell the rest? And if Gavin or Bo want in on it, fine. The more eyes tonight, the better." I went to scoop up Chloe from her bed, but she wouldn't budge. Sighing, I picked up the bed with Chloe in it and turned to go.

"Um, Charley, you can put this on my bill. Make it two. One for her now and one for you to keep on your counter for the future..." With a sheepish look, I hurried out the door.

Strolling into the kitchen, I found Mabel having a cup of tea with her feet up on the chair next to hers. A steaming mug sat beside her waiting for me to drink it. I put Chloe, still in her new bed, on the table and sat down across from Mabel, pushing the tea toward me.

"So, how's your day, Mabel?"

"Busy. I've had phone calls from no less than three people in the last three minutes telling me that they saw James kiss you," Mabel said with her eyebrows raised.

"Let me just say that yes, he kissed my cheek, but I managed to get most of the cooties wiped off."

"Good. Let me just be clear, that man is a sleaze at the very least and at the worst a murderer. I really don't think it's a good idea for you to be kissing him," Mabel said.

"I agree one hundred percent, but it's the only bait I could think of."

"Bait?"

"Yes, James and I will be having drinks at Sharkey's bar tonight. Eight o'clock. I'll be a bit late because I'll be breaking into his gallery. And, I've made plans." Leaning across the table with the mug still in my hands, I carefully laid out the plans for Mabel. I explained who the lookouts were and where they would be standing. Next, I explained about the flashes for signals and the two code words. Handing her a key chain, I instructed Mabel that I wanted her at Comfort Point to follow me and James as my back-up. Mabel sat back in her chair and stared.

"You're serious about this, aren't you?" she asked quietly.

"I need to know, Mabel. For Megan's sake and for my own. I keep feeling a sense of longing, urging, unease, I don't know what it is, but it won't stop until I do." I looked into her caring blue eyes, "Do you understand, Mabel? You are my scarecrow – I need you to believe me most of all."

"I understand, Dorothy. I'm just scared for you – for all of us. I don't want anything bad tonight."

"I know, I don't either. But this is the best I can come up with. Do you have any suggestions?"

"Yes, don't do anything too foolish and dress in sensible

clothing – practical for burglary, but nice enough to woo a madman," Mabel said, smiling into her tea.

"Great, good advice. I'll do that. Anything else?"

"Yes, I think it would be a good idea if we get Benji to come over here tonight and keep a watch for anyone who might want to harm the B&B or Chloe. I'll call Margharite and make sure it's okay with her. We can have Drew stationed at the Bike Shop entrance to watch both Margharite and Benji – a lookout for the lookouts." Mabel stood up and walked to the sink to rinse her mug. "Katy, I'm proud of you, it took guts and thinking to come up with this. I hope for all our sakes it works," she said and left to put the final plans in place. I gathered up Chloe in her bed and went upstairs to find some sensible sexy clothes to wear for tonight. Placing Chloe on her new bed in the picture window, I went to the closet to stare at my limited selection of clothes. I was just thinking of robbing a clothing store when my cell phone rang.

"Hello?"

"Katy, it's Dotty. The plan is in place and all players will be at their appointed positions by half past seven. Any other orders?"

"Nope. We are set to go. Benji will be here at Mabel's to look after Taffeta, Chloe and the Blue Heron – in case of any trouble. Drew will be at the side entrance of the Bike Shop to keep an eye on things as well."

"Excellent. Charley will go over about six and wait for James. He's been meaning to ask him if he wants to order any painting supplies."

"Does he normally do that?"

"Used to. I think mostly for Megan. He hasn't ordered any from us in ages. Never hurts to ask, though. Anything else?"

"Yes, if I live to see the dawn, can I sit down with you

sometime – I need new clothes. My vacation clothes are starting to bore me."

"Ha! Sounds typical coming from someone who is about to commit a crime and then date one. I'll see what I can do for you. Call me if you need anything. Be careful out there. Over and out." And Dotty was gone.

"That Auntie of yours is scary, Chloe. I know she's brilliant, but a little off, I think," I said as that little, fuzzy black face stared back at me. I went over and rubbed her tummy and scratched her ears, feeling the calm before the storm. Settling my nerves, I got up and showered to get ready for the evening ahead.

I was still standing at my closet when there was a slight tap on my door. Mabel entered handing me a hanger with a lovely black knitted sweater.

"Dotty sent it over. Said you called because you didn't know what to wear. She's adding it to your bill and said that you can use it as a tax write off – for burglary supplies."

"I'm so glad that all my new friends have a sense of humor – I seem to have lost mine – along with my mind," I wailed.

"You'll be fine. You just have a case of opening night jitters. Now go put this on. It's a little see through – might want to wear something under it – like burlap," Mabel quipped.

"… Kevlar or a bullet proof vest," I joked.

"Stop the drama. You want to lure your prey, not give him a heart attack!"

I slipped out of the bathroom and Mabel gasped. "My, you look lovely. Your fancy dress pants make you look slimmer and the sweater with all the frilly stuff looks very eye catching. Remind me to give Dotty my compliments."

"Thanks for the vote of confidence. Nice to know I'll look good for my mug shot!"

"Very funny. See, you've even found your sense of humor! Now, just so you know, the cast of characters is in place and James has just left his gallery and headed up the hill to the lighthouse. I'm leaving now to go to my post at the Point and Benji and Taffeta are downstairs in the front parlor. So, whenever you are ready..." Mabel rushed over kissed me on the cheek and walked out of the room and marched downstairs. I was double-checking my burglary kit to make sure my Swiss Army knife was in it when my cell phone rang.

CHAPTER 24

"Hello?"

"Katy, glad I caught you. This is Holly." Oh God, how does she know that I'm about to go marching into the lion's den?

"Hey Holly, what's up?"

"Thought you'd want to know what I found out at the Uptown School of Artistry."

"Really, you have news?" I asked surprised.

"Yep. Really interesting. It seems that James was a good student, but his teachers felt he didn't have the gift of passion and color, so they told him to go to Europe and he did. He met Anna while at the school and they flew off to Europe to live and paint. I asked if the school had any of his works or Anna's for that matter and get this. It seems there was a small fire in the records office about six months ago and all the records have been destroyed. Convenient, isn't it?" Holly said with satisfaction in her voice.

"Even weirder. Anything else of interest?" I asked, looking at the clock and trying not to panic.

"Just one more thing. They had a couple of Megan's works, nothing special, but she shows promise. She has the gift of color and emotion, but her technical abilities were lacking. Her teachers felt she could be good one day, if she applied herself. Unfortunately, there is nothing in the archives of her work now either," Holly concluded.

"Erased by the same fire, no doubt."

"Exactly. A very thorough job of whatever."

"Wow! Nice job, Holly. Thanks for the input..."

"Oh, I forgot, Andy wants me to tell you that he's been able to track down some old police reports – don't ask me how – and it seems that both Megan's death by fire and Anna's death by fire and/or drowning are still open cases. Apparently, Megan's body was too far gone to do a positive ID. Just an assumption based on a ring she wore on her hand and a necklace. Never any trace of Anna's body either. So, that's another positive feather to add to your hat." Holly sounded very pleased with herself.

"Excellent. Tell Andy thank you for the good work, and that I never want to know how he did it."

"Ha, I'll tell him. Well, must dash. Andy and I are going to drive into Denver for a meal at Le Central. I felt we deserved a dinner fit for royalty after all the hard work. Love you and will call tomorrow – bye." And with that, Holly was gone. I was relieved that I didn't have to explain my own plans for the evening. Gathering up my burglary kit, I kissed Chloe good-bye and headed downstairs into the dusk.

I waved to Benji, who was sitting in his deluxe wheelchair with Taffeta on his lap. He smiled and blinked his mini flashlight. I smiled back and eased myself out of the front door and into the shadows. I hurried past the Bike Shop and waved at Drew who was standing in the doorway.

"Good luck!" he whispered as I crept by. He blinked his flashlight. I proceeded past Margharite who stood straight and tall as she prayed into her hands. Waving and continuing past, she blinked her light as well. Passing by the pier, the glow of Dotty's sneakers was just barely noticeable in the shadows by her store, and her flashlight blinked as well. I kept walking, keeping to the north side until I got to the front of James' gallery. I heard a door squeak open and nearly jumped out of my new black sweater.

"Katy, it's Bo," said the low whisper. "I've knocked out the security system on our side of the pier. I'm here and the back door's unlocked if you need an escape route. Be careful." And the door softly closed. Great, I thought, a new member of the Black Cat Society. I'll make him pay dues for being our token male. I stepped forward and put the skeleton key that Andy had given me in the lock. With a few jiggles it opened nicely and I quietly made my way in, remembering to remove the key and lock the door behind me. Slowly, I made my way to the back of the gallery taking out my small mini flashlight. Playing the beam on the eight oils, my gut told me to try my favorite – the one of the lighthouse and the whole town. I gently stepped forward and grasped both sides of the painting, lifted and struggled to ease the heavy picture onto the floor. Squatting down, I gently leaned the picture against the back of the counter, getting a good look at the back, which was covered in brown paper. Pulling out the Swiss Army Knife, I released a section vertically from the frame and then horizontal forming a right angle. Thinking it was too easy to separate, I carefully lifted and folded back the paper. I could just barely see writing on the back of the canvas, but couldn't make out all the words.

So I released more paper until the whole message was exposed. It read:

James —

This one's for you. We will take this town by storm. May our work be like our lighthouse - a beacon to the world.

All my Love, Megan, your muse!

Breathing deeply, I slowly rolled the brown paper back over the back of the canvas, and reaching up to the counter, grabbed the scotch tape and gently reattached the paper. With a sudden spark of inspiration, I gently pried the frame off the canvas at the lower right hand spot. There, hidden by the ornate gold frame, was the signature I was hoping I'd find. Megan Harris. So, the pieces were in place. These were Megan's paintings. And that rat bastard James was selling her paintings as his. Quietly tapping the framing screws back into place, I was making sure that everything on the picture was in place. I was just about to stand up and hang the picture when I spied a movement out of the corner of my eye. I looked to the front of the store just in time to see a shadow of a person by the door. In an instant I had the picture hung and was quickly walking out the back door while sending a prayer of thanks to Bo for dismantling the security system.

I raced up the back deck toward the Mercantile and walked the few short steps to Sharkey's bar. I stopped to catch my breath and for a better look at the bar, having passed it several times, but never giving it much of a thought. The outside looked like a wooden matchbox made with logs from the same sailing vessel whose stern sat a short distance away, docked for eternity at Comfort Point. A sign to the right saying "Sharkey's Bar" hung in the middle of a large shark jaw strapped to driftwood frames. On closer inspection, pennies were placed haphazardly between the rows of shark's teeth. Puzzled, I headed up the two planks forming steps to the front door. Driftwood had been used for railings and as accent pieces on the ground. The entrance door was on the right next to a small window. A larger window toward the left held old beer bottles, while additional shark jaws were hung from the overhang.

Smoothing my hair and straightening my shoulders, I stepped into the bar. One lone table for four sat empty next to me on the right. The long, dark wooden bar ran parallel to the door, while several tables were placed to the left and up against the giant picture window facing the ocean. Old bar stools with black leather padding sat at attention in front of the bar. A large mirror was stationed behind the bar displaying various varieties of booze, while different types of glasses were suspended from metal racks chained to the ceiling. James lifted his hand to catch my attention.

I sauntered over and slid into the chair beside him with my back to the window. I gave him the brightest smile I could muster.

"Hello, James," I said in a low smooth voice. "Am I late? I didn't mean to be."

"No, your arrival was most timely. What can I get you to drink?" he asked suavely.

"Merlot would be wonderful."

"Fine, excuse me and I'll go talk to the barkeep. I won't keep you waiting long," James said as he slid out of his seat like a serpent and made his way toward the bar. I took the liberty of looking around the bar for my reinforcements. The place seemed empty for this time of night. Charley was sitting with a few bar flies on a beat up barstool toward the back of the place with a drink that shimmered like a pale ale in front of him. He slowly turned around and gave me a wink. I winked back. I spied a small door at the back of the bar next to the cash register – probably a small unisex bathroom. I shuddered to think what the inside looked like.

I stole a glance at the bartender as well. If this was Sharkey, he truly did resemble a man who likes sharks. Sharkey was all bulging muscle strapped into a black T-shirt with black jeans tight in all the right places. A belt with a silver buckle wrapped around his slender hips. He was bald, a shaved head I guessed, and with his shiny taut skin stretched over his scalp he looked like a reptile. But his shark eyes were ever watchful and searching. When he felt me staring, he turned his head in my direction. He did not smile, but a tug of amusement curled the corners of his full lips – like a predator spying a glimpse of his prey. Immediately I looked down at my hands on the table and tried to slow my breathing and gather my thoughts.

A Merlot appeared in front of me as James took his seat next to me. He reached for his drink; from the smell of it I guessed it was top shelf whiskey with no water and little ice. He held up his glass and said, "To art and its many shades and moods..."

"To art and its passions of the heart..." I said in my best Lauren Bacall voice as we clinked glasses. I sniffed my Merlot for rat poison, but it smelled fine. We sipped in silence.

"Thank you for meeting me tonight, Katy. I was hoping you were not avoiding me."

"Heavens, no! Just been busy taking in the sights. Now James, enough about me, I would love to hear more about you. Have you always been drawn to the art world?" I asked with artificial sweetness.

"Yes, I believe some are born to it. I love color, light and scale. I believe even my coloring books showed talent," James said seriously.

"Really? That must be wonderful to know what path your life will take. Was it easy to learn all the needed skills to become great?"

"Yes, I truly feel that to be a great artist, and I never said I was, you did, one must suffer for the arts. How else can you appreciate your talent and where your talent takes you?" James purred.

"Was your wife talented? I'm sorry, I'm just curious…"

"Well, she had rudimentary talent, but nothing on a grand scale. She tried hard, though, gave it her best shot," James said as he pulled on the collar of his gray silk shirt.

"I understand that Megan Harris was talented as well."

"My yes, she was a talent. Still new, still fresh, but she had the gift. I was pleased she chose me to be her mentor. I was able to pour every bit of help I could into her art. It was really quite gratifying," James explained.

"Then I guess it must have been so difficult when her tragedy occurred," I said, trying to ease into my interrogation.

"My yes, I was devastated," James began as he gulped the last of his drink and signaled Sharkey for another round for each of us. "I was completely torn apart. To lose Megan at the brink of her career as an artist was just… just… it was horrid!" James said rather loudly. Sharkey appeared at my side holding a small tray with our drinks. He leaned forward and set them down in front of us. As he straightened, he very gently stroked my hair, turned and slithered back to the bar. I cringed inwardly and sipped my drink, trying not to derail my train of thought.

"So, losing Megan and Anna … at the same time…" I probed.

"Yes, my Anna as well. She had grown sickly those last few months, but she was still my wife. It was just terrible," he shuddered.

"Then why, James, did you stay in a town so full of ghosts?"

"Where was I to go?" He answered in a still small voice. The first truly authentic sentence the man had said to me so far.

"So, you had nowhere to go, so the people of Comfort took you in and made you their friend?" I asked trying to draw the real James out.

"Ha! Their friend? I don't think so. They think of me as a murderer, a philanderer, and an artist. You must understand, Katy, that I am not an ordinary person and these are just… well…" he leaned forward and whispered, "…common people. I don't really have much in common with them." He straightened up and resumed his normal tone of voice. "Now don't get me wrong, I try to be helpful, been on several committees and things of that nature, but it is difficult. People keep insisting that I open the lighthouse. Never, I tell you, never!" James said getting louder with each swallow.

"Don't you want the lighthouse open for others to see…?"

"No! Of course not! It's not their lighthouse. I bought it fair and square. And it is my home. I'm sure nobody else wants strangers traipsing through their home at all hours. No, I tell you, I won't have it. The lighthouse is closed as long as I'm alive," James said as he banged his fist on the table spilling part of his drink. I simply stared at the man trying to piece together what he was saying and not saying.

"James, since the horrible events, have you been able to paint?" I asked, knowing I was swimming in the deep end.

"No, not a stroke. I tried to after her death, but I just couldn't do it. The passion for art left after she did. So, I resign myself to the few simple pieces I was able to produce in this lifetime and try to make a meager living from that," James said with a frown.

"I bet it more than pays the bills. I mean you do have quite a following..."

"Well, yes, I surely cannot complain. And with Anna's death, I was able to inherit a small sum from her trust left by her parents. It will get me by for these last years on this earth," James said sadly into his empty glass.

"I'm so sorry for your loss. I wish there was something I could do," I tentatively offered.

"There is," James said with his eyes piercing into mine. "Buy one of my originals, one of the jewels in my crown. It would mean so much to me, knowing that you have a part of me..." James leaned forward and grasped both my hands in his. "Please, do this for me. I think you understand me better than most and would understand what a gift it would be." And he reached down and kissed each one of my hands. Gads, I had had enough.

Withdrawing my hands I said, "James, I will seriously think on your offer. Give me a couple of days to talk with my financial manager..."

"You have a financial manager?" James yelped.

"Yes, I do. How about if we talk again in a few days? You get me a figure you deem is fair and I'll discuss the particulars with her," I bargained.

"I could talk with her instead, if you wish. Save you the time and hassle of haggling pricing and things of that nature. I wouldn't mind," James offered.

"No, really. I'd prefer to handle it myself. Thank you so much for the drink, but I must be going." I stood up, hastily shook James' hand to avoid more cooties and hurried toward the door. Sharkey stopped me on the way out and whispered in my ear, "Come back tomorrow. I'll have a piece of the puzzle about your friend James. I open at eleven." His breath was warm against my neck as he opened the door for me.

I got about two steps out the door when a pair of arms grabbed me and dragged me into the shadows of the outside deck. I gasped and tried to struggle free. The pair of arms circled me and drew me close.

"Stop squirming. If that creep had kissed anything more than your hands, I would have gone in and busted up the place, him along with it. What in the hell do you think you are doing, Katy?" he asked.

"Bo? Is that you?" I asked, trying to see his face that was completely in shadow.

"Yah, who else? Now listen. Be careful. Tonight you lucked out – had all your friends watching your back. But it won't always be like that. Stay away from him, Katy; he's bad news!" Bo warned.

"I'm being careful. What business is it of yours anyway?"

"I'm making it my business." His faced moved toward mine, his arms tightened around me and he kissed me. I didn't move and couldn't breathe. Bo released me and pushed me from him and walked into the bar. The door closed before I could see his face. Damn, damn, damn!

CHAPTER 25

I crept back to Mabel's in a daze. Great, I got cooties by a murderer, petted by a trophy-hunting bartender, and now kissed by the Invisible Man. God! Dotty better not buy me any more sweaters if this is what happens. I heard howling as I crept into the kitchen. Cherry, Wynetta, and Mabel were in the kitchen looking extremely worried. Chloe was on the kitchen table howling with all six pounds of her.

"Good Heavens, Chloe. What is the trouble?" I asked her. She took one look at me and jumped into my arms, snuggling on my chest. "What is it? Are you okay?" I grabbed a dry hand towel from the counter and wrapped it over Chloe who was now trilling and pretend suckling for all she was worth.

"What happened? Is she okay?"

"She has been howling and running from window to window since you walked into the bar," Cherry said. "Sakes alive, it sounded like the Hound of the Baskervilles in here."

"We couldn't do anything to calm her down. She even scratched the back door like a dog trying to get out," Wynetta added.

"I just don't understand it. She hasn't been this spooked since she was little," I replied as I stroked her. Chloe had calmed down and her trill had turned to a loud purr.

"I don't want to say anything, but you look like you're nursing…" Mabel said with a smirk.

"Very funny. So, did you all have a nice night?"

"Well, it was pretty quiet once you broke into the place," Cherry said. "Wyn and I couldn't see much, so we just waited until we saw Bo look through the front window and saw the back door open. After that we figured our part was over, we came over here to hang out with Benji."

"Remind me to kick Bo when I see him next. I had no idea who was at the front. I saw a shadow and made a dash out the back door. He nearly gave me a heart attack."

"We sent Benji home with Taffeta once we got here," Wynetta began. "Mabel joined us a few minutes later…"

"… I left my position after I saw you walk into the bar. I passed Bo who was hanging around out front. Came back here, walked in…"

"… and Chloe went nuts!" Cherry said.

"Well, she seems better now. I wonder what upset her. Did she know I was meeting James? She really doesn't like him." I leaned back in the chair and thought of the dead mouse in James' wine glass. "She played with Gavin's pens and sniffed his hand, so I think she likes him. She licked Bo – enough said there. Played stringy with Charley today and likes her new bed. Only person she didn't like was James – the dead mouse – the hand mauling… and now the howling."

"You don't think Chloe is trying to tell you something?" Cherry asked.

"Possibly. She's obviously upset. I just don't know why. She wasn't the one who got kissed by him."

"WHO GOT WHAT?" They all said in unison.

"James kissed my hands. Sharkey petted my hair and blew in my ear. And Bo kissed me!" I sighed as I said the last part rather quietly.

"THEY DID WHAT?" they yelled in unison. While stroking Chloe, I filled them in on my activities from the time spent at James' gallery to the note I found, as well as finding Meagan's signature. I also told them about James and Sharkey at the bar. And I reluctantly told them about what Bo said and about the kiss.

"Well, I never. That Bo is one yummy surprise!" Wynetta cooed.

"Thanks a bunch. I think he's gone off the deep end. And I still haven't seen his face!" I wailed.

"What do you mean you haven't seen his face? You locked lips?" Cherry shrieked.

"He was in shadow – I couldn't see a thing. He may look like a swamp monster and I'd never know. Great, I kissed a swamp monster," I whined.

"Well, I for one do not think Bo resembles a swamp monster. More like John Wayne in his younger days," Mabel said slowly with a smile playing on her lips.

"Great! Wonderful! I just kissed the Duke. What a nice way to end the evening. Is there anything else I need to know before I turn in?"

"Nope! All clear, present and accounted for. So, what are your plans for tomorrow? Need any help?" Cherry asked with a devilish grin.

"I'm going to go see Sharkey at some point tomorrow and find out about this puzzle piece. I think I'll take Chloe – if she bites him, we have another suspect."

"Good idea. Cats are so perceptive – I read somewhere they're psychic," Wynetta stated proudly.

"Really? Good, then it's settled – we'll visit Sharkey tomorrow. I might also see what James is up to and how to proceed. I don't know if I have enough evidence to tell the police yet. We do have police or something, don't we?" I asked Mabel.

"Charley is our deputy. That's why he was at the bar tonight – unofficially keeping an eye on you."

"Good to know. Well then, that's the plan. If I think of something brilliant, I'll let you all know."

"How about Bo?" Cherry asked with a wicked smile.

"Oh, I plan to avoid him for the rest of my life!" I teased, getting up from the table. "Thanks for taking care of Chloe, she'll be fine. And thank you all for watching my back."

"You're welcome. Glad we only have to watch your back..." Cherry began.

"...'Cause is sounds like Bo is watching your front!" Wynetta ended with a laugh.

"Lovely. I have a host of friends... Good night all!" I called back as I headed up the stairs.

Closing the door to my room, I settled down in the rocker and uncovered Chloe. She peered up at me with her gold eyes.

"Chloe, are you okay, baby?"

"Meeooo!"

"Is it James?"

"Aahhooww!"

"I'm okay. He won't hurt you. I'll make sure he doesn't hurt me either. Better?"

"Merp," she said and curled up on my lap to sleep. Covering her back up with the hand towel, I rocked her gently thinking of how to keep her safe and me as well. It was well after midnight before we both fell into bed. Chloe slept better than I did. I vowed not to tell anyone that I dreamed of a stranger in shadows with warm, moist lips.

The next morning we slept late and awoke to partial sun and clouds. Chloe must be feeling better, I thought, after spying the two pink mice on the floor. She was on her perch in the window seat happily licking herself.

"Morning, Chloe, feeling better?" She paused in mid lick and rolled over onto her back to show me her tummy. "Yep, you're feeling better." I jumped out of bed and headed for the shower, mentally planning my day. A stack of new clothes was sitting on the dresser as I stepped out of the bathroom. Choosing a lavender turtleneck sweater from the stack, I added jeans, purple cat socks and sneakers feeling ready to face my day. I said a silent prayer that I had enough clues to take to Charley so they could arrest James. Leaving Chloe sunning herself, I headed down for a late breakfast. A note was waiting for me on the kitchen table saying Mabel was in Uptown shopping and would return for lunch – and did I want to meet her at the Deli at noon. I wrote a big "Yes, my treat" on her note and made myself a bowl of oatmeal with cranberries and cream.

My first stop was Cherry's for a cup of really good coffee, seeing as how Mabel had not left me any. Cherry and Wynetta were in a fever of cleaning and rearranging. Another row of tables lined the wall close to the picture window. Cherry's tea shelves were half empty and Wynetta was madly unpacking new pounds of coffee and quickly adding them to the shelves. Cherry and Wynetta were wasting no time turning the coffee shop into a posh coffee house. I chatted with them briefly and left them to their furor of activity. Out of curiosity, I strolled around to the back deck area and over to Creature Comforts to peer in the window. Wynetta had been a busy girl. The place was empty of animals – four-legged, two-legged, crawling and slithering. Cherry had mentioned that Wynetta had a buyer, but I never thought it would happen so quickly. I nodded to myself imagining Cherry and Wynetta in business together running the coffee house. It felt like a good step forward for both of them.

I backtracked to Gavin's to ask a question that was none of my business. We chatted briefly. He reported that he and Miss Martha would be showing properties in Uptown and that business was picking up. He further explained that it would take a few more days for the leasing papers to Megan's studio to be ready. I asked how the leasing of Creature Comforts was going.

"Now, girlfriend, you know I can't tell you that. But it's really quite exciting," Gavin was rubbing his hands together.

"Really, Gavin, you can tell me. We have that whole client/ agent disclosure thing going. Anything we discuss, leasing, money, price, who is leasing Wynetta's place, whatever, cannot be discussed with anyone else. Surely, you know that?" I chided him.

"That's rotten of you, you know. How am I supposed to keep a secret?"

"How many other people know, Gavin?"

"Well, that's not fair either. Okay, but it's our secret – at least for a few more days until it closes. Any guess?" he tittered.

"Gavin! Spill it!" I growled.

"Well, the Deli guys are splitting up. One guy will run the Deli as it is with soups, sandwiches and lunch stuff. The other guy will be opening a supper club – after extensive remodeling, of course – featuring fine dining, fresh, natural and organic food depending on the season – using local growers. Just your style, I'd say, Miss Katy," Gavin beamed.

"Wow! What a great idea! That sounds perfect. I hope I'm still here when they open," I said while thinking I had just uncovered Cherry's secret. Must have been one hell of a poker game, I thought.

"Oh you will be. Saw you kissing Bo last night while I was playing lookout here in my office."

"You too? Is there anyone who doesn't know what I did last night?"

"Probably not. This is a small town, Katy. We know everything about everyone. That's why we get along so well."

"Because it's hard to blackmail people here when everyone knows everyone's secrets?" I teased.

"Hee-hee! No, because we all care about each other and look out for each other. Just about the most perfect place for someone like you."

"And what's that supposed to mean?"

"Someone who needs us as much as we need you, Katy! Now scoot, I have piles of work today, piles!" And Gavin turned his back, picked up his phone and waved as I left.

I spent some time at Comfort Point thinking about what Gavin said. There was truth in his words that warmed my heart. He spoke what my head had been telling me for some time. Family is more than the people you share blood with. Families are the people you choose who make your life richer and your days brighter. Maybe I could make this place my home – with a bunch of busybody misfits for friends, I thought with a smile. My hands rubbed the wood beams of the ship's back end. I felt courage, determination, and history running through my palms into my arms. Comfort had a history worth exploring and I hoped one day to learn more. With those thoughts in mind, I headed for the Deli promising myself I would not tell Mabel the big secret that I bet she knew already.

Mabel and I enjoyed a lovely lunch at the Deli. I had my usual clam chowder, sourdough bread and salad while Mabel had a meatloaf sandwich. We ate in companionable silence except for Mabel chiding me about my addiction to clam chowder.

"You order that every time we come here, Katy! They have other things on the menu, you know."

"I know, but I'm a part time vegetable-tarian. I eat veggies and other healthy stuff most of the time, but I just love their clam chowder. It's my way of splurging. So, I'm an addict. It's always good to have a vice and clam chowder is mine – the New England kind, not the Manhattan."

"Any other vices I need to know about?" Mabel teased.

"No, I haven't seen Bo all day, if that's what you're asking," I shot back.

"Really, Katy, if I didn't know better, I'd say you were warming to the guy."

"Warming? I'm steamed. How dare he kiss me? I don't even know him!"

"Pipe down! Now that the whole Deli knows, why don't you lower your voice and tell me what you're so upset about."

"I'm not ready for a man in my life. I still feel raw from my parents being gone and my being alone. I just don't want to open myself up to get hurt."

"Do you think that Bo would knowingly hurt you? Like you said, you don't know him."

"Well, that's just it – I don't know."

"Then, why not take some grandmotherly advice and get to know him – as a friend. You always have room for a new friend.

Then take it from there." Mabel said.

"But, what does he want? I just don't know – it makes my stomach hurt just thinking about it."

"Maybe it's the amount of chowder you just consumed," Mabel teased.

"Ugh, you could be right. I think I'll go walk around for a bit, then pick up Chloe for her date with Sharkey."

"Fine. Just don't make mountains out of molehills. Bo is a good person. You're a good person. That's all I'm saying." Mabel got up from her seat and tottered outside heading for home. I paid the bill and followed. After brushing my teeth, I scooped up Chloe, placed her in her halter with her purple lead, and headed out to Sharkey's bar.

CHAPTER 26

Chloe scampered about sniffing all the driftwood smells. I lifted her up to look at the shark jaw sign. Taking a deep breath, I slipped into the bar. It was deserted except for Sharkey, parked behind the bar, filling the cooler with bottlenecks. Placing Chloe on the bar I kept a firm hand on her leash. Sharkey wiped his hands on the towel hanging from his belt and held out a hand. Chloe sniffed it, sat and stared at him. Silently Sharkey placed a peanut shell in front of her. She looked at him, then the shell, and with one swipe of her paw brushed it off the bar. With a bark of a laugh, Sharkey picked it up and replaced it on the bar. Chloe swatted it off and looked over the bar to watch it settle on the ground. Sharkey gently scratched behind her ears and Chloe cocked her head and gave his hand a tentative lick. I let out the breath I was holding.

In one move, Sharkey was around the bar and standing in

front of me with that same amused smile tugging at his face.

"Did I pass the cat test?" he murmured while his eyes scanned me like an x-ray machine.

"Yes, it seems she doesn't think you're a threat," I said coolly.

"I'm no threat to her. I like cats. Had one once, a long time ago," he said with his eyes settling on my face.

"So, what's the piece of the puzzle you have for me?" I asked, trying not to inhale his musky cologne.

"Sure you want to keep this all business?" he asked too innocently.

"I think so. Do you have something for me?" I asked and instantly regretted my choice of words.

"Now that sounds more my style. I have whatever you want, Katy. Any time! Just remember that," he said, leaning forward and sniffing my hair. Places in my body were getting warm and I was having trouble concentrating.

"Thanks for that offer – first one I've had all day. I'll remember," I said while mentally yelling at my various parts to get a grip. Sharkey moved around me and reached for a small picture nailed to the wall by the door. He handed it to me and waited. The framed picture was a small eight by ten of the lighthouse sketched all in pencil. The proportions were good, the lines too, but the whole scene felt lifeless and mechanical. I glanced at Sharkey's face. He nodded with his head and pointed at the lower right corner of the frame. The initials JR were clearly visible.

"James Reinhold gave you this?"

"Yes," Sharkey replied, waiting.

"Did you see him sketch this?" I asked cautiously.

"Yes. He sat right at the table where you were last night."

"When did he do this?"

"A few months after he moved here with that new wife of

his."

"Why did he give it to you?" I asked curiously.

"I liked it. It fits me. All structure, no emotion," he replied, smiling.

"Ha, nice. I really don't think that's you."

"Really. Do you think you know me, Katy?" Sharkey asked, leaning forward.

"I think you are a good guy who likes to act badly."

"Are you sure?" He asked, tracing the line on my jaw.

"Pretty sure. Chloe doesn't lie," I said as she came up between us.

"Wow, saved by a cat. Nice one." He retreated back behind his bar.

"So, James gave you this – does he remember giving it to you?" I asked, trying to breathe.

"Maybe not. He and his wife were the worse for the wine they had. I doubt if he remembers how they got home," Sharkey said while picking up glasses to polish.

"Can I keep this for a bit?"

"You can have it – on one condition, of course," he said, pausing to look at me.

"What's the condition?" I asked, dreading the answer.

"Come in here one night – alone – when your little mystery is solved and let me buy you a drink."

"That's it?" I asked, thinking there must be a catch.

"That's it. Do we have an agreement?" he asked, reaching out his hand.

"Yes," I said with a sigh and reached out my hand. He took my hand and with his lips nibbled my knuckles. He kissed my palm with a bit of tongue thrown in and then let me go. We looked at each other for a moment before I hurriedly scooped up Chloe and the picture and bustled out the door feeling

Sharkey's eyes watching my every step.

I dropped Chloe off in the kitchen with Mabel and went upstairs to hide the picture Sharkey had given me. I'd look at it more closely later and decide what to do with it. Too many men were having a fascination with my hands and with me and it was starting to creep me out. To clear my head and gain some perspective, washing my hands again, I thought a visit with Cherry was in order. Making my way down to the pier, I sat in the middle of the bench and watched Cherry and Wynetta work. It was already late in the day as the sun gently touched the horizon, causing the ocean to sparkle. They were still at it — stocking, stacking and rearranging. I didn't have the heart to go in and interrupt them. I was just getting up when I felt a hand on my shoulder. Glancing around I saw James standing behind me with a piercing look that could mean anything. With his hand still on my shoulder, James walked around and sat down next to me pulling his arm around my shoulders. My insides quivered and turned to jelly.

"Miss Hawkins, how lovely to see you so soon," James said with his voice cool and low.

"Mr. Reinhold, since when did you stop calling me Katy?" I asked sweetly.

"Since you broke into my gallery last night," he said quietly.

"What?" I said, trying to wiggle out from his grasp.

"Just sit still, Miss Hawkins. I have a few things I would like to say to you. We are going to get up slowly and walk into my gallery. Understand?" he hissed.

"And why would I want to do that, Mr. Reinhold?" I sneered.

"Because of the gun I have pressing into your side. I think it makes very convincing motivation." With that, James stood up and pulled me up with him. He grabbed my arm, while still pressing the gun into my ribs and led me into his gallery where he pushed me away from him while turning and locking the door. Keeping his eye on me and holding the supposed gun in his pocket, James went to each window and pulled down the blinds. The room became very dark. I felt small and trapped. He motioned for me to go behind the counter as he walked toward me.

"Kneel," he said and indicated that I should kneel down behind the counter. I didn't. He kicked the back of my knee and pushed me to the floor. He quickly grasped my hands behind my back and started taping them with, from the sound of it, masking tape. I kept my hands clenched and rigid hoping there would be play when he finished. There was, but not much.

"Turn around," he said. I twisted on my knees until I faced him and saw only his eyes – half wild and half sad. "You have no idea what you have done, do you?"

"James, what are you talking about, I haven't done anything. Please, let me go," I pleaded.

"You are a liar. You left the bar last night with dust on your black pants. That made me curious, so I came back here to check – make sure everything was in order. And do you know what I found?" James asked, his voice rising.

"How would I know?" I snarled back.

"This," he said and held up my Dad's Swiss Army knife. "Now, I know that doesn't belong to me, so I began looking around. That's when I noticed the painting."

"What painting?" I asked, my voice trembling.

"The one you tampered with." He walked over to the painting, lifted it off its hinge and showed me the back where he had painstakingly replaced the tape I had used last night and had mended it with proper backing tape.

"It doesn't look tampered with to me. What are you talking

about?" I asked, my mind racing for a possible way out of this alive.

"I know it doesn't look it – I fixed it," he yelled at me. He replaced the painting making sure it was square, not crooked, something I should have thought of last night.

"So, I need answers, Miss Hawkins. And you will give them to me. If not here, then we will retire to the lighthouse. You will give me answers there – you will have no choice." James' body slowly rocked back and forth.

"Mr. Reinhold… James… let me go. It's over. Everyone knows that you did it. That you killed Megan."

"I DID NOT KILL HER! How dare you utter her name? You have no idea what you have done. Everything was fine until you came along. Now, do you want to tell me here or do we take a walk to the lighthouse?" His body continued to sway.

"I have no idea what you are talking about," I said, my heart beating madly.

"Then let it be on your head. I tried to save you. Stay there. I have a few things to attend to." James removed the gun from his pocket. It was a real gun and I wondered if he knew how to use it. He quickly crossed to his file cabinet, unlocked it and pulled out a stack of neatly bound money. He slammed the file cabinet closed and motioned for me to stand. I slowly got to my feet and leaned against the counter, my hands searching for anything I could feel on the counter to use as a weapon. Finding nothing to speak of, I glanced at James, who removed a tweed jacket from the back of his chair and came toward me to wrap it around my shoulders.

"There, no one will see that your hands are taped. Shall we go, Miss Hawkins?" He led me to the back of the gallery and we exited, making our way slowly toward the path that led to the lighthouse. We passed the Mercantile, Sharkey's Bar, and Comfort Point and saw no one. He had his arm firmly across my shoulders, in part to keep his jacket from slipping and part to keep me near him and the gun. My mind was racing with possibilities and attempted plans to escape. But the path was narrow and my choices few. We slowly made our way toward the lighthouse as the sun dipped below the horizon, shedding pale light on the ominous storm clouds approaching. Rounding a curve, I saw a wisp of fog floating before us. It was not comforting. I tried to still my mind from all the pictures running in my head. Then I heard it, floating on a distant breeze. Laughter. I shivered and prayed that someone would come.

The mist hovered and seemed to follow us as we neared the door to the lighthouse. A flickering glow graced the windows, but I did not feel welcome or warmth. James stopped and jerked me to him just in front of the door. He looked at me and his cold eyes danced in the flickering light. He turned the knob, pushed the door open and pushed me inside. Slamming the door behind me, I heard the lock turn. As my feet stepped forward I walked into a living nightmare.

The lighthouse was charred, blackened and smelled of smoke. Fumes from some type of solvent or paint thinner stung my throat and made my eyes water. Around the room were dozens of large candles sitting on wrought iron pedestals casting a ghostly flicker in the burnt out ruin of the lighthouse. I coughed and tried to breathe. Old wooden chairs and end tables were placed haphazardly around the room near the bigger candles. An easel, tubes of paint, brushes and rags were scattered on a large table. Blank canvases stretched on wood frames leaned against the far wall by the tower door. Drums of paint thinner and turpentine were placed under the table. A small sagging cot took up the far wall next to the tower door.

"James, what have you done? This place is supposed to be finished. You said it was remodeled, redone." He walked unsteadily toward the table and grabbed a box cutter with an exposed razor blade.

"You don't understand, it's never done. It will never be done." He was still swaying slightly from foot to foot as he moved to my side holding the cutter.

"James, please tell me what happened that night? I can get you help. Please, tell me..." I begged, feeling a tightness growing in my chest.

"What happened? I was reborn that night. I was given a new start. My life was FINE until you came along. I thought you were one of us. I thought you'd understand, but you don't. You're just like the others. They can't see past the pretty colors to see the real art. I had it all until you came," James rambled.

"How could you? You told me your life was terrible after Anna died."

"I did not. I would never have said that to you. Don't you listen, don't you understand?" he screamed. With one swift move James slit the tape that bound my hands.

"James, when I asked you why you didn't leave you said you had nowhere to go. You were alone..."

"No, I'm never alone. I can't leave this place – ever..." James' voice trailed off as he stared at a spot behind me while still holding the box cutter.

"James, why can't you leave? There's no one here now. Anna and Megan are gone," I said gently.

"They're never gone, don't you see? You're still here, aren't you?" James said. A harsh laughter filled the room and I spun around to see what James was staring at as the box cutter fell to the ground.

CHAPTER 27

A willowy figure wrapped in white gauze stepped through the tower door and limped toward me. A raspy laughter swirled around the room as it dragged itself forward. A candle lit up the face of the creature and I screamed at the sight. Where once a face had been, a mask of singed skin and burns remained. Eyebrows gone; lips, cracked and bleeding; nose just a pulpy stump; long strands of pale hair poked through the seared scalp. The folds of its ears were shriveled like dry leaves. The entire face was a map of scars and burns. I looked at the hands, which were twisted and gnarled like driftwood, noticing that two fingers were gone. My stomach gave a lurch as I stared at the creature before me with the smell of soot, ashes and singed skin stinging my nose.

"No, you are never alone, my love, are you?" the raspy voice whispered.

"No, my dearest. You have stayed by my side, always," James replied lovingly.

"Who is she?" the raspy voice asked.

"She is the one who broke into the gallery last night. She knows things," James said quietly.

"She did not know this. I live after another dies," the voice whispered. The form laughed and twirled in place.

"Yes, you live, my dear. But what are we to do?" James whined. The creature moved toward me, reaching out its hand, pointing at me with a stump of a finger.

"What do you know of us? What do you know of all this?" the voice asked, peering into my eyes. I coughed and sputtered and tried to catch a full breath.

"I know that Anna and Megan are dead and that James is selling Megan's paintings as his," I said, trembling.

"You are wrong. One of us is very much alive. And the paintings are his," the voice whispered.

"It's clear to me now that one of you is alive. But the paintings are Megan's. I saw the back of one of her pictures – the one with the note – and I found her signature."

"You are still wrong. The paintings are his. Megan is just a vessel. He is the master. Always was," the voice whispered louder. My stomach turned and I found my hands shaking. I heard the words, but could not understand what they meant. With every bit of courage, I asked the question I didn't want to ask.

"Who are you?" I asked, quietly peering into the face, staring into its eyes. The creature turned away from me throwing up its arms and laughed the lung-seared laugh of the truly insane.

"You mean you don't know? You still haven't figured it out?" the voice chided me. From behind the creature, I saw the wispy mist floating beside it. I stared from one to the other and my heart lurched when I reached my own answer. I looked to James who was staring at the creature.

"You see it, too, don't you, James?"

"Yes, it's been with me since that night," James said simply.

"What do you see, dearest? Is there someone else here?" The creature whirled around looking for others.

"I know what he sees," I said to the creature.

"What do you see? What do you think you know?" the creature chided.

"I see Anna," I said. The creature screamed and whirled around sweeping its arms, grasping and searching the room for the ghost that hovered beside her all along.

"Do not speak that name – never that name!" The creature went to James' side and grabbed him.

"What did she say? What did she say?" she pleaded, shaking him.

"She sees her, my dearest. She sees Anna," James moaned.

"You are Megan," I said to the creature. "And… I think I can tell you what happened that night. You killed Anna, I don't know why, and placed her body in your studio. Then you set the fires to cover your tracks. Am I close?" I asked Megan, who had released James and was limping toward me, her breath rattling.

"You don't understand. Anna was going to have James break up with me. Me! I'm his vessel, his muse, his soul mate. Because of me, he could paint. He taught me everything – color, dimension, forms, harmony, and passion. He paints through me. He poured his gift into me, so I paint – his paintings. I couldn't have that. Couldn't have her ruin his work. James was mine – I am his." Megan stopped, rasping for air. "They came – together – to my studio. How dare she? She is no artist, has no style. I was furious at her for making James break it off.

I grabbed her around the neck and smashed her against the wall and shook her. I squeezed that scrawny neck of hers and crushed her until she gasped... her... last... breath," Megan whispered. From behind her, James put his face in his hands and wept. He looked up at me like a boy lost in his deepest nightmare.

"So, you killed Anna?" I asked Megan.

"Yes, she was going to part us – we cannot be parted," she reasoned.

"Then you set the fire to cover..." I began.

"...I set her on fire to destroy her like she was going to destroy me," Megan screeched.

"How did you move the paintings? No one saw you," I asked James.

He cleared his throat, "I had been storing them in my gallery, which at the time was closed to the public. We only had to move a few pieces." He looked back down at his hands.

"Then you set the place on fire and came back to the lighthouse, both of you?"

"Yes. I needed...we needed time to think and plan what to do," James said, looking at the floor.

"Then what happened?" I asked as I edged myself closer to the door.

"Yes, dearest, tell her. Admit your sins and be forgiven," Megan chided him.

"I thought it best that we leave this place... make a run for it. Megan wouldn't leave. Didn't want to leave her paintings – our paintings. So, I told her I was going without her and went to pack." James lapsed into silence. Megan appeared before me and motioned me away from the door, standing between it and me. Trembling, I backed further into the room.

"And...?" I prodded.

Megan began to laugh and whirl around the room until she was again by James' side.

"A blaze of glory…" Megan whispered. "I decided to go out in a blaze of glory."

James got up and came to me with pleading eyes. "She started the fire while I was packing. When I came back into the room the place was ablaze – raging, flames everywhere, smoke… couldn't breathe. I reached for her, but she pulled me toward her, toward the flames. I panicked, pushed her and ran out. The next thing I remember, I was walking on the beach and had no memory of what happened or how I got there. I saw the lighthouse was in flames and ran to help, I found Megan curled up outside the tower door leading to the beach. She was smoldering, burned and smelled of…" James retched and hung his head down. "I didn't know what to do. Megan would be blamed for Anna's death. I needed her, needed her talent. Her art was everything I ever hoped to be." James ambled over to the chair and sank down – a lost and broken man. Megan had stopped laughing and was pulling a huge can of paint thinner from under the table. Before James could stop her, she had unscrewed the top and tipped it over, causing it to spill on the wooden floor, splashing her feet. She laughed and splashed in the puddle at her feet. The fumes were strong and made breathing even more difficult. James wrestled with her as she dove under the table for another can, knocking the brushes and paints to the floor. She had another can unscrewed and upended before he pushed her away from him.

"Enough!" He barked at her. "I HAVE HAD ENOUGH!" Megan looked at him and cocked her head.

"We are together forever, my darling. We shall never be parted," Megan declared.

"Yes, yes, my dearest. But stop this." James looked around at the huge puddles on the floor, his eyes watering, nose running, and pants drenched. I held my sleeves up to my nose to block the fumes. The mist appeared beside Megan and hovered. It was hard for me to think of it as Anna, but I knew it was. As Anna floated next to Megan, I could almost see them together. Megan so tall and willowy – like a reed in the breeze, Mabel had said. Anna, small as a frail bird, hovered beside her. Anna floated to one of the wrought iron pillars and with a puff of mist tilted the iron pillar, causing the candle to crash to the floor. In an instant the entire floor flashed and was on fire with James in the middle of it. He started toward the door, but Megan wrapped her arms around him, stopping him and pulling him back into the center of the room. James looked over at me and yelled, "Run!" I stumbled past them toward the door, fire licking at my feet as the flames got higher and the fumes thicker. I sank to my knees as I reached the door. Fumbling with the lock, I jerked the door open and fell through the opening. I turned for one last look to see the fire encircling James and Megan, with flames licking at their clothes. They clung to each other, inseparable in death as in life. I heard sounds coming from inside. It sounded like the screams of two souls eternally damned.

My eyes were watering and my vision blurry. I was too close. My chest was burning and nose stung from the toxic fumes. I couldn't breathe. I felt hands pull me up and push me further out the door. I was fighting for every breath and losing. As darkness closed around me, I heard a "Merp" and felt my face being licked.

CHAPTER 28

The pain in my shoulder felt like the pricking of pins and needles and my chest was heavy as I opened my eyes and looked around me. My eyes were still blurry, but I could hear the unmistakable sound of purring. Chloe was sitting on my chest, kneading her claws into my right shoulder. I was familiar enough with the Blue Heron to know that I was in the front parlor.

"Chloe, you and I smell like an ashtray," I said weakly.

"Oh good, you're awake," Mabel said and she wiped my face with a warm cloth. "I wasn't sure what to think when Bo came crashing in here carrying you, with Charley following close behind holding Chloe. You had me scared half out of my wits."

"What happened and how in the hell did Chloe end up at the lighthouse?" I asked, wishing my head would clear.

"Well, it seems Gavin saw James sit down with you on the bench by the pier. He didn't like the way James was looking at you and when you both stood up, Gavin ran across and told Bo. Bo waited until you left the gallery and he followed you both as you made your way to the lighthouse. Bo sent Gavin to tell Charley and then me. Then Chloe started her chirping, so I figured she would know where you were going. I harnessed her and gave her to Charley. She was like a bloodhound following your scent," Mabel explained.

"Good grief, she could have been hurt when the fire started," I moaned.

"Not with Charley looking out for her. He's developed quite a fondness for that cat of yours. I wasn't worried about Chloe."

"So, then what happened?" I asked, sitting up and settling Chloe on my lap where her claws would do less damage.

"So, Charley and Bo listened – Charley needed proof of James' wrongdoing in order to prosecute. They were trying to figure a way to get in and you out without anybody getting hurt when they saw this flash of light as the fire started. Then all hell broke loose. They tried the door, which was locked of course. When you opened it, they pulled you through and brought you straight back here. They're out there now trying to put the fire out."

"Well, you might want to tell them that there are two bodies, not one," I said quietly.

"What?" Mabel gasped.

"James hasn't been alone in the lighthouse all this time. He's had company."

"Who?"

"Megan."

"What? No. That can't be. She died in the fire at her studio."

"Nope, that was Anna. It seems James was going to break up with Megan that night and Megan did not want to. She killed Anna in cold blood and started the fire to cover her tracks," I said, shaking my head trying to clear the pictures in my head.

"But, what happened then?" Mabel asked. I went on to explain how James had wanted to run away, but Megan wouldn't leave her paintings. I further explained that we were right, James was selling Megan's paintings as his and Megan was okay with it because she was 'his vessel, his soul mate and his muse.'

"Isn't that something?" I got dizzy rolling my eyes as I said that part.

"Very. All I can say is that Megan was one unstable person. I would never have thought her capable of such a thing," Mabel said sadly.

"I got the feeling from what she said that James was her whole world. And that he was so obsessed with her art that she took it for love and acceptance. James is one sad shell of a man. I think he truly loved Anna. Unfortunately, Megan got hold of his soul and wouldn't let go."

"Poor Anna. She always seemed like a nice girl, just fragile somehow."

"Well, I wouldn't worry too much about her now. Anna started the lighthouse fire."

"What? That can't be – she's dead," Mabel exclaimed.

"Yes she is. The mist you and I have been seeing since the fire was Anna, is Anna. And the laughter we've heard was Megan out for a moonlight madness jaunt. It's amazing no one has seen her in all this time," I mentioned very gently, looking into Mabel's face. My vision was still blurry, but I could tell she found it hard to believe. "Anna's a ghost. James saw her too. Anna was there with us at the lighthouse. She followed us up.

When Megan poured the paint thinner on the floor, Anna's ghost walked over to a huge cast iron pillar with a candle sitting on it. She's the one who tipped it over and started the blaze."

"I can't blame the poor dear. What are we going to do, Katy?"

"About what?"

"Anna. I don't know anything about being a ghost whisperer, but can you do something?" Mabel asked.

"Well, when my head, vision, and smoke has cleared, I thought I'd take a walk back to the lighthouse and see if she was still there. Or if, in burning her killers, she left. I don't get a sense either way. I may have inhaled too many fumes."

"Well, then you and Chloe march up to your room and get cleaned up. I'll start a nice hot bath for you. And I'll get a dryer sheet for Chloe. Maybe if we rub her down she'll smell Spring Air scented and not like a pack of used smokes!" Mabel stood and marched upstairs to run my bath. I scooped up Chloe and gingerly limped up the stairs. I didn't know why my body hurt, but I felt sore all over. I stripped and soaked in rose scented bubble bath until the trembling stopped and my skin was all pruney. The bath water turned soot colored. Dressing in my black stretch pants and big fleece shirt, I felt better and warmed both inside and out. My mind kept replaying the final scene in my head – of James and Megan, their arms wrapped around each other, as the fire circled around them consuming them like some demonic monster. The sound of Megan's laughter mixed with the crackle of the blaze. I couldn't bring myself to tell Mabel that I had seen Anna dancing in the flames as well – almost as if she was fanning them.

CHAPTER 29

Hearing voices, I took a quick look for Chloe and figured she was downstairs eating her fill of tuna as a just reward for being a bloodhound. Slowly, I crept down the stairs and into the dining room, following the sound of voices. Seated around the table were the original members of the Black Cat Society, as well as Gavin and a charcoal covered Charley, holding Chloe.

"I see we are holding a meeting welcoming the new members of the Black Cat Society," I said with a smile.

"It seems appropriate given tonight's activities," Dotty said, patting her husband's hand. "We've been waiting for you so we could do an official vote. All those in favor of adding Gavin – for his bravery as a spy and courage for alerting us to you being in danger – say Aye!" Seven voices rang out with a resounding yes, followed by one "Merp."

"Thank you, Chloe, for your approval," Dotty said,

laughing.

"All those in favor of adding Charley to our membership – seeing as how he's our deputy and saved Katy's life," Dotty continued. Eight voices and one cat rang out a heartfelt yes.

"And finally, I think we have one more person to add. He isn't here because he's with the Fire Marshall and keeping an eye on the hot spots at the lighthouse, but I also believe Bo should be added..." Dotty stated firmly.

"...And for saving my life as well. And for keeping tabs on me while I tried to solve this mystery. I second the vote," I said quietly. Again, eight voices yelled "aye" followed by a cheerful chirp from Chloe. "Then I think we have a full membership..." I proudly announced.

"Not just yet," Charley chimed in. "I have to be getting back to help the Fire Marshall and Bo, but I think we have one more to add."

"Who?" I asked.

"Sharkey," Charley said.

"What? Are you crazy? Do you have any idea...?" I sputtered.

"I have every idea what you are thinking. But, he has been keeping an eye on you, too. Keeping me informed on behaviors of certain people and he gave you the picture James drew. Yes, Mabel told me about that as well. I think he has exhibited all the characteristics... Ah, there you are, Ray, just the man I was talking about..." Charley said as Sharkey sauntered into the room. He was covered in grime as well and smelled like it.

"Thanks for your kind words, Charley, but I can't stay. Just wanted to see that Katy's okay and unharmed. And to tell you that the Fire Marshall needs to see you," Sharkey said.

"Then we'll be quick," Dotty said. "All in favor of Ray Sharkey joining the Black Cat Society say 'aye.'" Nine voices sung a chorus of 'aye's and again, Chloe chirped her own approval.

"Congratulations, Sharkey," Charley said standing up and putting Chloe on Dotty's lap.

"Thanks, I guess. Not sure what any of this means. But I'm sure you can tell me about it later, Charley. Good night folks. Take care, Katy," Sharkey said as he and Charley walked out, leaving a trail of smoke and dirt in their wake.

"So, are you going to tell us the whole story or are you going to keep it a secret?" Cherry cried. "I'm bursting! What happened? And what is this about a ghost?"

So, sitting down at the head of the table, I told them all about what I knew, what I had learned and what had happened tonight. While I talked, Chloe was being passed around like a peace pipe. It was easy to tell she loved all the attention. Mabel had quietly gotten up and passed around wine glasses filled with a light Napa Valley Merlot. When she returned from the kitchen, she had scones, brownies, and date bread arranged on a huge tray. We munched and sipped our way through the rest of the evening. I was amazed to realize that no one thought it odd that Comfort had a ghost. I still couldn't tell if Anna was with us, but I hoped I would see her one last time. We talked well into the night, reviewing facts, reciting clues, offering up ideas and speculation on why one person would hurt another. As I listened, my mind started thinking about if there were other ways to help this community from what happened. I had a strong feeling I would be having a long conversation with Holly in the morning.

The Society broke up well after midnight. Bo called and talked with Mabel. He said that the few remains had been recovered, though there wasn't much to salvage, and that Charley was heading home to take a much-needed shower. Bo was going to do the same. Dotty left shortly after, followed by the others. I gave each of these wonderful people – Cherry, Wynetta, Margharite, Dotty, Gavin, and lastly, Mabel – a hug of gratitude and love. Had it really only been ten days since Chloe and I had arrived in Comfort? It seemed like a lifetime ago. Chloe and I gingerly walked upstairs for a long overdue sleep.

Rain pounding on the windows woke me the next morning. The dark clouds of yesterday had arrived this morning in Comfort, bringing a steady downpour. Washing away the troubles of the past, at least I hoped. Showering and changing into my heavy red sweater and jeans, I headed downstairs for breakfast. Mabel was grilling French toast and had bacon and eggs already on the table.

"Are we expecting company?" I asked, hugging her around the waist.

"No, I just figured you would be hungry after last night. I woke up starved this morning. And so did the princess. She ate one complete can of tuna. Can you believe it? Your six pounder is gradually approaching a seven pound ball of fluff," Mabel teased.

"Yeah, but it's all muscle and brains," I joked.

"Right, just go on believing it. So, what's on your dance card for today?" Mabel asked not meeting my eyes.

"I thought I would take a walk to the Point and seek some Comfort and possibly a ghost. And if necessary, a trip to the lighthouse to erase any ghosts I may have hovering around in my own head."

"You sure you're up for the lighthouse?" Mabel asked gently, sitting beside me with the huge plate of fresh toast.

"Yes. It's just a building. And I would like to know what condition it's in. I'm glad the rain came. It will help with the hot spots. It would be a shame if it's not repairable. Not that James did any of it." I explained to Mabel about the scorched and burnt condition of the lighthouse and how it seemed Megan had been our firebug not just at the pier, but at the lighthouse as well.

"I just can't understand why James never repaired it. It makes no sense," Mabel said.

"I think he tried to and Megan kept setting it on fire. I bet she became a living terror to be around."

"Well, I have to say I'm glad this whole business is behind us. It will be nice to move forward. Speaking of forward, I had another call from the flower shop people saying that as soon as the weather changes they will be out to landscape my scorched yard. Really, Katy, the things you do. You have a way…" Mabel began.

"…Of treating people well and being full of surprises. Yes, I do try. And I would like to thank you for noticing. Now, let's just eat. This is delicious, by the way."

"I have to admit I'm looking forward to the new bushes and flowers, but really, Katy, you are too much," Mabel said with a maple-smeared smile.

We finished our breakfast in peace. Grabbing her rain slicker, I headed outside and made my way toward Comfort Point. The rain came down in light sheets and the heavy gray clouds hung low over the ocean mixed with a few patches of low lying fog. With my hands grasping the wooden planks of the old ship, I bowed my head and whispered a silent prayer for James and Megan. I harbored no ill will toward them. I figured wherever they journeyed ahead, karma would be far crueler than any emotion I could come up with. I prayed that somehow they would find their peace. Lifting up my head, I felt the rain touch my face, anointing my head.

Turning, I saw a silver shroud of mist beside me. It hovered near me and immediately I knew it was Anna. I wondered how long she had waited there. Smiling, I breathed deep, centering myself, and listened. I felt more than heard Anna's words of gratitude and thanks. She seemed sad about James but resigned to his fate – and maybe hers. I felt Anna's spark of anger toward Megan and knew it was fueled by jealousy, envy, and disbelief. I couldn't help but understand – jealousy from a woman scorned, envy for a talent that wasn't hers, and disbelief that someone would do such harm.

In my heart, I asked her if she was staying or did she know that she was free to journey on. She knew. She had stayed long enough for someone to find her killer. And to tell me and the others a sincere and heartfelt thank you for easing her pain. As we listened and shared the silence, a ray of sunshine poked through the bank of clouds above us, shining a beam directly onto the lighthouse. I smiled. The mist that was Anna rose up and twirled around me. As I watched, she changed from her silvery gray to a warm golden white, and with a laugh that might have been my own, she soared up into the beam and melted into the sun.

"Godspeed to you, Anna. May you find peace in this life and comfort in the next," I said wiping tears mixed with soft rain from my eyes. Closing my eyes, I said, a prayer of blessing for Anna and her journey.

The rain had made the path to the lighthouse muddy, but I trudged ahead. Smoke hung in the air, but the rain had settled the ash to mix with the earth. Nature's compost. The lighthouse looked as sad as a wet kitty. Black scorch marks licked at the frame of the front door and up the outer wall. I stepped inside and glanced around. All the furniture had been removed or burned – it was hard to tell which. The inside was just a damp, dingy shell. Charley walked out the tower door toward me.

"Hello, Katy! I saw you when I was up in the tower. Thought I'd meet you and let you know that the tower itself is undamaged," Charley said, wiping his hands on his dirty slacks.

"That's great news. How about this part of the house?"

"Oh, I think with a bit of muscle, it can stand up for another hundred years. The Fire Marshall thought the blaze real interesting – lots of flame, but not much damage except in the center where they stood. Couldn't bring myself to tell him a ghost did it," Charley said with a wink.

"Yeah, I bet he wouldn't believe you either. So, this place will be okay?"

"Yes. Given time and someone's attention," he said. We walked around the outside and looked at the structure. It was a fine building and I felt it deserved some tender loving care – and a good paint job. After surveying the area, we headed back down to the pier talking little, where I dropped Charley off at his shop. I took the path down to the beach and perched on a rock letting my mind wander. In a way, I felt sad that Comfort had lost its resident ghost. Chuckling to myself, I wondered if there wasn't another one ready to take her place.

I had come here to vacation and find a way to heal from a sad and lonely year. Instead I had found death, a mystery, and flames. And along the way, friends, kindness and laughter. I thought about paths chosen and roads not taken. About family and friendship and the ties that bind people together or, in some cases, tear them apart. With a deep happy sigh, I pulled out my cell phone and made the call I'd been thinking about since late last night when the visions of ghosts, flames, and paintings swirled around my head. Boy, would Holly be surprised – she's always the last to know.

EPILOGUE

It's hard to believe a month has passed since the phone call I placed at the beach and how so much has changed. Not just from that day but from the people of Comfort. I've always believed change has a way of healing the soul and fortifying the spirit. Well, the town folk of Comfort have taken that thought and put it into action full throttle. I peered out my bedroom window looking out at the pier and all the little shops that had become part of my new home and daily life. The town was getting on with the business of living and it made me smile into the full length mirror. Dotty has really good taste in clothes, I thought, as I swirled around admiring the deep purple calf-length skirt while smoothing out my fancy black see-through sweater.

"I'm glad I put her on retainer as my personal shopper, Chloe." I told my fuzzy little companion. "She knows what looks good on this busty body of mine." I scooped Chloe up and nuzzled her shiny black coat, adjusting her purple halter and leash to ensure she wouldn't get unhooked and scamper away into the night. I skipped down the stairs and out the kitchen door to join the party. Mabel had declared this night the First Annual Black Cat Society Gala. "I don't know what that means exactly," I whispered to Chloe, but with the amount of wine I saw on the table in the kitchen, I knew one thing – it meant I'd be cooking my own breakfast tomorrow.

Rushing out the kitchen door, I placed Chloe on the ground for her to explore the newly landscaped side yard. The kind folks of Comfort Flowers had made quick work of Mabel's once burnt out side yard. Planters of geraniums outlined the new outdoor dining area in colors of white, pink and red. Flagstone pavers were fitted together with reddish tan sand to form a lovely geometric base for the huge banquet table currently holding residence. Honeysuckle, Bougainvillea, and several different colors of Hydrangea bushes added accents around the yard that wrapped around toward the back of the Boardinghouse. To me, it looked like a picture from the pages of *Better Homes and Gardens*. A few feet away, Mabel, in a lovely periwinkle blue dress, was humming. "I feel pretty" – something I've heard her hum since the work was completed yesterday afternoon.

The table looked magnificent in a coastal cozy way. A light blue table cloth with dark denim colored napkins accented the simple white dinner plates. The citronella candles placed strategically in the planters cast shadows and sparkles on the crystal wine and water goblets. The silver flatware arranged just so was ready and waiting for the feast that was being laid down by the Blooming Idiots Catering staff – namely Cherry and Mabel with Wynetta filling water goblets. Wynetta looked like

Patsy Cline in a black western shirt with red piping and a full black tiered skirt. The outfit matched her black and red cowboy boots. Cherry's burnt orange tunic and matching wide legged pants shimmered like an Arizona sunset. This was their first official catering gig and, from the sheer volumes of food and the mixture of exotic and tempting aromas, it was set to be a huge success.

"Can I pour you some wine, Katy?" Sharkey purred in my ear, eyeing the holes in my peek-a-boo sweater.

"Love some. Looks like a nice night for a party."

"Any time's a nice time for a party – don't know why I got voted into this club, but glad I did. You look lovely in the moonlight," he said quietly.

"Thank you," I said into my wine glass while eyeing his black silk shirt with the first three buttons undone, tucked into his slim charcoal gray jeans. I thought the gray snakeskin boots were a nice touch.

"Haven't forgotten our deal, have you?"

"What deal?" I asked as I sipped the wonderful red Merlot from a local winery.

"One night... one drink... my bar... you and me... remember?"

"Oh, that. But I gave you your picture back..."

"Yes, but a deal is a deal. We shook hands on it..." Sharkey smiled into my ear, "I collect on my agreements. No hurry... some things are worth waiting for...I'll be here..." He kissed my ear while his hot breath tickled the base of my neck. I shivered.

"Well, I never back out of an agreement, either. I'll stop by one night..." I breathed deeply trying to cool the fire in my underpants.

"Like I said... I'll be here..." Sharkey sauntered away to

pour the rest of the glasses.

"What did he just say to you? You're as flushed as that glass of red wine you're holding?" Cherry asked while stealing a sip of wine from my glass.

"Just welcoming me to the neighborhood," I lied.

"Looks more interesting to me – like he was reciting a recipe and you were the main ingredient," Cherry said, giggling.

"Very funny. Sharkey is a lovely person. He's the type you flirt with, but not the type you bring home to mother."

"Right. I think of him as a fast car you'd love to drive, but the speeding ticket would be painful." I burst out laughing at the visual and hugged Cherry to me.

"All right, what's all the whispering about?" Mabel asked holding her own glass of wine.

"We were just swapping old car stories," I said. "You know, how the fine is always worse than the offense." Cherry choked on my wine and went looking for a glass of her own.

"So, Mabel, how many glasses have you had so far?" I asked sweetly.

"This is my first and I will not be treated like an addled senior. I know my limits and will not exceed them – speaking of not wanting to pay the fine. Ah, here's the Taylors – now try to behave yourself. I know perfectly well you and Cherry are up to something." And with that, Mabel marched off to welcome Drew, Margharite and Benji. I noticed that Taffeta was wearing a rhinestone studded halter with a black leash. Smiling I wondered how much I'd be billed for that. Benji, dressed in a simple navy blue polo shirt and jeans, positioned himself at the table and had Taffeta attached at one side of his chair and Chloe to the other. He waved hello and proceeded to pull out cat toys from the various pockets of his wheelchair, much like a mother with her diaper bag. I wandered over to Drew and Margharite and smiled to myself when I noticed Drew's relaxed expression. It was nice to know that he no longer had reservations about me. It appeared that I no longer was an outsider. His brow was no longer creased and his shoulders were not hanging around his ears holding up the weight of the world. He wore a simple pair of khaki Dockers with a white shirt and brown sweater vest. Margharite was a vision of loveliness in a safari print tunic with slim black Capri pants. We chatted while Drew went in search of their drinks. Margharite explained that it's been a joy and a challenge adjusting to Benji and his new found freedom. It seems a useable and well built wheelchair can lead to a mischievous and adventurous boy, she said while beaming motherly pride in Benji's direction. I told her about the many times I had seen her son zooming down the side streets and around the pier – usually with Taffeta in tow. I didn't mention the time he nearly ran me over. After giving Benji a Coke, Drew ambled over holding wine glasses for Margharite and himself.

"Have you seen the Bike Shop lately?" Drew asked.

"No, when I've walked by it looks closed and locked up. Everything okay?"

"Just fine. I got rid of all the bikes and bits and pieces. Had enough – didn't make me happy working on them anymore. I read about a guy who builds bikes for underprivileged kids. Gave him the whole lot. I'm turning the Bike Shop into a club house of sorts for Benji and his new friends!" Drew proudly announced.

"And if Benji gets his way, we will be adding a basketball court, too. With that new chair, there's nothing he can't do. I feel so blessed!" Margharite smiled into her wine glass holding back tears in her eyes. I made a mental note to call Holly and have her figure out how to get a basketball court built while not knowing all the red tape and hurdles it would take. I knew she would prevail.

"It looks like Cherry and Miss Mabel like their new job catering. The food looks so tempting, too," Margharite said.

"I'm starving. Mabel seems to be enjoying her new lease on life. First, a new Boardinghouse with only two guests," Drew said, lifting his glass in a toast.

"And second, she cooks for us officially now," Margharite said, raising her glass as well.

"And third, to Chloe's and my new home where I get a room and really good board. I think it's a win-win for everyone!" I raised my glass and we toasted Mabel, who was now adding more platters to the already groaning table.

"Did you hear the news about Cherry and Wynetta?" Drew asked as he motioned for Sharkey, who was acting as bartender, to refill our glasses.

"No, what happened now? I know that they officially reopened the shop except that they kept the name – Cuppa Comfort – something about a good omen," I volunteered.

"It seems they've been having a bit of a spat lately," Drew leaned in and whispered.

"A spat? About what?" I leaned in and whispered back.

"It Cherry. She wants to bring in her birds – for company. Says they are lonesome," Margharite whispered while smiling wickedly.

"But the Health Department…" I stammered.

"… Is a friend of Cherry's. Wynetta says it bad for business – too smelly. But, the business is booming. I hear you have the same drink every day. Standing order," she teased.

"Well, I'm trying to be generous and help them out. But Chloe would have a field day if Fran and Ollie were in there. Can you imagine?" I said laughing at the images in my head.

"Okay, what's the joke?" Charley asked, walking up beside

us. He was smiling broadly and holding a half empty glass of wine. He was dressed in the same blue and white pinstripe shirt, confirming my suspicion that he either only owned one shirt or several of the same shirt. However, he had dressed up by adding black dress pants. Dotty, dressed in a dusty rose twin set and black skirt, looked very stylish as she stood behind him holding her own glass in one hand and Charley's hand in another.

"We were talking about Cherry's plan to have her parakeets inhabit the coffee shop," I explained.

"I don't care if she went to school with the Health Inspector, I just can imagine it. It's just not right – on several levels," Dotty offered.

"How's my grankitten?" Charley asked, jumping in.

"She's with Benji and Taffeta," I said, pointing to where Benji was seated at the table dangling a piece of string for Chloe to swat.

"Looks like the boy could use a hand. Please excuse me," Charley said as he moseyed over to play with Taffeta and Chloe.

"That man has taken to Chloe like a Navy Seal to his sniper rifle. I've never seen anything like it," Dotty said.

"Well, if you ever want him to have a kitten of his own, say the word. I have a source that can score you any cat of any kind, day or night," I offered.

"Really? I may have to think about that. His birthday is coming up…" Dotty said thinking out loud, the wheels in her head already spinning.

"Just let me know. By the way, I've been meaning to tell you, I love all the baskets hanging in front of the shops. It looks wonderful," I said.

"Thank you. I think Comfort Flowers outdid themselves this year. And just look at what they've done with Mabel's yard. It's paradise!" Dotty exclaimed and we all agreed.

"Hey, Katy! You have a phone call!" Mabel called from the kitchen. I excused myself and went to see who could possibly be calling me. Walking into the front parlor, I grabbed the phone.

"Hello?"

"Katy? It's Bo."

"Bo? Where are you? You sound like..."

"... I'm at the airport. Look, something's come up and I can't make the party tonight."

"Oh..." I said, trying not to show my disappointment.

"I'm sorry, Katy. But I wouldn't do this if it wasn't important. I hope you can understand," he explained.

"I guess so. Are you okay, Bo?"

"Yeah, I'll tell you about it sometime. Listen, I wanted to tell you two things before I go."

"Yes?"

"First, I found your Swiss Army Knife at James' gallery. I gave it to Mabel to give back to you."

"You did? Oh, thanks, Bo. That was my Dad's, he carried it with him all his life – it means a lot to me."

"Glad I could help."

"And the second?" I asked.

"I do not look like the swamp monster..." Bo laughed into the phone.

"What? I never... who told you... Bo?" I stammered. He laughed even louder.

"Look there's my jet, gotta go. I'll talk to you soon. Oh, and Katy? Look on your bed." And he was gone. Damn, damn, damn. I still hadn't seen his face! I frowned into the phone, slammed it down, and stomped my feet like an irate four year old having a tantrum in the candy aisle. I looked up at the ceiling visualizing my room on the second floor and frowned. What did he mean look on my bed? Doesn't he mean under it?

I vowed to ignore his request until I had had a second glass of wine.

With that thought, I hurried back outside looking for my wine glass to drown my sorrows and stopped dead in my tracks. Gavin and Miss Martha had made their entrance, and what an entrance it was. Gavin was dressed in a blinding white clingy sweater, white leather pants that looked like they were sprayed on, and white platform pumps. Who knew that they came in a men's size twelve, extra wide. Miss Martha was wrapped in a white vinyl cape and white beret. The look was, well, blinding. Everyone was gathered around looking somewhat stunned and searching for something to say. Personally I thought he looked like a giant bleached white incisor or upper molar.

"Now there's someone who knows how to dress for a party!" I yelled as I rushed up to Gavin. I gave him the biggest hug, kissed Miss Martha on her petite head and smiled. "Finally, my date has arrived!" I said, tucking my arm in Gavin's.

"I've come out of the closet," he whispered quietly in my ear.

"And bolted the barn door behind you, I see," I whispered back. "You'll be fine…"

"Are we late? I simply could not decide what to wear. I stuck with tried and true – Nancy Sinatra never disappoints."

"I agree," Cherry said and we all clapped idiotically.

At that moment, Mabel saved the day by announcing, "Dinner is served." We all clambered to the table to join Benji, Taffeta and Chloe. Sharkey refilled our wine glasses and sat down next to Wynetta. Mabel was perched at the head of the table next to Sharkey and I again took the foot of the table as the others filled in around us. As we all settled in, Mabel raised her glass to propose a toast.

"To the Black Cat Society and its members and our mascots

– Chloe and Taffeta." We all raised our glasses and drank. I didn't correct Mabel. I figured the Black Cat Society accepted anyone, regardless of cat affiliation or not. And that we would not discriminate against breed, fur type and color either.

The feast was sumptuous. Three different salads; a marinated vegetable salad, Italian house salad dotted with sweet peppers, and a Caesar made with homemade dressing. The centerpieces to the meal were the entrées. A light veal Parmesan, a multi layered vegetable lasagna, and manicotti stuffed with a whipped ricotta and spinach filling was mixed in between multiple heaping bowls of pasta marinara. The meal was filled with laughter as old friends mingled with new. Stories were passed around as quickly as the garlic bread. Sharkey would occasionally whisper something to Wynetta, which would send her into a fit of giggles. Dotty, Charley, and Drew got into a complicated discussion over possible weaponry used at the space station, while Mabel and Cherry kept revising recipes – out loud. Chloe and Taffeta finally gave up, climbed into Benji's lap and fell asleep. Margharite, Drew, and I kept up our end of the table chewing over the other changes happening at the pier.

I told everyone that I had learned that the Uptown School of Artistry had taken over the selling of Megan's prints and were using the proceeds to fund scholarships for future artists. I thought privately that Anna would have appreciated that. Shortly after the case was closed, I had given the two rough drafts, liberated from the bank, to the school as well. I didn't want them in my possession any longer.

Gavin joined our conversation and mentioned how it would be exciting to see what the future had in store for the two empty shops at the pier. The Reinhold Gallery stood empty now waiting for a new owner, hopefully one with a good heart and a plan to do good in the community. When Margharite asked about Megan's studio, Gavin just smiled and said that remodeling was taking place and that the new owner would be along in a few short weeks to open for business. He kept a straight face the whole time and only once did he slyly turn to me and wink. I was surprised and proud of Gavin. He had kept his word and did not spill my secret.

"How can you, dressed in blaring white, possibly get through a whole dinner without spilling marinara sauce on yourself?" I heard Wynetta mutter to Gavin from the far end of the table, while dabbing her wet napkin on the sleeve of her shirt.

"I'm gay, darling, not a klutz," Gavin purred back, sending the whole table into another fit of laughter. I was surprised that this diverse group of people had come together as a team, a community and at how well they truly got along.

Well, I had a few surprises of my own. When everyone had slowed down and pushed their plates aside, I took my knife and politely tapped it on my glass to get everyone's attention.

"Folks, I have a few things I'd like to say, if I may..." I began.

"Speech... peach..." Mabel slurred.

"First, I would like to thank the lovely Blooming Idiots for our wonderful feast – you outdid yourselves!" We all applauded. "Next, I would like to thank Sharkey for acting as bartender – and keeping us all plastered!" There were more cheers and applause.

"And last, my heartfelt thanks to all of you sitting here before me. Thank you for taking me in, for being my friends and giving me a purpose. And most recently, for keeping me safe, saving my life and giving me a new home that I welcome with open arms," I said as I nodded to Charley and Drew who got up from the table and went into the front parlor. "After much deliberation, some tricky maneuvering and sheer cussedness on my part, I have gifts for you – with thanks and gratitude for your bravery, courage, and friendship. All I ask in return is that you never ask how this all came to be, no questions. Just believe me when I say, Anna would have wanted it this way. Agreed?" I insisted, looking at each person seated before me. Mabel kept her head down so as not to let on that she knew my financial status.

"Agreed," they replied in unison. I then nodded to Charley and Drew as each emerged from the parlor carrying seven of the eight crown jewel paintings. There was a collective gasp when they saw the paintings.

"How in the world…?" Cherry muttered.

"Katy? What on earth?" Mabel stammered.

"Remember, she made us promise," Margharite said her eyes sparkling.

Slowly, Charley and Drew walked around the table asking each member to select one for their very own. They were all dumbfounded. I waited as each person, or couple made their selection.

"But there's one missing," Wynetta said having counted.

"The last one I'll be giving to Bo when he returns," I said as Sharkey snickered. "I made arrangements with the Uptown School – again don't ask. They were pleased with the exchange. So, enjoy them, my friends. You deserve to have them as a reminder of the good you did for the town and for the beauty in all of you." I sat down and sipped my wine. Mabel got to her feet and cleared her throat.

"I, for one, am speechless. I think this is amazing, Katy. But I will never ask how or why, like we agreed. I believe these should be a reminder to all of us as well. We need to remember to help those who are in need and to take care of each other. And not to walk away but to do what is right, not just what is easy. Every time I look at this, I will think of that wisp of mist, Anna, and say a prayer that I will be a better person for what has happened here in Comfort. And I will strive to be the person Katy sees in me. Thank you, dear." Mabel sat down and wiped her eyes with her napkin. Many throats cleared and chairs squeaked.

"Nice downer of a party, Katy, girl," Gavin said as he hiccupped. I laughed, Miss Martha barked and the tension and emotion broke loose like an afternoon thunderstorm. Sharkey got up and turned on the radio that had been conveniently hidden in one of the bushes. Nancy Sinatra began to sing … "These boot were made for walking…" Gavin got up and started to dance with Miss Martha, shaking and shimmering around the yard. Sharkey walked over to Cherry and pulled her to her feet and started twirling her around the table. Drew grabbed Margharite and began waltzing to their own music. Wynetta and Mabel joined hands and jitterbugged. All the while, Benji slept with two precious kitties on his lap. Chloe looked up from his lap and winked at me. I winked back and nodded my head as she nestled back down to sleep.

As I glanced around the yard and leaned over to drink in the charming town with its Victorian homes, beach bungalows, and simple cottages, I was filled with a sense of gratitude and awe. I was grateful for finding a town full of kind and generous people, and in awe, like someone finding a gold nugget at the bottom of a gold miner's pan. I felt grateful at my fortune for stumbling across this place with Chloe. This town had given me far more than friendship and healing and I looked forward to the days ahead.

Staring up the cliff at the lighthouse I felt a stirring sense of pride. Though only in the beginning stages, I knew Holly would convince the town's Historical Society to allow me to purchase the lighthouse, restore it to its former glory, and then donate it back to the town – along with a Trust for upkeep and maintenance in the years to come. I would make a point of having the beacon restored as well, to once again shine its light guiding ships home to safe harbor. I couldn't help but feel that the lighthouse had already done that for me.

But, honestly, I thought to myself, as I rubbed the sore muscles in my shoulders, this town is still missing one thing to be perfect. With a wicked smile, I got up, walked into the kitchen and headed up the stairs to my room to place a phone call and start a ball rolling.

Opening the door, I noticed two things at once. First, someone had lit a hurricane lamp and placed it on the dresser. The second thing I noticed took my breath away. There, nestled on my pillow, was a red rose with a piece of antique ivory lace wrapped around it in a bow. Bo, I thought as I reached for the rose. A photo was propped up on my pillow. Framed behind a background of familiar snow capped peaks and tall green pine trees was a well-muscled cowboy sitting tall in the saddle on the back of a equally well-muscled sorrel horse. The man's well used straw cowboy hat was pulled low so most of his face was in shadow. All except his mouth, which was smiling. I touched my fingers to my lips and thought of a kiss I had from those lips. The kiss from the cowboy!

Smiling, I placed the photo back on the pillow, sniffed the rose and placed it on my dresser. I wonder how Bo got this up here, I thought.

"Merp," Chloe said from down around my ankles.

"Why do I have a feeling that you had something to do with this?" I asked her as she jumped on the bed and nosed

Bo's photo.

"Merp," she said as she snuggled down next to the photo and pretended to sleep.

"Now what did I come up here for in the first place?" I asked myself more than Chloe. I stretched and absentmindedly rubbed the sore muscles in my back. "Now I remember – the one perfect thing this town is missing!" I said to thin air. Grabbing my cell phone, I began to hum while dialing, knowing I had a sneaky smile on my face. Money can't buy you everything, I thought, but it can keep you … in Comfort.

THE END

ACKNOWLEDGMENTS

To Mark, Chloe, and July – my family – thank you for supporting, accepting, and encouraging me and for filling my life with love and laughter. I love you all – you make my world complete!

To Cassie (the best horse that ever was) – I miss you and all the love and hay we shared. Thank you for teaching me to love unconditionally. I love you, Cassie Girl!

To Chance – Thanks for keeping me company all those nights while I dreamed and plotted this book – your purrs and snuggles were greatly appreciated. I miss you, little buddy!

To Joyce and Charles Towne (aka Mom and Dad), thank you for your support, love and for being great parents. Thank you for being there.

To Ethel Bianchi, for the privilege and honor of having you in my life as a dear friend, I thank you and love you – you are an inspiration.

A heartfelt thank you to Nancy Atherton for all her guidance, advice, wisdom, and support.

A special thank you to Sarah Petkus for a wonderful book cover. Visit her at www.foxhollowart.etsy.com.

A huge thank you and sigh of relief to Amanda Ingalls for layout and formatting of this book. You are a treasure! Visit her at www.fromatozstudio.com.

And to the many others who have given me courage, support and great ideas, a big thank you to you – especially: Betsy Carson, Jerry Casados, Jodi and Bob Eaton, Geri Rutz, Carol Rourke, Beverly Holmes, Howard and Merle Smith, my amazing and loyal clients, and to all those who listened to my ramblings as they turned into chapters – I truly am blessed to have such wonderful people in my life!